Receive a signed book-
plate with proof of

purchase.

Details:

http://fierceinkbooks.com/
collectors-edition-content/

FIERCE
INK
BOOKS

Aptitude

Natalie Corbett Sampson

CANADA | est. 2012

Aptitude
Copyright © 2015 Natalie Corbett Sampson
All rights reserved

Published by Fierce Ink Books Co-Op Ltd.
www.fierceinkbooks.com

First edition, 2015

Library and Archives Canada Cataloguing in Publication information is available upon request.

ISBN: 978-1-927746-88-2

Edited by Allister Thompson
Cover design by Emma Dolan

For LAR, who only knows love.

1

Not

The sound of footsteps started as uncertain whispers and grew into a hurried, pounding rhythm that reverberated through the hollow tunnel of the hall toward my cell. As the volume increased, my heart leaped and sped so that when the footsteps halted outside the door, my heart felt lodged in my throat. Silence. Then the hum of the security palm panel replaced the echoing footfalls, and I held my breath to find out who was on the other side of the door.

The door slid aside with a burst of lemony perfume on hot, stale air and admitted two people. A tall, lanky woman in a blue suit pushed her way in first before the door was all the way open. Her jacket fell neatly to the width of her hips and gaped to show a lighter blue blouse underneath. Her pants were fitted but held a crisp crease falling straight down the front of each leg to point at her shiny black shoes. The two-inch-wide band sewn into the upper sleeve of her right arm was bright blue. She was a Judician. Her dark hair was short and meticulously placed, sweeping away from her face into a swirling spiral over her right ear. The particular style drove me to thrust my fingers through my own hair that hadn't been brushed in... I couldn't say when. I tucked the flyaway strands that had fallen loose behind my ears and tugged at my gray shirt to smooth the wrinkles that must have been there.

Behind her stood a shorter, rounder person, a man who looked younger than me. His Judician band, of thinner material, made the sleeve of his jacket sag askew against the arm hanging at his side. He was bald except for a circle of dark hair hedging the top of his head. One hand held a briefcase, the other pushed his glasses up his rounded, reddened nose. He stank. As he

stepped through the door, a thick whiff of body odor cut through the lemon scent hovering around the woman, and I concentrated on not wrinkling my nose.

The door slid shut, and I was trapped again, this time with the severe, gangly woman and her opposite. The room was not big enough for the three of us.

The woman strode toward me and thrust out her hand with a force that propelled me in a diffident step backwards until my calves met the edge of the bed. I don't know why, but I noticed right then that her nails were immaculate, painted red and filed to a fashionably sharp point. Mine were chewed, curled up and hidden in my palms.

"Hessa Black. My name is Counsel Gallie. I'm the prosecutor assigned to your case." I didn't take her hand. She dropped it to her hip and turned her attention to the screen she'd placed on the small table. "Your turn," she said without looking up from the screen.

My turn? But then the round man stepped forward. "Hi, Hessa. I'm Counsel Finch, I'm your representative." His eyes were watery and brown. He looked at me too straight, too long, and I looked away first.

"Sit," Gallie said as she waved her blood-colored claws to the chair opposite the one she had claimed.

I hesitated long enough to earn a loud sigh and a pointed glare, but I had nowhere else to go. I slunk into the chair at the table, but I leaned against the back to gain as much distance from her as I could. In the corner of my eye Finch looked from Gallie to myself and around the tiny room. When his gaze fell on the corner, his face scrunched up and he took a step away then perched on the edge of my bed. He took out his own screen from his case and laid it across his knees, fluttering his fingers over it. The light from the screen glowed up on his face, leaving dark shadows in the hollows of his eyes.

Gallie's screen flashed as it flicked between pages, following the commands of her fingers. Her eyes fluttered under her lids, painted to match the identifying blue strip on her sleeve. She said nothing but occasionally emitted an audible release of air that carried exasperation. For long, silent moments I studied them while they studied what must have been *me* documented in text and photos on their screens.

My fingers worried at the three inches of skin on my lower arm smoothened by the constant presence of my missing communicator. I didn't trust them. Hell, I didn't trust anyone. Not since they came the night before and demanded I go with them. If only Toan had been there … what would he have said? What would he have done? Would I still be here?

It was late when they came to the door, past social curfew and into my favorite hour of the day. I loved the calm quiet of late evening, keeping the lights low and the scenters on relaxing lavender, scrounging to find a few more minutes of productivity in the day. I had just opened my students' assignments on my computer in my home office. The columns of numbers on the screen threw shadows around the small dimly lit room. The intercom in the wall startled me with "unregistered person at front door," and I jumped, knocking my hot tea across the screen. I took just long enough to strip off my sweatshirt and drop it on top of the mess, hoping it would sop up the tea before I hurried down to the front door in my gray T-shirt. So when I answered the door, I had a glare on my face and a smartass remark on my tongue that I swallowed when I saw them. I wonder if the mess is still there, if my computer still works or if the tea seeped into the circuitry and destroyed it.

There were three of them. Protectors, dressed in dark gray uniforms with thick black vests, dark hats and dark glasses. I couldn't see their eyes; instead, the reflection of my stunned face looked back at me from each lens. Their faces were unyielding masks with drawn-in brows and pinched, closed mouths. One met my startled greeting by grunting my name: "Hessa Black?" I nodded just a bit and unknowingly sealed my fate. A second man held out his communicator, showing identification.

"You'll come with us," he said. It wasn't an invitation or a request.

"Is someone hurt?" My mind flashed back to an emergency call on a dark night years ago, and I shivered in the warm air.

"You'll come with us," the same man repeated, as if I hadn't spoken at all.

"I — I need to change." My voice sounded feeble and lame, and my uncertainty was proven by the fact that I stood still in my house clothes, waiting for their permission instead of turning away to go get dressed.

"There's no need. We'll leave now."

Maybe I should have protested, but they were the law, and as naive as it sounds now, I didn't realize I was in trouble.

I folded my arms against the cold and stepped into the night. The house door slid behind me, and out of habit I said, "Lock door" to the security system. I followed one Protector while two followed me. Too close, so that I smelled the garlic on one Protector's breath. Beyond the halo of our door light, the night was dark. Our movement toward the road initiated the streetlights, and they slipped on, illuminating a long black car parked at the curb. I had only ridden in a private car once before; it seems luxury transportation only comes with very bad circumstances. My breaths shortened, and my heart raced until I felt dizzy, and the car and street and houses seemed to tip in front of me. I stopped. Cold fingers curled around my elbow and pulled me forward. As we approached, the rear door swept up and open, and I had no choice but to fold myself in and sit on the cool seat facing the back of the car. It smelled of bitter old smoke, and my throat pulled even tighter against the noxious taste carried through the scent. The seat belt snaked with a whir from my right shoulder to my left hip and snapped into place. I didn't feel safer; my chest bone was squeezed between the pressing seat belt and my pounding heart.

One Protector slid in after me. He sat opposite, riding forward, facing me with his body but keeping his shielded eyes turned away. The car was big, but with him in the space I felt crowded. I folded my arms and tucked my legs under me, trying to make myself small. As the car shifted into motion I asked again, "Is someone hurt?" but he didn't even acknowledge my presence, let alone my question. From then on I kept my eyes on the window, watching the lights behind us switch off as we passed out of their sensor range and my street fell dark. I tried to remember if there was somewhere I'd been or something I'd done, or said, that might have triggered a warning through my

4

communicator trace. Some kind of suspicious misunderstanding to warrant their reaction, something I could explain easily enough if they'd just give me the chance. Or a slip. But the evidence was gone, disintegrated into nothing. Within moments they whisked me away through the empty streets and echoing halls to the room where I now sat waiting for the Judician antitheses to tell me why I was there.

The cell was small, three meters square, if that. One corner hugged a mattress on a metal frame that squeaked each time I moved on it. The mattress was wrapped in stiff white sheets and a scratchy red blanket. The pillow was hard and flat. I'd tried to fold it in half, thinking if I lay still it wouldn't flip open, but when I got that close, it reeked of something unfamiliar, something sour. I threw it to the floor, where it landed under the table, and laid my head on my arms instead.

Gallie and I sat in the opposite corner of the cell, at the heavy silver table. The top of the table was shiny, with metallic grain running through. I'd spent the morning sitting in the chair, running my fingers along the cool grain lines, studying them as if they were a map illustrating my route into that hole. Or maybe out. Overhead, the white-lit ceiling hummed, which was usually the only sound, except when someone walked by the door. I think that was the worst of it —— they had taken my communicator, and I missed its frequent beeps. There were no screens that whirled or muttered, no distant hover whoosh, no sirens, no voices. Just the even hum of the ceiling.

In the third corner a small oval was barely visible on the floor. The outline was a thin crack in the otherwise unmarked surface of the shiny black floor. I hadn't even noticed it at first, until my anxiety drove me to pace. When I stalked to that corner, I heard a whoosh of air, and the oval split in two, each half sliding aside under the floor to leave a dark hole. An odd stench, a combination of sewer and chemical cleaner, wafted up to meet me. Walking away from the toilet made the oval slide closed again. I'd limited my pacing closer to the door in the fourth corner of the room after that.

Like the table, the door was metal and solid, cold and smooth when I pressed my hands against it after it closed be-

5

hind the Protectors who left me there. It didn't budge. A transparent square at eye level was almost always closed by a cover accessed from the outside. Along the length of the opposite wall, above the bed and toilet, was a thin strip of window to the outside. It was only three inches or so tall so that the light it let in was limited to a bright sliver that had traveled across the floor over the bed and toward the door since I woke early that morning. I had stood on the bed to raise my eyes to the window. There was nothing but concrete walls with jutting corners and edges that must contain miles of mazed hallways, just like the one outside the cold door.

"Do you know why you're here?" Finch now asked, and my shoulders jerked up as he brought me out of my trance.

Gallie's thin fingers swept off her screen, and it turned black. She looked up and studied me for an uncomfortable moment before taking a deep breath. I turned my head in an almost indiscernible denial. She tapped the sharp point of her fingernail on the table, the other three curled in against her palm so tightly the skin was white against her knuckles. "I told you." She blew out on her pent-up breath, and in the still of the cell I felt her exhalation brush warm against my face a second after I heard it. I smelled peppermint then onion. "He's dead, Hessa, and you are being held responsible."

"Toan?" The whisper fell out of me as if forced out by a punch. "Toan's dead?" My cracked voice pricked my throat, and my stomach heaved up pressing against my heart. If I had eaten the food they offered, I'd have vomited all over Gallie's pristine suit. Toan's wide, boyish smile flashed in front of my eyes as the cell and the two Judicians blurred through instant tears.

"Excuse me, Counsel Gallie, but you are here to observe, not to intervene. You will have your chance in court." Finch's watery eyes blinked at Gallie, and his eyebrows tipped inward. Gallie shrugged and waved her hand palm up at me.

Finch sighed and looked at me a breath too long before he said, "No, not your match." For a second I could breathe, but then he went on. "Aubin. Aubin Wallace is dead."

Aubin. The shock of hearing his name aloud momentarily cloaked the implication of his other words. My ears hummed.

Aubin. Who was this man to say *his* name to me? How could he possibly know? I squinted at him. I pinched my lips together in defiance and bit the inside of my cheek until I tasted metallic blood. I hated him then. I willed them both away. I wanted them to leave, even though it would leave me alone. But they sat still. Gallie's eyebrows raised and her head cocked as a sneer inched slowly across her lips. Finch looked at his hands, fingers woven together and resting on his screen in his lap.

And then the rest of his message caught up. *Aubin is dead.* I broke. My heart, that I had spent the last many months piecing back together, blew apart into shards that cut me as they flew. Aubin was dead. I was trapped, and Aubin was dead.

"See? I told you she didn't know." Gallie's voice had a hint of a laugh to it. "Perhaps you had better start over, Counsel Finch."

Finch looked from Gallie to me and nodded. He sat up a bit straighter and fluttered his fingers above the screen again.

"When was the last time you saw Aubin Wallace?"

I knew the exact date, the exact hour, but sharing less seemed safer. "Eleven," I managed to squeeze out of my tight throat.

"Eleven of last year?" I couldn't speak again, so I nodded. His simple question ferried me back in my memory to a moment that was so intimate, only the two of us knew it existed. Now just one, just me. I had told no one, of course; it was too dangerous. And wrong. I had walked away stiffly, my false bravado carrying me away from his wet blue eyes and his haunted insistence.

I forced myself back to the present, where I was locked in the metallic cell. "What — what happened? Why am I here...?" I whispered.

"He is dead, that is the truth we know as of now," Finch said. "The Authority has evidence that you know information which will explain the circumstances of his death further. Information that you kept secret. The Authority maintains that had you shared the information, his death would have been avoided. You are being charged as culpable in his death because of that evidence, and your failed responsibility to share it. That warrants a charge of murder."

Murder. The word bounced around in my brain, and I shook my head to try to clear it. Aubin. Just months ago he was

7

full of curiosity and hope and wonder… How could he be…? But he was dead. What reason did these people have to lie? Aubin was dead. Murder. Could it really be my fault?

"Hessa, I thought you knew all of this." Finch leaned toward me from his perch on the bed but turned to glare at Gallie when she snorted.

I wanted to scream '*How could I?*' but I kept silent, staring at the grain lines in the table, tracing their swirls with my eyes. "We need to prepare for your trial. Counsel Gallie will be narrating and presenting the evidence." He looked at her when he said this, and Gallie smiled brightly, nodding. My jaw throbbed, and I made myself release the clench. The pain only rose into my temples and pounded there instead. "I am your representative."

"But I … I didn't…" I was going to say "I didn't hurt anyone," but that was far from the truth. "Why do they think it's my fault?"

Gallie answered, her voice sharp and fast, cutting in while Finch took a breath. "There is irrefutable evidence that proves you are to blame for Aubin's death. I have shared the information I have with your representative, so he knows the futility of challenging—"

Finch stood and closed the half step between himself and Gallie. His face was flushed red and his hands were fisted, shaking. "Counsel Gallie, I must remind you of your role in this meeting. You asked to be present solely to ensure no undisclosed truth was revealed. I ask you maintain your silence." They stared at each other as if I was no longer in their midst.

"Of course, please proceed," Gallie finally said. Finch sighed and turned back to look at me.

"Hessa, your trial will be presented through Narrative Summary Trial by Counsel Gallie. She will present the information to the judge, I will be there to ensure the information is submitted with objectivity. If you are found culpable and therefore guilty of murder, your certification will be stripped and you will be convicted to oddout containment." He glanced at Gallie, and she flashed him a wide smile. "We will start in one week."

"One week?" I managed to push out on a panicked breath, and then swallowed down another mouthful of bile.

Finch returned to his screen, tapped and stroked the cover, then swept his fingers toward the wall. I kept my gaze locked on the metallic lines of the table, but in my periphery the black wall lit up with white letters that spelled my name. I avoided looking up.

"Yes, timing is essential in a Narrative Summary Trial. Research has indicated that an immediate summary is the most reliable method to obtain the highest accuracy of truth, and testimonies are most precise closest to the event. The system moves quickly so witnesses don't have time to forget details or generate alternate truths. Any delay in proceedings raises questions and doubts in the truth presented."

"So you will tell my side?"

"There are no sides, Hessa. There is no indication of conflicting facts. The Judicial Authority is confident it knows the truth. Counsel Gallie's responsibility is to provide the structural questions that will elicit the facts, and my role is to make sure those questions are not delusive or subjective. Your responsibility is to tell the truth." He blinked, twice, and his lips twitched as if he was failing an attempt to smile.

Gallie stared at me so steadily, I hoped she didn't see me shiver. My head pounded with questions. What facts? What truth? What did I know? As if she could read my thoughts, she smiled at Finch and said, "May I?" but leaned forward in her chair and rushed into her next breath before he could protest. "You will need to provide your concealed information that our evidence demonstrates you have. The judge will determine your guilt and liability in Aubin Wallace's death. If you are found guilty, you will be incarcerated and submitted to the Authority's medical sustainment program."

"That is it!" Finch growled.

"Yes, that is all I have to say." Gallie smiled sweetly at him and stood to face him, nose to nose. "Are we finished here?"

Finch narrowed his eyes and stood his ground. "Not quite," he spat, a spark of spittle flying off his enunciated 't'. Gallie grimaced and forced her smile wider before she stepped around him to stand by the door.

"Hessa, do you have any questions?" he asked, his voice

lowered as if he could whisper to me unheard.

I had questions. Thousands of questions. So much was unknown that I didn't know what to ask. My throat was closed, and I concentrated on pushing air in and out. My jaw locked closed, tight again, bulging pain from my teeth to my temples. I couldn't loosen the grip and suddenly I realized if I did, I might start to scream and not stop. I shook my head.

"I will be back tomorrow. Now that you have met Counsel Gallie, the audio surveillance in the room will be sufficient to exclude the need of her invigilating our meetings."

Gallie smiled with one last pitiful look in my direction, faced the door and placed her hand on the palm panel of the wall. Her barbed red nails stood out against the dark wall. The door slid open. "Are you coming, Counsel Finch?" she asked sweetly. Finch was still looking at me, his wet eyes locked onto mine until my cheeks started to burn. I looked away.

"Until tomorrow," Finch whispered and stepped through the door after Gallie. The door closed with a mechanic thunk behind them, leaving me alone with the documents on the screen glowing on the wall — and my thoughts.

I followed my finger along the grains for a while, resisting the urge to read through the information glowing on the wall. I desperately wanted to see what it said, but I was terrified to look. The Judicians' whirlwind visit had left me with more information but even more questions.

I had only encountered one other person since the officers had left me there. A stooped old man in a dark green oddout uniform that matched the green bruise dripping from his eye had appeared twice to deliver my meals in a plain flask of liquid nutrients. The first time he came, shortly after I arrived, I tried to talk to him. As soon as he walked through the sliding door, I pummeled him with questions, asking where I was and why I was being kept, but he only looked away as he shuffled to the table to put down the flask, and then back to the palm panel to request his exit. That morning he had shaken his head before I even opened my mouth. As he shuffled out, a sarcastic, hollow laugh echoed in my head when I remembered the character in an old movie Toan insisted we watch for compulsory arts hour.

I decided to call him my butler.

The butler slid in again, interrupting my standoff with the screen. He put the flask on the white 'L' reflecting on the table, and I heard him sigh. He hesitated, and I thought he shifted just a bit in my direction, but his communicator buzzed, and he must have thought better of whatever he had been about to do. Or maybe I had imagined it. He turned and left without looking back. His appearance and disappearance pushed me to act. I grasped the flask, opened my meal and looked up at my name on the wall.

I hadn't even noticed the screen on the wall, but a rectangle of the dull gray fabristone had been replaced by a polished black background against which my white name glowed. The background was glassy, like the deep lake I remembered from the holozoo, so still I could see my reflection. The 'ac' of my last name cut across my forehead just above my eyes, staring back at me. I was a mess. My dark hair that was always neatly tied back was frizzy and loose; it was pointing all directions around my face. The amber orbs of my eyes stood out against wider, red-rimmed whites. Frantic. Even with the limitation of the black screen as a mirror, I could see my face was pale enough that my hated freckles glowed. My eyes were puffy, making my lips look even narrower than usual, and more so as I pressed them together. My gray house clothes —— T-shirt and sweat pants —— were shapeless and hung from my frame. My wild appearance made me feel even more out of control. I wished I could get dressed and brush my hair. Put everything back in place.

I held my fist up in front of the screen on the wall and twitched my fingers open. The screen flickered and my name dissolved into a white rectangle with black text: a formal document with the Authority crest at the top. My name was bolded in larger font, standing out from the rest of the message. Down a line and halfway across the screen, also thick and enlarged, was Aubin's. There we were, officially tied together by mention in a legal document. And the worst possible words linked our two names: *is charged with murder due to interference and manipulation resulting in the untimely death of.*

I knew two things: Aubin was dead. It was my fault.

2

Mbili

Court Representative for the Authority – Let the court record indicate the following: I am Counsel Gallie, Prosecuting Judician of this Narrative Summary Trial of the accused, Hessa Black, in the death of Aubin Wallace, Creator.

Court Representative for the Defense – Let the court record indicate the following: I am Counsel Finch, Objective Judician, representing the accused, Hessa Black.

Gallie – Thank you, Counsel Finch. Would the court please consider this narrative to now be open; all information provided henceforth should be considered during judgement. Accused, please place your hand on this screen and state your classification and profession, name and age.

Defendant – I'm, uh, I'm certified a Quantifier, and I'm a math teacher. Hessa Black.

Gallie – And your age, please.

Hessa – Nineteen.

Gallie – Let the records indicate that palm print analysis confirms this identity. And what is your Aptitude Lineage?

Hessa – My parents are third generation Quantifiers.

Gallie – What level do you teach?

Hessa – I taught the Intermediate students.

Gallie – The academic year is not complete. What do you mean by 'taught'?

Hessa – I was removed from my position.

Gallie – Removed. By whom?

Hessa – I was detained by Social Authority.

Gallie – When was that?

Hessa – Eight days ago.

Gallie – And since then?

Hessa – Since then what?

Gallie – What have you been doing since you were detained?

Hessa – Waiting in a holding room, what else?

Gallie – Why were you detained? Why have you been held?

Hessa – I was told it's because Aubin is dead. And that it's my fault.

Gallie – Please be more specific, Hessa, for the record of the court transcript. Who told you this?

Hessa – You did. You and Counsel Finch said Social Authority has determined I am responsible for Aubin's death.

Gallie – Yes. Thank you. And now you are here on trial by narrative for murder.

Hessa – That's what I've been told.

Finch – If it please the court, we are all well aware of why we are present for these proceedings.

Gallie – Are you matched?

Hessa: Yes. I'm matched to Toan Whitley.

Gallie – Is he here today?

Hessa – Yes. He's sitting there.

Gallie – Let the record show Ms. Black has indicated the man in the first row, seat nine, who identified himself to Security as Toan Whitley, Quantifier and Professor of Maths. How long have you been matched to Toan?

Hessa – Almost two years.

Gallie – Two years. And how long ago did you write your Proofs?

Hessa – Almost two years.

Gallie – Were you matched directly following your Proofs?

Hessa – Yes.

Gallie – Was it an arranged match?

Hessa – No, we chose it.

Gallie – But so soon after your Proofs. How long have you known Toan?

Hessa – All my life. Our parents are close friends. We grew up together.

Gallie – It's unusual that you and Mr. Whitley were raised together but not arranged to be matched.

Finch – Your personal opinion is not objective in this narrative, Counsel Gallie.

Gallie – Yes, excuse me. Why did you choose to match with Toan?

Hessa – Why? Because I loved him. I wanted to be matched to him.

Gallie – You loved him?

Hessa – I love him. He is my best friend.

Toan was my perfect match. Everybody knew it. Even now, if I think of an age, any age, it's Toan's face that represents that time of my life. In my earliest memories, he has big, round cheeks that he'd push up when he smiled so that his dark brown eyes would tip inward with a squint. His nose was straighter when he was younger, before he tripped and broke it during his compulsory run when we were twelve. No one else seems to notice the slight shift to the left, but I do. When we were ten, he insisted on growing his hair long so that it would fall into his face in shiny honey waves. He developed a habit of shaking it to the side, out of his eyes, with a side-tipping toss of his head. When he scored third on a test, Uncle G took him to the barber and had it shaved short. He got a perfect score on the next test and has kept it trimmed neat ever since. But he denies superstition. His boyish features have grown strong and angular. His upper lip is roughened by stubble by evening, when he kisses me goodnight. His wide, easy smile is infrequent, replaced by a studious look and solemn eyes. I miss it. I miss him.

My mother used to tell me she knew even when we were toddlers fighting over an old abacas or counting blocks. My father would laugh, then, and say he was the first to know because he was sure of it that night they had dinner with Toan's parents and we both wailed from my crib in the next room. I cried louder just to be heard. He'd shake his head and remind me that I was never one to be outdone. I figured he'd tell the story at our Matching Appointment, and he did, but he left the last part out, the part about not being outdone. He hasn't said that since we wrote our Proofs. And everyone laughed and nodded because they knew it too, including Toan and me sitting with his wide hand squeezing mine. We were the perfect pair.

Our fathers grew up together in the same row of houses. They studied together and wrote their Proofs on the same day. Toan and I would play nearby while they sat and challenged each other at synced math games on screens at our ancient wooden table or sipped tea in the matching orthochairs Uncle G and Aunt Sara had in their living room.

"Gauss, you must be getting old. You don't remember your Proofs score, or mine."

"I remember them very well. Don't lie in front of your daughter, Nim. Your score was well beneath mine!"

"No, mine was higher. You were lucky to have scored in Second Stat at all; I was very nearly in First Stat."

"Is that so? Then how did you end up appointed at such a dismal employment position?"

"What the—" and here my mother, or Toan's, would interrupt before their slurs became cluttered with profanity.

They'd laugh and wink at Toan and me watching nearby. We never figured out who was telling the truth. If our mothers knew, they kept their secret safe.

By the stories they told, everything was a competition between our fathers. Even their height — Uncle G was proud of the inch he'd ultimately gained over my father. They were both appointed to good jobs. My father worked for the Financial Department as an actuary managing investment risks. He was very important. Uncle G claimed to be more essential, managing interest accounts for the bank. He would sometimes take Toan and me into his office, when he had a quick task to complete or an errand to run. It was high above the city on the 127th floor. Toan and I would stand with our toes and noses pressed against the cool window so that the glass itself fell from our vision, and we felt we were standing in the sky. The blue and green shining high rises around us reached up past the old brown stone buildings at the waterfront and dwarfed the archaic still clock on the hill. The grass on the hill surrounded the clock in the same deep green that dotted the streets at measured intervals. We could see the clear hover tunnel cut through the city from north to south, and if we were lucky enough to be watching at just the right moment, we'd see the strip of red flash through. Black patrol levisoars hovered between buildings, flown by Protectors watching from the sky. The new sky bridge stretched below us between two green glass cylinders, and we could see people walking between the two buildings.

"Look, Hessa!" Toan said, his finger bent back by the smooth surface. "There in the clouds. That one looks like a horse, don't you think?"

Before I could find the cloud he was pointing out, Uncle G made a raspy coughing sound and stepped up behind us. I felt a heavy hand on my shoulder and saw one land on Toan's as well. "You mustn't waste your time. Time is valuable, and to waste it is theft. You are Quantifiers. Let's count the windows, eh, littles? Do you think you can count that high?"

Count the windows? That seemed as impossible as counting stars at night. And what made *one* window? The buildings linked by the sky bridge were all glass; were they each one big window? I could hear Toan whispering numbers beside me, so I started counting too. I got to 314 before Uncle G found what he was looking for and said it was time to go.

By the time we reached our higher grades, Toan and I were inseparable. We were a good balance. Toan kept me straight and focused; I made him laugh.

Our friends knew us as an indivisible unit. Once, I met some friends at the Central Database for a study meeting. As I approached the table, Keene smiled at me and looked over my shoulder. Her eyes searched and her face grew a frown. My stomach twisted, fearing there was a threat right behind me. Had the CDB librarian seen me peek at the paintings someone had left open from their search? I felt cold, and my heart started to race. I dreaded to but forced myself to turn and scan the wide open room — the glass wall separating us from outside, the sliding doors that had shut behind me. Nothing. "What? What is it?" My voice cracked.

"Where's Toan?" Keene whispered. She was genuinely concerned.

16

"Oh, home." I exhaled relief. "He had to finish the week assignment before studying for the test." Keene's frown turned to me. "What?" I asked again.

"How'd you find your way here without him?"

"Oh, shut up," I groaned as she laughed, but I didn't have much else to say in my defense. It was true; we were never apart, and I had missed holding his hand walking to the CDB alone.

The summer we were sixteen, we shared an apprenticeship as statisticians for the local baseball team. One night we were leaving the office and took a short cut through the field. The sky was dark, but the stadium lights were still on, lighting up the field as if it were daytime. I found a wayward ball lying on the plastic grass beside the painted white line. In the time it took me to investigate and pick up the ball, Toan's long-legged strides had taken him several meters away. "Hey, Toan! Wait up! Let's play catch." My voice echoed in the wide space.

He turned back to look at me but shook his head. "I'm a Quantifier, not an Athletic. I can't throw."

"How do you know you can't? Have you tried? You're not a Quantifier *yet*. Maybe you have secret Athletic skills buried in your Lineage."

Toan's lips whitened in a pressed frown, like they always did when my joke missed its mark. "Hessa, you shouldn't talk like that. Someone might hear you."

"So? What if they do?"

"They could terminate your employment, for starters. Fine you for wasting time or even charge you with fraudulent impersonation."

"Yeah, right." I shrugged in feigned indifference that hid the shudder his warning caused. He was right, of course, and that was the least they could do. But there was no one in the field. "One throw, you catch it. I wanna see if I can do it."

"Hessa, really let's go."

"Oh, c'mon, Toan, don't be so serious. There's no one here. Go back a bit, I'll throw it and you catch it. How hard can it be?"

His stare was heavy and lasted a bit longer than was comfortable, but he humored me by putting his hands up near his

17

chest. I smiled at him, glanced around once more to make sure we were still alone and pulled my arm back the way I had seen the Athletics on the baseball team do it. With an awkward half step, I swung my arm forward. The ball crashed to the ground a meter in front of me and bounced well short of Toan's half-assed target. I laughed and rubbed my shoulder. It burned from the unfamiliar pull. Then he laughed too.

"See? You're a Quantifier too. Admit it, I'm stuck with you." He waited for me to catch up and slipped his hand around mine, pulling me close and stealing a kiss.

"And I'm stuck with you," I whispered and kissed him back.

So I don't remember a me without Toan.

Jelu

Gallie – Did you ever consider writing Proofs for another certification?

Hessa – My parents are Quantifiers.

Gallie – I'm not asking about your parents, Hessa. Did you ever consider seeking certification in another Proficiency Class?

Hessa – No, of course not.

Gallie – And why not?

Finch – I protest the nature of these questions. The answers are general knowledge; children of certified Quantifiers write Quantifier Proofs.

Gallie – Indeed. I am endeavoring to be thorough.

Finch – I request the court that you move on, Counsel Gallie. There is no discordance with this information.

Hessa – My parents are Quantifiers. I am meant to be a Quantifier.

Finch – I implore you, Ms. Black, to refrain from answering such questions.

Hessa – I have nothing to hide.

Gallie – Our participation in this trial suggests otherwise, Ms. Black.

Finch – Again, your opinion is not pertinent, Counsel Gallie.

Gallie – How did you score on your Proofs?

Hessa – I was in the Second Stat.

Gallie – Congratulations. And Toan's score?

Hessa – First Stat.

Gallie – Indeed. That is quite an accomplishment for both of you. Your parents must have been very proud.

```
Finch - Counsel Gallie.
Hessa - I guess so.
```

I thought the anticipation of writing the Proofs was difficult, but it was nothing in comparison with the wait for our results. I spent weeks reviewing my class work, re-memorizing the concepts and figures, equations and theories and approaches. My parents expected high marks, but my intrinsic pressure to succeed was greater. The Proofs were the passage to my future, to my job, our home and the family we wanted. To earn housing, we had to certify in the top three stats, and only the highest skilled personnel were allowed to apply for Lineage Progression. We needed to score within the top two stats to be approved to have children without genetic improvement. Genetic improvement cost thousands of dollars and took years of applications and processes. We both wanted children, Toan even more so than me. I was more worried about failing Toan than letting my parents down; he had so much more to lose. I knew it was shameful for parents whose children scored low on their Proofs, worse yet for the ones who failed the Proofs altogether. At stake was our future: matching, meaningful jobs and housing allotments. Toan's dream of being a father. I couldn't lose that for him.

No. In comparison, the short wait from when we finished writing to when the scores were reported was terribly worse than the weeks of study leading up to the Proofs, because there was nothing more I could do.

I finished first and arrived at the old oak where we had agreed to meet to find myself alone. That made me nervous. The oak stood in the middle of what used to be a large field in the middle of campus. Years ago, when students of all certifications studied there, they used the space for the Athletics. The front office walls displayed framed pictures through the years of the school campus as taller glass buildings were built beside the old squat brick ones creeping closer to the tree, stealing grassy area for more space to study. Now the tree was surrounded by a quad that would be too small even to land a levisoar in, probably only five meters square, and an octagonal iron bench with a plaque that celebrated the age and success of the Quantifier school.

Too nervous to sit, I stood by the tree and ran my finger along the scratched groves. Long ago, someone had scraped away the top layers of the bark, leaving weakly shaped letters behind. One was a 'T', I could tell from the straight horizontal and vertical lines, even though the vertical line did not meet the horizontal one right in the middle as it should. The other was too careless for me to decipher. A 'B' or an 'R', maybe? Even a 'P' was a possibility, if that short lower curling stroke was inadvertent or not part of the letter at all. I wondered why someone would mark on a tree. The letters made no words and carried no meaning.

I soothed myself by stroking the smoothened letter with my finger, trying to keep my doubts in check. How could I have finished the test ahead of Toan, who always had all the answers locked away? Had I missed a question? A screen? Had the computer somehow provided less than the full test? My throat was dry, making it hard to swallow. Tears pooled in my eyes that pricked and stung as I blinked them back. One snuck out, unbidden, and I tasted the salt as it slipped between my lips before I brushed the trail away. I rubbed my palms on my face savagely so the hurt on my skin was worse than the cramping in my stomach.

By the time Toan sauntered toward me down the paved lane between the senior and junior buildings, I had forgotten my earlier confidence and was convinced I had failed. His smile was long and poised as he approached, but it faltered the closer he got.

He stopped close enough that his familiar scent eased me a bit. I breathed it in, deeply, trying to slow my heart. "Hessa? What's wrong?" He put his hands on my arms and squeezed just a bit, searching my eyes. I felt instantly better, if only marginally. It wasn't close enough. I stood on my toes to wrap my arms around his neck, clamping tightly until he slipped his arms around my back and patted me like a frightened child. "What is it?" he whispered between kisses near my ear.

"I ... I don't think I passed. I failed, I'm sure. I was done too quickly. You never take longer than me. Maybe I missed part of it?"

Toan pushed me back and held my face in his hands. He smiled and shook his head, and then he kissed me. My panicked breaths grew slower and he pulled back, slipping his arms around my waist. "Don't be silly, Hess, you can't miss part of it. The program wouldn't have let you finish. I'm sure you did fine. I checked over all of my answers. Did you?"

I finally smiled up at him. "No. You know I can't, it makes me too nervous and I start doubting my answers. I didn't check any of it."

"And you're always right the first time."

"Not always."

"Okay. Usually, then." I shrugged in capitulation and nodded reluctantly. "See? You did fine, I'm sure of it." Toan pulled me close for a hug. I sagged against his chest and breathed him in, relaxing just a bit more. His T-shirt was soft and warm against my cheek, his heart bounced against his ribs with a reassuring rhythm. If he said it would be okay, maybe...

"Well, I'm glad one of us is sure," I mumbled into his shirt. I took another deep breath of his familiar smell — a hint of sweat covered by cotton and the soap I'd sniffed once in the washroom at his house. I wished I could capture it in a scenter to keep it near me, to calm me whenever I was stressed.

"Where do you want to go now? I'm sure we have some time to wait until the scores are released. Are you hungry?"

"No. I could throw up, really. But you are, aren't you?" I knew Toan could eat any time; I never understood how he stayed so lean. He was vigilant about his compulsory runs even then, but his appetite was insatiable. I felt him nod his head against the top of mine so I stepped back out of his arms and took his hand. "Let's go down to the Old Coffee Shop. You can find something to snack on there."

His warm hand around my cold one kept my panic in check. We walked in silence through campus and the few blocks past the row of stone houses to the corner eatery frequented by our peers. Through the window I could see it was crowded with fellow students who must have had the same thought as us: to find a place to hunker down and wait out the posting of the Proof results. It was a period establishment where they tried to recreate the atmosphere of coffee shops from two hundred years ago. They played music created by oddouts, before people were genetically delineated. Maybe they weren't oddouts then, if there weren't any Proficiency classes. The furniture was all wooden and the tables were just tables, with no embedded screens. The coffee synths were covered by facades that looked like old time machines. If you wanted to pay more and wait longer, the staff could make coffee out of one ancient coffee maker. Toan tried it once and said it wasn't worth the wait, at least thirty seconds. A waste of time, really.

The door slid open as we approached, and we stepped into cooler air that was filled with the warm aroma of roasting coffee. Someone had left the scenters on too high, and my stomach churned a little. I followed Toan as he wove through the high tables and chairs to an empty table at the back of the room. A few of our friends waved as we passed, but the mood was muted and somber, smothered by the importance of the Proofs.

The top ten percent of students would score in the First Stat, the ultimate achievement that opened all doors, not just Proficiency Classification. First Stat academics were appointed to careers in important and classified fields. I had been aiming for Second Stat; I'd be guaranteed a good job, maybe with the government or teaching, and still be approved for Lineage Progression through natural genetics. If I failed that goal and ended up in Third Stat, I'd be placed in a professional job but would only be able to apply for Procreation Permits if Toan scored in First Stat. And only then through genetic improvement assistance.

If I scored lower than Third Stat … I swallowed the thick slime that rose at the thought.

The bottom sixty-nine percent of students became Band oddouts. Band oddouts found their own jobs, usually menial work. They had to finance their own housing, health care, grocery rations and utilities on their minimal jobs. They could only match with another oddout in an unofficial ritual and could not apply for Procreation Permits. Unpermitted children were identified as oddouts and given minimal life-skills education. Band oddouts were ostracized even by the Chosen oddouts.

There was a time that oddouts were invited to write Proofs, but now that Lineage students were so much stronger, the government decided it was a waste of resources to test students destined to fail. Tough jobs, little money, not enough food, no education, no housing allotment... No one wanted to fall below Third Stat.

Toan brought me a tea, but I couldn't drink it. My stomach churned too much. Our futures were written; we were just waiting to learn the results. I knew Toan would score high — he was always one of the strongest students in our classes. I had been too, but I couldn't shake the growing doubts. If I scored lower than Second Stat, maybe Toan wouldn't want me. Maybe he'd want his children more. And if I fell into oddout status, we couldn't be matched. That would make it easier for him to choose. My parents' Lineage would be truncated, and all their investment in my future — the private schooling, the hours of studying, the tutors and counselors — would be for nothing. Right then, everything rested on the Proofs.

I only felt worse as the time crawled by. The Proof scores were posted an hour after the last student finished his or her test, but no one knew when that would be. One year they waited twenty-three hours. After that year the government instituted an eight-hour limit. They reasoned anyone who took longer than eight hours to complete the Proofs wasn't skilled enough to be certified anyway. I watched Toan sip his coffee and chat with the people around us. He was serious and subdued, but his face was relaxed and he smiled brightly when he caught me looking. He squeezed my hand. Every few minutes his laugh startled me out of my stewing, but I couldn't follow the conversation. All of my concentration was focused on keeping my heart rate level, my stomach in place and the tears from my eyes. I studied the whirlpool that followed the turning spoon in my tea and kept myself in check.

Toan's arm draped over my shoulder, and I looked up and forced a failing smile. "You did fine," he whispered, his breath hot in my ear. I nodded, unconvinced. "You should drink that, it'll help." He tipped his head toward my tea, but my stomach jumped at the thought. I nodded again and raised the warm mug to my lips, pretending to take a sip. He flashed me his 'I win' smile and turned back to his friend. I went back to my stirring.

In the end we only waited a little less than four hours, though it felt like a lifetime. With a deafening reverberation, everyone's communicators buzzed in unison. I jumped in my seat, and Toan laughed at me. He turned over his wrist and pressed his thumb to the face of his wristcomm. I couldn't see it from my angle but could read his face as his eyes scanned the screen and his smile grew wider. I knew that look.

"Well?" I asked anyway.

"First Stat!"

For a moment my anxiety was extinguished by excitement for him. "Toan! That's incredible!" I stood from my stool and threw my arms around him, kissing his smile so that my lips met his smooth teeth.

"Yeah, unless you scored oddout and we can't be matched," he said through his smile against my lips. I stepped back. I felt my face fall slack and my head spin. He must have seen it. "Hessa! I'm joking! Check your score. I know you did great too." He grabbed my wrist, but I pulled back and held it against my chest.

"That's not funny, Toan."

He reached down to peck my frown. "No, it's not funny at all. I'm sorry. Check your score." And when I didn't move, "I mean it! I'm sorry. Check it."

But I couldn't. The flashing from my wristcomm glinted in the corner of my eye against my chest, pulsating slower than my heart. I couldn't turn my wrist over and read my future. "I can't. You tell me." I didn't move.

Toan rolled his eyes and shook his head at me, but his smile lingered. He took my hand slowly and brought my knuckles to his lips before turning my wrist over to see the communicator screen. He bypassed my thumb ID with my pass code. Of course he knew it; he knew everything about me. Again his eyes flickered and his smile grew. He turned my wrist to face me so I could see the blue screen and red letters:

Hessa Black, 94 percent, Second Stat Quantifier.

The room spun, and I blew out the breath I didn't realize I

had been holding. The heat of the coffee smell became stifling, and I needed some air. I looked from the screen to Toan's grinning face. "Told you so," he laughed.

"You're always right." The sarcasm I meant didn't make it to my voice.

He leaned toward me and kissed me, then whispered close to my ear, "We can be matched! We'll get good jobs and find a place of our own. Hessa, it's all coming together!" I could feel myself being swept up in his excitement. His enthusiasm filled me as my anxiety slipped away. I kissed him, long and deep, and when I pulled back he smiled with his eyes half closed.

Around us the mood fractured as our peers learned their fates. Celebratory shouts pierced through moans and sobs, faces ranged from white through pink to red in shock, excitement, anger, embarrassment. When a fight broke out between a muscled boy and his wispy friend close enough to knock over the table and two chairs beside us, Toan grasped my hand tightly and said, "It's time to go." We pushed against our peers who were trying to see the fight until the current of those who, like us, would rather avoid the chaos swept us up and spilled out onto the street just before the Protectors stormed in.

The day had grown dark while we waited in the café, and the glow of motion streetlights spread away from us as students scattered toward separate destinations.

"I'm surprised they didn't call," I said as we walked to the hover station. My parents and his mother would know the results were in; the announcement would have been made on their central panel.

"Some news is better in person," he replied.

The street was closed to cars for the safety of pedestrians and bikes. It was hard to believe that everyone used to drive everywhere. Licenses were limited to professionals who needed to drive: Medics, Protectors, people who needed to move quickly. I remember telling my mother I'd have one when I was grown up, and she laughed and said "Quantifiers do not need cars." But that was before I'd driven in one. Now I've been in two, I don't want one anymore.

The hover station was only a few blocks' walk. Students

waited quietly on the platform, the lights from the floor lighting up the angles of their faces; chin, nose, over their eyes. I tried to read their faces with glances short enough to be polite. Some were easy, thrilled or devastated, but most were stony or hidden. I gave up and watched the central panel instead, even though I couldn't hear what the faces were saying. No one in the station talked. The wind blew through the tunnel, whistling hollow notes. When the hover arrived, we were lucky enough to find a paired bench in a corner and huddled. I smiled while Toan chattered about all of things we had to do next: apply for a Matching Permit, housing allotment, professional placement. He must have noticed my smile slip to painted because he squeezed my hand and said, "It's overwhelming, isn't it?" I nodded and leaned against his shoulder, safe in his understanding.

The walk to my home was too short. The streetlights flashed on ahead of us and off behind us, shifting our shadows around under our feet. I wish I could reach back and grab onto the feeling I had that night. The air was cool and fresh and open, and it felt like anything was possible. *Everything* was possible. Our life together was finally secure, safe, determined. We didn't talk as we walked, but every so often I'd look up at Toan and he'd smile down at me, and I knew, because I knew him, that he felt the same way. I was disappointed when our walk ended halfway down the row of identically faced houses. Only familiarity and habit let us know which flight of steps to take without looking at the number lit under the window. I turned to go up, but Toan pulled me back by my hand and kissed me. Embarrassed, I scanned the windows to see if our parents were watching, but they were all darkened, so I couldn't tell.

"What if they see?"

"What if they do?" He was right, so I kissed him. He was always right. We stalled on the steps, kissing and whispering plans until our wristcomms buzzed simultaneously with the same text message: *Well?*

We found my parents and his mother waiting in our gray living room. My father lounged in his orthochair, seemingly interacting with a show on the central panel. His fingers fluttered over the touchpads on the arms of the chair, his eyes focused a

little too intensely on the central panel. Our mothers sat facing
each other, playing a game of Roundalls. Usually they played
with such intensity, they would be locked in their own world,
the screen flashing on the low table projecting shifting holo-
grams as their strategies played out. But when we entered, all
three heads turned to us with a synchronization that betrayed
their ruse. My father didn't attempt to conceal his impatience; he
folded his lanky frame forward and stretched it to standing,
flicking off the central panel with a swipe of one hand and
smoothing his thinning hair with the other as he demanded,
"Well?"

Toan's grin was wide, reminiscent of his childhood squint.
"First and Second Stat!"

Our mothers rushed to hug us, their faces split with smiles
as they squealed acclamations like, "Oh, that's wonderful!" and
"I knew it!" and "I am so proud!" I wasn't sure I saw my mother
brush her fingers across her eyes until I felt her cheek wet
against mine when she squeezed me tightly.

Over my mother's shoulder I could see my father rooted, his
face pinched with his black eyebrows pulled down and in, drawing a darkness into my excitement. "Who was First?"

"Oh, Nim! What does it matter?" My mother broke her hug
from me to step back and swat my father's upper arm, across
the steely gray band he wore, even in the house. "They scored
well enough to be certified, to be matched *and* to qualify for Lineage Progression with a Procreation Permit!" She smoothed
down the dark flyaway strands around her face and tucked them
behind her ears.

Toan laughed aloud at that, but his eyes were warm on me.
"That's two years away, Aunt Sarah." His gaze lingered; I knew
he was happy about that too, in spite of his attempt at mollifica-
tion.

"Who was First?"

I turned from Toan to face my father, petrified in his demand of a response. His hair stood angularly, defying his habitual
leveling. His eyes were amber, so much like mine that it was unsettling when I imparted disappointment. "Toan achieved First
Stat, Poppa, I only scored ninety-four percent."

He nodded once at me, his eyes hooded with disappointment, reminding me of when he caught me wasting my time using my graphing markers to draw a picture of a cat instead of making charts, as they were intended. The words he had hissed echoed in my head: *'You ungrateful and selfish, girl, don't you dare waste what you've been given'*. I was relieved that he turned now to smile at Toan. He did not see me blinking furiously to keep the tears in. "Gauss would have been very proud of you, son." His voice cracked just a little when he spoke Uncle G's name, as it always seemed to do.

Toan's smile faltered as he glanced from my father to me and back. "Thank you, Uncle. I hope so."

The silence only lasted a moment, but it fell thick and warm and suffocating in my mother's spartan living room. Toan stepped closer and took my hand, giving it a squeeze and dissipating the pressure surrounding me. "Let's eat, then?"

I forced a laugh that was tight and sharp. "You just ate, Toan!"

"I want to celebrate. Celebrating makes me hungry."

Our mothers laughed at him and twittered around us, but I didn't hear their words. I chanced a glance at my father. He was watching me, and when caught, he winced and looked away.

4

Ceithir

Gallie –You have been detained by Social Authority
for the past week, is that correct, Ms. Black?

Hessa – (inaudible)

Gallie –Louder, Hessa, the court must hear your
answer.

Hessa –Eight days. I've been detained eight
days.

Gallie –My error. What was the status of your
lifestyle before your detainment?

Hessa –I don't understand the question.

Gallie –You said you chose your match. You had
a good professional appointment and you were allo-
cated housing in a preferred neighborhood, correct?

Hessa –Yeah, I guess.

Gallie –You sound uncertain. Were you or were
you not happy with your circumstances?

Finch –Counsel Gallie, are you arguing with the
accused?

Gallie –I am asking if she was happy with her
choices before being detained a week   excuse me,
eight days ago.

Finch –Ms. Black, were you happy?

Hessa –Yes, I   we were happy   before.

Within two weeks we were matched at the Judicial office. We
spent the three days and nights of our Matching recess holed up
in the hotel room, learning about our new relationship. I was
shy, Toan was gentle. We spent hours curled together, whispering about the plans that were becoming reality. It seems so long
ago now — a different lifetime, those first weeks when I knew

30

everything was as it should be. Most of all, I remember feeling safe.

Once we were matched, we applied for a housing allotment and spent a day touring through the three choices we were offered. On the hover, we traveled out of the city past the old neighborhoods where houses had irregular, rolling shapes like stout brick knolls. When government home allotment replaced private sales, they mandated the smallest footprint possible was necessary to build enough for everyone. As the city grew outward, new government homes grew thinner and taller. Toan's First Stat classification allowed us a private home instead of an apartment in the high rises. I was happy we'd have our space.

The first option was worn and beaten. I felt my adrenaline-paced heart slow as we explored it, a sinking feeling in my chest. There was nothing wrong or broken, just a chip in the siding in one place, paths worn in the floors, colors faded on the walls. With our classification and our match, our new life was new and exciting, but the house felt used.

"The next one will be better," Toan said, reading my mind as usual.

We followed directions on my wristcomm from the hover station to the second address. "Here." I pointed to the house with the 1717 lit on the address sign under the window. It was five stories, stacked high and thin and sandwiched between identical homes, 1719 and 1715, only different by the colored doors. Ours was blue, which may have won me over right then.

Toan led me up the walk between the small patches of synthetic grass. No maintenance. He put his hand against the palm panel, and when the house system identified him, the door slid open. He smiled back at me and offered his hand. I took it.

We went through the entry into a small kitchen to the side; the walls shimmered with new color-shifting paint. All of the appliances were new, heating and freezing systems, food synth and incinerator. I glanced my fingers along the counter's black edge, cool and smooth. I opened the incinerator door, and heat swept up into my face on a belch of air. The same gust that would later disintegrate all traces of the truth.

"Hessa! Up here!" Toan's voice carried from an upper floor.

31

The stairs led up out of the entryway, opposite to the kitchen's entrance. I went up slowly, trying to sense if they felt like mine, if it felt like home. Toan was standing in the middle of the empty media room. The walls were dark gray. The large central panel screen on the wall was on but idle, showing an image of liquefied clocks and a horse's corpse.

"Ugh," I groaned before I could stop myself.

Toan's smile slipped and his shoulders fell. "You don't like it?"

"No, no! The room's great!" I rushed. "But what is *that*?" I pointed to the wall where the picture of the melted clocks had slid away leaving a two-sided picture in its place. One half had a bulbous figure, the other a hand holding an egg between the thumb and first two fingers.

Toan laughed. "We'll change that," he said with a shrug. "Look, there's enough room for both of the chairs your parents gave us." And I could almost see the shiny black polyleather furniture filling the two corners between his outstretched hands.

"Let's go upstairs." I turned and climbed up another flight, knowing he'd follow. The stairs ended in a hallway that split the floor in half. Two closed doors, one at either end, at either side, of the hall. "Offices," I said, excited. "But why aren't the doors facing each other?" I didn't know it then, but I would become grateful for the time that hallway gave me between his door and mine. Toan stopped to look in each room, but I kept going up the stairs. The next floor had a small landing with a closed door. I went in and discovered the first master bedroom. A small room with more shifting paint, it had a closet on one wall and a bathroom through the door on the other. I backed out and climbed to the top floor that matched the fourth in layout. The bedroom was blue when I entered and darkened to purple. I stopped and stared out of the window. Over the tops of the other roofs, I could see the ocean — just barely, but it was there. The sunlight glanced, shining, off the water as it met the horizon.

Toan found me there, watching the light bounce in the distance. He slipped his arms around me and kissed my shoulder. "Do you like this one?"

I nodded. My heart was fast, the smile stretched across my face uncontrollably. "Which room do you want?"

"We could share one... Dad told me once that matched couples used to share a bedroom." He squeezed me against him as he said it, and I turned around in his arms with a nervous laugh.

"Yeah, but how often did those matches last back then? No wonder, if no one had their own space." I don't know if I really saw his face shift in disappointment then, or if my memory has added the cloudy eyes and slight downturn of his lips with all that we've been through. "We could share some nights."

"Yeah?" He smiled and kissed me, then mumbled against my lips, "What about the first night?"

I laughed. "It's a plan."

"Well then, you can have the one with the view," he said softly, standing beside me and looking out the window too. "I'll take the one with less steps to climb." And while there were still documents to sign, to me, that's when the house became our home.

At the end of our Matching recess, we were assigned our professional appointments. I was given my first choice of jobs, teaching the secondary students calculus, combinatorics, dynamical systems and algorithms. It was enough variety to stay interesting, enough consistency to build confidence. It was a subordinate program servicing Third Stat Lineage families, so it was a challenge to work with them to maintain or promote their classification.

As First Stat, Toan continued studying towards professorship, so he didn't waste his high aptitude by limiting himself to lower learning. He was assigned a mentor who, by chance or design (we'd never know), was a classmate and friend of our fathers.

"Gauss would be happy." My father nodded when Toan told him the news. "He was always top of our classes, and I've heard that his work is very important."

I wasn't sure what he meant by that. Professors' research was classified by the government, of course. I was sure the details of his work placement was the first secret Toan kept from

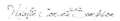

me. He said he hated not being able to talk to me about it, but it didn't seem that hard for him to do. I tried not to let it bother me, but it was unnerving that Toan knew something that he couldn't, and wouldn't, share with me. Maybe I was more disconcerted that he was so good at keeping it a secret.

Both of our jobs were in the Municipal Education Department. I had seen the new building from the hover but hadn't realized how big and intimidating it was up close. The building was designed through collaboration of an architectural Creator and a Quantifier who specialized in Ford circles: two adjacent spheres, one that housed the research department and the other the public school with spheres in decreasing sizes nestled between them as meeting rooms and offices. The buildings were surrounded by three concentric rings of generated trees. The trees were genetically designed to stop growing at predetermined size, with perfectly spherical crowns of leaves that never needed to be tended and artificial spring aromas seeping from the scenters.

We fell into a comfortable pattern in our own new home and new life. Toan liked to choose and heat our meals, so I cleared our dishes into the incinerator and wiped up the kitchen after supper. He gathered our clothes for cleaning, I retrieved them from cleaner and hung them back in our closets. He took my communicator when I forgot to put it on the windowsill to charge. I pointed out when he forgot to report his compulsory arts hours.

Each day we would get up and do our compulsory run together before breakfast. We couldn't talk; our quickened breath was devoted to filling our lungs and feeding our muscles. Each evening before bed we'd complete our mandatory arts practice together, watching a play or reading silently curled up in his bed or mine. I enjoyed the time of quiet companionship, counting the trees to measure out our distance or laughing at the same joke from the screen.

After breakfast we rode the hover to work. I had always loved the hover. I imagined it must feel the same as being on a boat: the gentle, buoyant bounce and rock you felt when it stopped for passengers in the station, then the sway as it picked up speed until it was moving too fast to feel it moving at all. When I was little and my parents would take me into the city where the stops were so frequent that the forward back sway alternated with the side-to-side bounce without time in between, I would pretend I was on a pirate ship back when pirates stole gold coins to count. I once told my father that if I stole gold coins, I'd find something more fun to do with them than counting, but he told me to stop being silly and went back to his textbook.

We walked from the hover station to the Education Department and parted ways in the round front lobby. He'd tug on my arm just before he let go of my hand, and I knew he wanted a kiss. I always looked around to make sure no one was watching before I glanced over his waiting lips with mine. We would head our own directions — he went left through the body scan into the secured research wing, I turned right to be hit by the cacophony of teenager-filled halls.

I loved my work. The students challenged me with their questions when they tried to understand the truth of the equations. I strove to present the obligatory lessons in a way that kept them interested and engaged. I suspected a few of them could have passed their Proofs and been certified as Quantifiers before their tenth birthday, but most struggled to keep up with the pace of our lessons. Either way, most were as driven in their studies as Toan and I had been in ours. I could see Toan and I in the two who sat in the back corner of the room, huddled with our heads touching and whispering over a problem. I was proud of my students' success rate; my assessment measure was the highest in our district that first year. Forty-two percent of my students placed in the top thirty percent of the district; three of those were in the top ten percentile. Any good Quantifier knows that one year is hardly a reliable sample for a trend, but I was proud of them. This year I was determined to improve on those numbers, but I'll never know.

I would take my lunch in the staff room, a wide white room with no windows full of fabristone tables where the other teachers assembled as their schedules allowed. Sometimes Toan would join me, though with increasing frequency he spent his break time discussing his secret research in the restricted area.

The divides of Lineage reached into our break room: Quantifiers sat with Quantifiers, Protectors with Protectors, and so on. There was an occasional debate between Preservers and Deciders about which was more important for our future, the past or the present, and of course everyone had something to say when the Athletics brought up our district teams. But most discussions were trapped to each round blue table where we clustered to compare notes on the day.

At the end of the work day I'd wait for Toan in the common lobby so we could take the hover back home together. He would come rushing through the security doors long after the sunlight had left the curved glass ceiling, closing his bag as he went.

"Sorry, Hess, I got caught in a meeting," or "Hessa! I'm sorry I didn't know the time!" or, with a head shake, "I just can't get my head around this one problem." He'd hug me and kiss the top of my head when I relaxed against him, and it wouldn't matter anymore that I had to wait.

With the race to the hover behind us, we'd settle side by side and he'd slip his hand over mine. "Tell me about your day, Hessa." He knew the names all of my students, knew which were promising and which were likely headed nowhere, despite their best efforts. I think he really felt for the ones who would end up as oddouts, even though he didn't know the kids.

"Quan solved a page of problems in three minutes." Or "I don't know how to get Naren to understand." Or, "Will is working so hard, I hope he sees it in his assessment results."

Toan smiled at me. "You'll get through to them. You know how to teach so they learn." His words made my cheeks grow warm.

"Tell me about *your* day," I'd joke.

He'd laugh, but it was more bitter than funny. It bothered me that his classified status meant that he couldn't tell me anything about his work, but I think it bothered him more. He'd shake his head with his jaw clenched. Sometimes he'd say, "I wish I could, Hessa," in a voice that was unfamiliarly soft before he changed the subject to plans for our next day off or to ask what I wanted for supper. His days piled up, one after the other, in an existence he couldn't share and I couldn't understand.

When we got home we would putter about; Toan would prepare our meal from the rations in the freezer, I'd tidy our clutter or start working on my lessons for the next day. Toan liked to make a big deal about dinner. He insisted we eat together at our table. "Good habit to get into for when we have our children," he explained. He'd turn on a candle set to an appetite fragrance and insist I sit while he brought my plate to the table.

"Why do you bother with all this?" I blurted once and regretted it when I saw his face fall.

He shrugged and paused for an uncomfortable moment. I tried to will my words back. "I just want it to be nice, Hess. We work hard all day, and I don't even get to share that with you. I want our time together at home to be happy. I want you to feel special."

"I do! It's very nice," I assured him. He didn't seem convinced, so I kissed him. I think soon after that he programmed a playlist for dinner into the house system.

We applied to have the same day of the week off, but there were employees at the Education Department with higher seniority, so our request was not approved. Toan had Saturday off, and I was given Monday. Once he finished his mentorship, he'd be able to choose his day off, and I couldn't wait. I was lonely when he worked and I was alone. We were starting a life together but had never spent so much time apart. Mondays I'd get up with him to do my compulsory run, but he'd head off to work and I'd stay home. Our grocery ration was delivered on Monday, so I had to wait at home until the delivery oddout arrived. While I waited I'd catch up on work, grading or planning or completing reports. Other times I'd watch the media until my guilt pushed me out of my chair to find something more productive to do. Once the groceries were put away, I would head out to do some shopping or meet my parents for lunch. I liked to be home by the time Toan returned from work. When he smiled at me and asked about my day, my shoulders fell back into their rightful place. I was content again.

5

Gallie – Did you trust Toan?

Hessa – Yes, of course. We trusted each other.

Gallie – How much of your experiences did you communicate with him?

Hessa – I told him everything. I didn't have any reason to keep secrets from Toan.

Gallie – And how much did Toan tell you of his day?

Hessa – He told me what he could.

Gallie – What do you mean by that?

Hessa – His work was classified, so he couldn't tell me about it.

Gallie – Did that inequity cause friction in your match?

Hessa – Why would it? It wasn't his choice.

Gallie – That wasn't my question. Did it bother you that your match kept much of his life secret from you?

Hessa – I didn't like it, but there was nothing we could do.

Gallie – Creating your own secret might be fair retribution for his concealment.

Finch – Again, Counsel Gallie, your judgement is out of line at this time. Please strike that from the record.

One night Toan was sullen on our hover ride home. He kept his eyes tuned to the screen in his lap and didn't once offer to read the parts he found interesting or funny out loud. I wanted in, I wanted to know what he was thinking and feeling and couldn't tell so long as he kept his face averted.

38

"Toan, what's wrong?" I whispered, my voice wavering just a bit.

"You know I can't tell you that!" he snapped without looking up, in a tone I hadn't heard before. I leaned back in my seat, away from him, and turned away, blinking back tears. I heard him sigh, then felt his hand land on my knee. I couldn't help but look back at him. His eyes were irritated before he could blink his restraint back into place. His smile was minute and sad, and it told me without words that he was sorry, but he needed some time alone. I smiled back, trying to reassure him, and turned on my own screen to read the news.

We arrived home and he went through the motions of getting supper ready. To his credit, he tried to reply to my attempts at conversation, but I could tell his mind was stuck in whatever had happened that day. After supper he escaped up to his office while I fulfilled my compulsory art hour watching a show on the central panel. It was all I could do not to follow him up. He seemed so far away on nights like that, and they were happening more frequently. I wanted to know what was bothering him, wanted to know if I could do something to make it better. He had always been the first person I went to with my own struggles, and I hated having the confidentiality of his work between us, blocking me from helping him through whatever was weighing him down.

I must have fallen asleep on the couch because I was startled when the lights came on and he walked into the room. The central panel had reverted to sleep mode, and flashes of colored fish swam through their digital ocean with faint splashes and puffs of salt air from the scenter. Toan held two glasses half filled with viscous blood-red liquid and propped a long, thin bottle under his arm. His eyes were rimmed red and sagging with fatigue. He sat beside me and handed me a glass. I thanked him with a smile and took a sip. Tart, cold, wet — and way too strong — it smelled metallic and burned its path to my stomach.

Toan's swallow was longer and emptied half the glass before he turned to look at me. "I'm sorry I've been difficult tonight," he said, even though he didn't have to.

"You must be really sorry to open our monthly ration this

early." It was only the first week of the month, and he appeared to be serving the strong alcohol neat from the bottle. "Aren't you going to dilute that?"

He shrugged with a small laugh. "No point in drawing it out." He tipped his glass back and gulped another mouthful to finish the glass. "Besides, it was a horrible day." I nodded and waited, feeling guilty even then because I didn't change the subject. I should have. He poured more wine concentrate. I ached to know what could have happened to drive my cautious, conservative partner to drink engineered wine straight and undiluted. "I wish I could tell you. You wouldn't believe what Adam did."

I didn't even know who Adam was, just that he wasn't his mentor. I started listing possibilities in my mind: A supervisor? Another doctorate student? Another professor on the team? Toan glowered at his hands, wrapped around the delicate glass. I remember worrying he might crush the tumbler in his hand if he squeezed any harder.

"I guess what's done is done, and it doesn't matter anymore." He grumbled this without looking up at me and then downed the entire contents of his glass. I tried to breathe silently so as not to remind him I was there. He sighed again and shifted, swaying, to reach the bottle off the table. It was thin, narrow, only a few centimeters in diameter, but it was tall and finished off with a spiral neck at the top. I watched the red liquid roll over through the spiral until it fell free from the bottle into Toan's glass in thick, round drops. He took another mouthful. "I wish I could tell you, Hess, I really do. I mean, who would know that I said anything?"

I knew Toan. I could see his defenses thinning as if he was walking towards me in a haze, creeping closer with each gulp he took. I knew I should try to stop his secrets from seeping out. I didn't want to. "What's so secret, anyway?" I asked, trying to keep my voice casual instead of challenging.

He glanced up at me, suspicious and sharp, but his look shifted to bemusement when I smiled. It caught him off guard. "You're pretty," he slurred with a smile.

"You're drunk." I laughed, and he laughed too.

My shoulders relaxed a bit when he laughed, but my throat was still tight and sore, guilty for prying. I opened my mouth to suggest we put the wine away and go to bed when he blew a resigned huff. I could smell the wine on his breath. "It's weapons, Hessa. That's why I can't tell you."

I sat still and silent, though part of me was screaming to stop him, to stand up, to leave now that he was talking. If anyone knew he told me even that much, he would lose his job, maybe even his classification. The housing, grocery rations. Our match. But I couldn't move.

"I'm in the physics research department, and we're developing equations that will replicate interactions of organic compounds with fabricated systems." I stayed silent, stifling my shock. I couldn't rectify the thought of my gentle Toan working with biological warfare. "The Authority won't tell us why we need them, but I think it's the Chosen oddouts. They have camps outside the city, and they are planning to take down the Authority."

"What? Why?" My whisper startled me.

"I don't know for sure, but some say they think Lineage Selection is unnatural and ungodly and they were chosen by their God to teach everyone else how to live. Crazy, I know, *those religious zealots*." He spat the last words with a vehemence that I'd never heard from him. He shook his head and stopped talking for a moment. Then he took another swallow of wine. I held my breath.

"And Adam, he…" His voice trailed off as he tipped the last of his wine into his mouth. A drop escaped from the corner, and he caught it with his tongue. He stared down into the glass as if the remnant sticky rings encoded his answer.

"What did Adam do?" I whispered.

He kept talking to his empty class. "I guess the Eastern Continental Federation are trying to help the oddouts. They sent agents, and Adam… I don't think he knew what they really were after. He said they were ECF journalists who wanted to learn about our classifications, our education system and social governing. He didn't know … he didn't know."

"What happened?" I gasped, louder than I meant to, and I

41

think my disbelief percolated through his drunken fog.

He glanced up at me, looking like he was surprised to see me sitting there. He grinned then, in a sloppily angry manner; the slice of his mouth cut slowly across his face. "Oh, Hessa, I've said too much. It's ... it's over, anyway." He started to stand but was unbalanced and fell back in the chair threw his glass across the wall where it smashed. "I hate this, Hessa, I hate not telling you. I feel so far away from you most days and I..." His voice caught as if he swallowed a sob and he squeezed his eyes shut.

"Toan, Toan, it's okay. It doesn't matter. I don't need to know anything. We're here together now. That's all that matters." My throat was tight and sore from keeping my own tears in check. I couldn't let him see me fall apart.

His eyes sprung open. He looked at me for a long moment while I waited. "I still hate it. I miss you." His eyes welled and one tear slipped out to slide down his cheek, his anger seeming to have slipped away as well, leaving a pathetic drunken slump back in his chair.

I put down my own glass, still full except for my first sip, and stood up, reaching out to him. "C'mon, Toan, let's get you upstairs."

"You're taking me to bed?" His attempt to be lewd was lost in the slushy inaccuracy of his sounds.

"In a sense," I agreed, taking his hands and pulling him to his feet. I followed him up the stairs toward his room, though I don't know what I would have done if he had fallen back. It's not like I could catch him, but I had to be there behind him, ready just in case. He slumped onto the bed and was probably already asleep when I slipped off his house shoes and pulled the thin blanket up to his shoulders. I couldn't resist brushing my lips against his warmed cheek, and his face twitched to that side as if he was winking at me. Instead of heading to my own room, I crawled over him into the bed and pressed up against his warm back, wrapping my arm around him. He sighed in his sleep.

The next morning I left him sleeping and went up to my own room to get washed and dressed. Toan was at the table when I entered the kitchen. He held his head in his hands, hung over the mug of coffee. When I wished him good morning, he groaned unintelligibly.

"How much did I drink?" he managed to croak when I brought my tea to the table and sat opposite him.

"Um, three fourths of the wine." When he frowned I added, "The wine *concentrate*. Straight."

His eyes widened. "Not diluted?"

"Nope. You said you couldn't be bothered." Toan shook his head and then caught it in his hands and held it still. I raised my mug to hide my grin. "Are you going to be okay to work?"

"Yeah, I have to. I need to go in. I need to be there today." I watched his thoughts flash across his face; his pained eyes grew, still locked glazed on his coffee. "Hessa. What did I say last night?"

"Nothing," I said too quickly in my effort to avoid hesitation.

"But I remember talking."

"You must have been dreaming."

He raised his eyes and studied me, and I felt like he could see right through me, right into me, past the sweat gathering on my skin to my racing heart, to see the reality I was trying to protect. We sat still, our gazes locked, each unwilling to look away first. He scrutinized me. I knew he was looking for a sign that would give away the truth, so I stood still, holding my breath and locking my eyes on his to make sure I didn't give him any such indication.

He blinked first, and I started to breathe. He stood and stepped closer, to brush a kiss on my cheek and slip his words in my ear. I smelled stale alcohol and bitter coffee on his whisper. I held myself still, concentrating so hard on staying unresponsive that the only movement was furious blinking to clear my flooded eyes. He strode away to toss his mug in the incinerator and head upstairs to get dressed for the day, but his words echoed behind him like a prophecy: "You're too good at keeping secrets, Hessa."

6

ye Assát

Gallie – Last month Aubin Wallace was found deceased in the residence he shared with Lindsen Collard. How did you know Mr. Wallace and Ms. Collard?

Hessa – I knew Aubin. I've never heard of the other person.

Gallie – Lindsen Collard. You claim you didn't know her?

Hessa – No.

Finch – This question has been answered.

Gallie – Then how did you know Aubin Wallace?

Hessa – He was a teacher in my wing of the Education Department.

Gallie – A maths teacher?

Hessa – No, a language teacher. He taught writing.

Gallie – So he was not a Quantifier.

Hessa – No.

Gallie – What was his classification?

Finch – The court is well aware of Mr. Wallace's certification. Only a Creator would teach writing. Move on, Counsel Gallie.

Gallie – And when did you first meet Aubin?

Hessa – Almost a year ago.

Gallie – Can you be more specific? What month?

Hessa – In Seven.

Gallie – And where, specifically, did you meet him?

Hessa – In the lounge at the Education Department, back right corner table. He was in the third chair from the door counting clockwise.

Gallie – Sarcasm is not useful here, Ms. Black.

44

What was your impression of Mr. Wallace when you
first met him?

    Hessa — He was friendly.

    Gallie — How often did you see Mr. Wallace?

    Hessa — He was in the lunch room most days.

    Gallie — Did he sit with you?

    Hessa — Sometimes. He liked to talk to everyone.

    Gallie — When you met, did you tell him you were
matched with Mr. Whitley?

    Hessa — Not when we first met. It didn't come
up.

    Gallie — You didn't bring it up. Did he tell you
he was not matched?

    Hessa — No. We talked about teaching. Our match
status wasn't relevant to our conversation.

    Gallie — 'Wasn't relevant'. When did he learn
you are matched with Toan Whitley?

    Hessa — I don't know.

    Gallie — Did you ever tell him?

    Hessa — I don't know how he first learned, but
he knew I was matched to Toan. It wasn't a secret.

    Gallie — If you didn't bother to tell him, how
are you sure he knew?

    Hessa — He met Toan several times.

I stormed toward the staff room the day I met Aubin. I just
couldn't get Jane to understand the sequential orientation when
quantifying divergent assumptions of temporal concepts, and
she seemed to be giving up. I'd spent the past twenty minutes
going over the lessons with her, and I didn't know what else to
do. My head was pounding and my teeth hurt from gripping my
jaw tight. I was hoping Toan would take his lunch with me so I
could ask his opinion. He was particularly good at that equation
set. I touched the palm panel, but the door didn't open. The
panel felt cool, not warmed by power. I pressed my hand against
my thigh and rubbed hard to the point of pain then pressed my
hand against the panel again. Still nothing. I balled my fist until
the nails pressed into the pads and my fingers hurt, and then
punched my thigh instead of the smoky glass door, and the door
slid to the side. He was on the inside, dropping his hand from

the interior panel and smiling at me.

I noticed his eyes first. I'm sure that sounds ridiculous, but it's true. His were the first blue eyes I had ever seen. I know it used to be common for people to have blue eyes a long time ago, but I'd never seen it. The blue was disquieting, somehow open and piercing at the same time, as if the barriers between his mind and mine were less substantial because his eyes were light. And I remember that was a strange thing to think. I stood still and stared at them through the open lounge door, my frustration dripping away to burning embarrassment that he had seen my tantrum.

"Are you coming in?" he asked, startling me out of my gaze. He laughed, and I felt my face grow warmer.

"Um, yeah, thanks." I gathered my senses and brushed past him through the faded lunch smells to escape to the table in the corner, where the Quantifiers typically sat. I tried to swallow my disappointment when he followed me to the table and sat down beside me. The room was large enough, with six or seven round tables to choose from. He didn't have to sit there.

"I'm Aubin. I just started today." He held out his hand, and I shook it, careful to avoid looking him in the eyes. His hand was cool, but his grip was strong.

"Hessa Black."

"Nice to meet you, Hessa Black."

There was a full pause while I felt his eyes on me. I could see in my peripheral vision that he was smiling, and I was sure he was enjoying my agitation while I searched for something to fill the silence. Not blinded by his eyes, I could see the rest of him: light brown hair worn longer than a teacher should, crisp white shirt and dress pants. Being on his right, I couldn't see his armband.

"I didn't know they hired a new maths teacher." It was a stupid thing to say, but all I could think of. I forced myself to look up again, determined not to be foolish about meeting someone with blue eyes. Just eyes. They saw just the same as mine. But the blue startled me again.

He turned and raised his left arm, pointing at his bicep with his right hand: red. Creator. "I wouldn't know, being new myself. I'm a language teacher, mostly writing." His grin remained through his words, and I felt my jaw tightening again. I couldn't decide who I was most angry with, myself for being so nonsensical, him for enjoying it or Jane for putting off my mood to begin with.

"Oh, a language teacher. They sit over there," I heard myself say and swung my hand in the direction of the opposite corner of the gray room, where a few Creator teachers sat huddled together. As soon as the words were out, I wished I could take them back. How rude. My ears were hot. I couldn't believe I had said it aloud.

"I can move…" His smile faltered for the first time.

"No, no, don't be silly." Nice advice. "I just mean the maths teachers sit here, the language teachers sit over there. Usually. There's no *rule* about it. You're welcome to stay."

His smile returned, and when I glanced up, his eyes seemed to glow. "I think I will, if you really don't mind."

"You are free to do what you want, Mr.?"

"Wallace. *Aubin* Wallace. Thank you, Hessa Black."

There was a moment of silence in which I hoped our awkward interaction was over. I turned on my screen and pretended to scan through text. I hoped he'd see how busy I was and leave me alone.

"How long have you worked here?"

I looked up again into his eyes. I wasn't startled that time, but I did feel funny, kind of dizzy and out of breath. Mesmerized? What did that feel like? "I've been here almost a year."

"And what do you teach? Maths, obviously, what level?"

"The first year of the pre-Proof programme. You?"

"Middle year, literary creation. I moved here from Toronto, where I wrote for government circulation, mostly works for the compulsory hour curriculum."

"You were a writer?"

"Still am. It won't leave me alone." He laughed with his whole head, his jaw opened up and back instead of down and his eyes closed just a bit. But I didn't understand the joke. "I, uh, I guess I needed a change, so I requested a transfer out here.

47

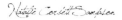

They said this position was the only one available, but I think I'm going to like it."

How could he be a writer and a teacher at the same time? How was he still a writer if he hadn't been placed in that employment? I wasn't sure what to say, so I smiled and nodded to cover my confusion.

"Do you like teaching here?" he asked.

"Yes, I do. The students are smarter than I expected, being a subordinate program. They try very hard."

"You didn't seem to be enjoying the job when you first came in."

I felt heat flash from my chest into my face at his reminder of my stomping and fussing. I stared hard at the screen and shrugged. "Just one of those mornings." Then the words started tumbling out against my better judgment. "I have one student who works really hard, but I just can't get her to understand. I'm worried if I don't get through to her soon she won't do well enough to progress forward towards her Proofs."

The silence was just thick enough for me to lament sharing so much.

"She's first year? It's the beginning of the year, and her Proofs are still three years away. I'm sure you'll both do fine. You must be a good teacher if you already care that much about one student in Seven."

His encouragement and unexpected compliment made me feel strange again; an unfamiliar lurch in my stomach, a tingling in my chest. I glanced around the brightly lit room to find a new topic that had nothing to do with me. "What is that?" I asked, swinging my hand from my tablet to the blue folder he tapped his fingers on. I could see what looked like papers laid unevenly inside, the sharp corners poking out of the folder at different angles, curling up to points.

"This? This is mine. Poetry. I was going to work on it until you came in."

"Is that paper? You don't work on a screen?" It seemed my rational brain had cut itself off from the part in charge of spurting out words. I couldn't stop asking stupid questions.

"I prefer paper when I can find it." His gaze on me was steady.

"Oh. I'm sorry to interrupt your work." I could feel my cheeks burning and tried to build resentment toward him for making me embarrassed again.

"I'm not." His tone was light, and I could hear the laugh that played on his voice. I dared to glance up again, and his blue eyes were watching me. Then I realized I was smiling back. Looking back now … I know I should have stood up and walked out right then. But I didn't. Maybe I already couldn't.

The second time I saw Aubin, he was sitting at the Quantifiers' table in the lunch lounge. I had hoped to escape uncomfortable small talk from the day before, and the sight of him drove an exasperated sigh out of my lungs. But there he sat. He greeted me with a wide smile and a dramatic wave from the table where he sat with two of my Quantifier peers. They looked up at me with expressions that asked if I knew why he was sitting there. I forced a smile back, took a deep breath and walked toward the table.

By the fifth day my face didn't burn when I saw him anymore, and by the next week I realized I didn't dread seeing him at lunch anymore. I walked in on Friday of the second week and was already smiling at the back of his head when he turned to welcome me in.

"Hi, Aubin."

"Hessa, hi, I'm glad to see you. I couldn't remember which day you had off."

It was a statement, not a question. He wasn't asking for the information, but I provided it anyway. "Monday."

"Hey, me too. I usually end up working or writing anyway, but it's nice for a change in location. Cedar Park has tables to work at, have you been there?"

Toan and I ran through that park sometimes, but we hadn't stopped long enough to notice any details. I shook my head.

"You should go. It's beautiful, lots of flowers to count." Somehow Uncle G's voice shimmered in his words. My eyes snapped up to his to see if Aubin was making fun of me. He was smiling, but it was sincere.

49

"I'll have to go check it out."

I started to look forward to our lunches together. Sometimes our colleagues would be there, sometimes it was just us. I don't remember when, maybe sometime the next week, my fellow Quantifiers started sitting at another table. Aubin was often already there when I entered. I told myself it would be rude to leave him sitting alone. However it happened, the routine became that Aubin and I sat together at the corner table while our colleagues came and went from the others, depending on the conversations.

It was three weeks before Aubin met Toan.

"It used to be a library — a real one full of books." Aubin was telling me about a museum he loved in Toronto.

"A building full of *books*? That's it? What a waste of space."

"Only one floor is set up as a library now. It's probably as big as the Athletics gymnasium, with shelves and shelves of books."

"Really?"

"Really. And the smell, Hessa, when you walk in—"

"Ew. I can imagine."

"No, it's not bad at all. It's something else ... dust? Maybe? Paper. Sweet and warm, somehow — if something can smell warm. Soft."

I rolled my eyes. "Doesn't sound very clean to me."

His mouth opened as he started to say something more, but we were distracted by the door sliding open. Toan strode through, smiling as he met my eyes. I smiled back. I wondered why my stomach twisted just then, and I was worried the meat in my sandwich had turned bad.

"Hi, Toan, I wasn't expecting you!" I turned my head up to receive his kiss and then turned to Aubin. "This is my match, Toan."

Aubin stood, and his chair clattered to the floor. He put his hand out toward Toan. "Hi, I'm Aubin Wallace."

Both men turned to look down at me in my chair and seemed expectant for me to say something. I had no idea what they wanted to hear and felt strangely trapped by their height hovering over me. "I'm glad you could join us for lunch," I said, and it seemed to break the spell. Toan smiled and Aubin righted his chair under himself to sit again. Toan stepped around me to sit on my other side.

"I'm really sorry it's been so long, Hess. It's been busy over there. I wish I could come more often."

Aubin's brows raised in question, so I explained, "Toan is studying for professorship. He does research in the restricted wing."

"Impressive," Aubin said. "I'm sure it's very interesting."

"And classified," I explained before Toan had to.

"Yes, I know." Aubin's voice seemed flat.

"It can be interesting." Toan's smile tainted his voice, making it light. "It's a lot of work, though. The deadlines are tough. I usually end up working through my break so I can leave on time." He laughed and looked at me. "Even that doesn't always work, though, does it, Hessa?"

I shook my head in agreement and said, "Pretty much never." I meant it to be a joke, but my tone sounded forced, even to me.

"That's why I've seen you waiting in the lobby," Aubin said, and I nodded.

Toan winced, so I changed the subject. "Aubin is a language teacher. He teaches writing."

"Really?" Toan looked at Aubin over his sandwich, and Aubin nodded. "Writing was something I could never get. Give me numbers and equations any day — it's always the same, just a problem to solve. There are too many words. How do you work without limitations? And why?"

"I feel it," Aubin almost whispered.

I felt myself frowning at him, trying to understand what he meant.

"Wha'?" Toan asked at the end of his laugh with his mouth full.

Aubin shook his head. "Never mind … Creator humor." He pulled himself upright in his chair. "I guess I'm as intrigued as you are. I marvel at you Quantifiers. I've tried to learn some math, but I just don't understand it."

I was confused again. "What do you mean you've tried to learn some math?"

"In Toronto, I used to sit in on my friend's class."

"A Quantifier class?" I imagined Toan's bewildered face mirrored my own. "When? In school?"

Aubin shook his head and worked to swallow the food in his mouth. "Nah, just a few months ago. My friend was a maths teacher for final year, so I asked if I could sit in on his class, and he agreed. But he might as well have been speaking Latin for all I could understand."

"Latin?" Toan asked. I had never seen Toan so perplexed. I might have laughed had I not been so baffled myself.

"What's Latin?" I asked instead.

"Latin is a lost language. No one speaks it anymore. But it is the basis for a lot of our English words, probably even some of your Quantifier terms."

"Huh." Toan's grunt was the most unintelligible thing I'd ever heard him say. I laughed then and he turned to me. "What's so funny?"

"I dunno." I couldn't curtail my amusement, and Aubin's smile had grown. "I think it's that I've never seen you so confused before." There was a moment that my stomach dropped when I worried I embarrassed Toan in front of Aubin, but then he started to laugh himself.

"Well, I guess my head is full of numbers; there's no room for other thoughts."

"There's always room for more," Aubin sobered enough to say, earning a long look from Toan. For a moment they watched each other, and I wondered why I was wringing my fingers around each other.

"You are interesting, Aubin," Toan said, but the laugh had left his voice, leaving it heavy.

"I've been called worse," Aubin replied as Toan collected his garbage for the incinerator.

"I'm sorry to cut this short, but I promised to be back early for a meeting." Toan stood, looking at me. "I'll see you after class, Hessa? We have dinner with your parents tonight, remember?"

"How could I forget?" I joked and stood to kiss him.

"Nice to meet you, Aubin. I'm sure I'll see you again."

"I'm not going anywhere," I remember Aubin said, in just those words. Looking back now, I should have been concerned, but I didn't hear his warning then. When Toan left the room and the door slid closed behind him, Aubin turned to me as I sat down again. "You didn't tell me you were matched."

I was taken aback by the directness of his comment. He wasn't accusative, but his voice was even and pointed, without its usual humor. I was caught staring at him for a moment before I narrowed my eyes and tried to keep my voice level. "You didn't ask."

Aubin returned his attention to his food and shrugged.

His indifference made me feel obligated to say more. "It never came up." He shrugged again, and then I needed a response bigger than his shrugs. "Well, aren't *you* matched?"

"No." He looked up from his lunch and trained his eyes on mine. Icy. I wished I hadn't asked. I forced myself to hold his blue stare as long as I could before it started to blur. I turned away to collect my own garbage. I stood and without looking back at him crossed the room to dump my lunch remnants into the incinerator. I returned to the table to gather my screen, muttered a parting and slunk out of the room, grateful that the palm panel worked on the first swipe.

I stewed the rest of the day. And I had no idea why.

As we rocked on the hover that night, Toan was excited about a new development his team had made. He spoke in circles and with a vagueness that protected his secrets. Without telling me anything, he told me about the enthusiasm his team had shared in their meeting. "Just wait, Hessa. If the right people hear about this we could be documented as the initial founders of the theory. I wish I could tell you. The applications are tremendous. My team may earn first options for any project coming out of the government this year. I couldn't believe it when we got to the end and I saw — well, I can't tell you what I saw, of course, but you'd be impressed, I'm sure." I could see his haunted, drunken eyes from the night he told me about the weapons, but I couldn't question his change of heart then without admitting what I knew. I hoped he was talking about a different project.

"I am impressed, Toan. It sounds very thrilling for you."

"For *us*, Hessa! Who knows where I'll end up, and of course you'd come with me." I smiled and nodded, not sure I wanted to be anywhere else. "Listen to me go on and on. I'm sorry, Hessa, tell me about your day."

With that question, Aubin's glare came unbidden in my mind. I shrugged.

Toan always seemed to read my mind, but I was still startled when he asked, "That character at lunch was an interesting guy. What was his name? Aaron?"

"Aubin."

"Yes, Aubin. Interesting."

"He's friendly. I was thinking we should invite him over sometime — I don't think he has any family or many friends around here."

Toan looked up from his screen at me. "What on earth would we talk about? We don't have anything in common with him. He should find some Creators to spend his time with."

"There's no law against being friends with other classifications, Toan. I like talking to him."

"He does have some different perspectives, doesn't he? Be careful you don't get caught up in any trouble he causes."

"Trouble? He doesn't cause trouble, he's a language teacher."

"Well, I dunno about Toronto, but around here it's unacceptable to waste time on activities that don't contribute. If he had time to take classes, he should have found some that would strengthen his own aptitude, not fool around with things he knows nothing about."

"I'm sure he was just curious, Toan." I bit at my fingernail and hoped the irritation I felt did not come out in my words.

"Then he's not collaborating enough." Toan's logic was infallible. His conviction was usually soothing for me, but just then it made me annoyed. I didn't know how to argue with him. He was right, so I said nothing at all. For a few minutes we sat silent in the hover's swaying hum until he finally reached over and took my hand. "If you want to invite him, that's fine with me. You always want to be everyone's friend. I guess we can talk about Athletics or something." He smiled at me and touched my hair. I smiled back and felt my shoulders fall just a bit. "And speaking of contributing, they've asked me to join the Recreation Board as Quantifier representative. I thought you could join with me?"

The hover slowed as we entered our station. I was relieved that our imminent exit cut short my opportunity to answer as I nodded and said, "I'll think about it."

7

Luiknek

Gallie — What did you discuss with Aubin Wallace?

Hessa — We talked about a lot of things.

Gallie — Can you give us some examples, please?

Hessa — I don't know, just what people usually talk about.

Gallie — But what would a Quantifier have to discuss with a Creator?

Hessa — We talked about our jobs, our students, told stories about growing up.

Gallie — So Mr. Wallace was easy to talk to?

Hessa — I could tell him anything.

Gallie — Anything? That hardly sounds appropriate.

Finch — Opinion, Counsel Gallie. Do you have an objective question?

Gallie — I'll rephrase, of course. Did you discuss topics that were improper?

Hessa — No, of course not.

Gallie — 'Anything' is a wide definition, Hessa. Just what did you discuss?

Finch — You've asked this question.

Gallie — I argue she has yet to answer it specifically.

Finch — Perhaps a more specific objective question will result in a specific answer.

Gallie — Did you discuss topics that would generally be of interest to Quantifiers?

Hessa — I don't know what you mean.

Gallie — Did Mr. Wallace ask you about math or numbers.

Hessa — He asked some questions, yes. He wanted

to understand math concepts.

Gallie – Did you answer his questions and explain the math to him?

Hessa – I tried. He was interested, but he couldn't understand my answers.

Gallie – Because he was a Creator.

Hessa – No, because he did not have the foundational information to understand the concepts. He never studied math.

Gallie – He was a certified Creator, his parents were Creators. He did not have the mind to understand concepts of a Quantifier. Isn't that right?

Hessa – No.

Gallie – No? He wasn't a Creator born of Creator lineage?

Hessa – Yes, but it wasn't because he was a Creator that he didn't understand math. He would have been able to understand the math if he had studied the foundational concepts. He was smart.

Gallie – How can you know that?

Hessa – I knew him. He was smart, smarter than me anyway. He could have understood everything I do, if he had the same education.

Gallie – That's an interesting opinion, Ms. Black, quite contrary to the theory of Aptitude Lineage. So you had some conversations about math with Aubin. Aubin was a writer. Did he discuss writing with you?

Hessa – (silence)

Gallie – Please answer the question, Ms. Black. Did you discuss writing with Aubin Wallace?

Hessa – No.

Gallie – No? Never?

Hessa – No.

Gallie – Well, why not, Hessa?

Hessa – I wasn't interested.

As I approached my classroom the next morning, I could see a figure silhouetted by the light of the wide window at the end of the hall. He was leaning against the wall by the door to my classroom. I could only see his outline, but I knew it was Aubin. I stopped, and the figure turned and waved. Backlit, I couldn't see his face. I didn't know if he was smiling. I forced one foot in front of the other and concentrated on taking regularly sized strides. As I got closer and the light filled his face, I saw a smile twitch on his lips, but it didn't stay there. I realized I was holding my breath.

"Good morning, Hessa."

"Hi, Aubin, you're here early."

"I wanted to speak with you for a moment. Do you have time?"

I didn't. I had final preparations to make for my lesson and had to sort files to be returned to the students. And I was suddenly feeling a bit queasy. I put my palm to the panel, unlocked the door and heard myself say, "Sure, come in."

I strode to my desk to set down my tea and my bag. Aubin slipped more slowly into the room, looking around as someone does when seeing a place for the first time. I followed his look around the stark white walls, where charts on the screen-covered wall exhibited the students' grades and progress towards their Proofs. The Education Department knew that comparison between students was an effective tool to delineate success; those who could would be inspired by the competition and strive to succeed, those who could not would realize their ineptitude in time to avoid unexpected disappointment. I wasn't so sure about it, but who was I to question their research-based methods?

Aubin had said something. "I'm sorry?" I asked.

"This room doesn't look like you."

It was a strange thing to say, and I didn't know what he meant by it. Of course it didn't. How could a room look like a person? "Oh," I finally said. Aubin had made it to my desk and was standing across from me. He was much shorter than Toan, but still a bit taller than me, so when I looked up from my desk I could look into his eyes without tipping my head. He was looking at me but didn't say anything when our eyes met. It was unnerving; my stomach clenched and my breath hurt. I pulled my eyes away to watch my hands flick over the screen on my desk, as if looking for something important. "Aubin, I have to get ready for class."

"Yes, right. Hessa, I wanted to come by to apologize for yesterday."

I wanted to look up but couldn't — I kept my gaze on my hands as I flipped randomly through charts on the screen. "Apologize? For what?"

He moved, and his hand shifted into my line of sight. It covered one fidgeting hand and fell on it, drawing both of my hands still. His hand was warm, and the energy of that heat seeped into my hand like a slow current. My breath caught and I looked up. He let go and the current stopped.

"I wanted to apologize for being so rude yesterday." He was sincere. "It surprised me when Toan came in, and I spoke impulsively. I am sorry."

My head shook before I could stutter the words, "N-no need to apologize, Aubin, really it's nothing." I could feel a slow burn creep up my neck into my cheeks.

He smiled, and I smiled. The light shimmered in his eyes, and I imagined it was a flash of the current I felt in his hand.

"Well then, that's good." He took a step back. "I had better go get ready myself. Have a good morning, and I hope to see you later." Before I could respond he turned on his heel and strode out the door.

I watched him go and then sunk into my desk chair. It felt as if all of the air in the room had left with him. I put my face in my hands and counted my breaths until they came at a regular rhythm again. With a renewed determination to get on with my day, I moved my bag off the desk. That's when I saw the envelope. It was small, maybe ten centimeters square. The yellow front was marked with black ink scroll that I recognized as handwriting but couldn't read; one short word. I slipped open the envelope and removed a stiff, folded card. The outside was unmarked and white, with a woven texture that felt raised to my fingers. The inside was lined with more script, thin and leaned to the right. I couldn't read it, but my eyes were drawn to their movement. Stationary, they leaned and pulled my eyes from left to right, with their tails and wings looping up or dropping down, round in small circles, swung back and forth. I hadn't seen anything like it. I was still staring at the static movement of the letters when my first students startled me back to the action of preparing for class.

At lunch the door slid open to an empty lounge, empty save for Aubin sitting at the table in the corner. I let a sigh slip through my lips as fingers slacked out of fists. He turned when I stepped through and smiled. "Hi."

"Hello." As I walked to the table, I held up the envelope he had left behind. "You forgot this on my desk this morning."

He nodded. "I left that for you."

"Why?"

"I wanted you to read it." He laughed, and I felt my cheeks burn, so I frowned as I sat. "Did you?"

"Did I what?"

He shook his head at me. "Really, Hessa, for a Quantifier of Second Stat you can be quite stupid, can't you?" I glared at him, but he laughed and I couldn't hold onto the insult. "Why didn't you read it?"

I lifted my shoulder and lied. "I didn't know you meant for me to read it, I just thought you dropped it and left it behind." I watched my fingers fidget with the crust of my sandwich to avoid his gaze.

"But it has your — oh." He stopped talking, so I looked up at him. His eyes shifted as I watched him think. "You can't read handwriting, can you?"

"No, why should I? What use is it when a screen is much more efficient?" I turned away in irritation.

"Well, if you could, you could read this note I wrote you, for one."

"What if I don't want to?" Even in my embarrassment and irritation I could remember the flitting lines on the page. Even without knowing what the fluid lines said, the loops and swirls had me transfixed. Decoding the message they conveyed sounded fascinating. I was intrigued, but interest in handwriting wasn't productive for a Quantifier, it was a waste of time to spend looking at a useless ancient tool. I cursed myself inwardly for my weakness and negligent curiosity. Such a waste. I clenched my jaw and focused on opening my lunch wrappings, reeling in my interest, pretending indifference with a dismissive wave.

"Okay, I'll read it to you." He went on as if I hadn't replied, as if I wasn't sitting beside him storming like a petulant, defiant child. "Look, this is your name: H-E-S-S-A."

Against my will, I looked up from my administrations to my lunch. His nail-bitten finger pointed to the short word on the front of the envelope. I shrugged again, and he laughed.

"I'll read the inside:

'*Hessa*' — that's you." I tried but couldn't keep the corners of my mouth from tipping up.

"'*I hope you can accept my apologies. I fear our new friendship is at risk of becoming farpotshket if I stumble in my efforts to make amends.*'

"This last letter is 'A', for Aubin. That's me." He finished with his finger tapping on the isolated triangular mark tipped to the right and drawn with a long right tail. I couldn't help it, I laughed.

"What does farkop —— what was that word?" I leaned in, squinting at the scrawl as if I could discern meaning by looking more closely.

Aubin pointed out one string of letters. "'Farpotshket'. It means making more of a mess of something that is already screwed up by trying to fix it. It's from a lost language."

"Fartopshept?"

"Farpotshket."

"Whatever. Is it Latone?" He laughed again, and I punched his arm.

"Latin. No, it's not Latin. This language was called Yiddish."

"How do you know all those languages?"

"I don't," he said with a slight turn of his head as he folded the card and placed it back in the envelope. "I like studying words that have no translation, no equal, in English. I find words that are a whole thought, a concept wrapped up in one ancient word. It started as a project I shared with a Preserver who was looking at historical cultures. Now that's what I write; I try to write poetry around the lost words I find."

"Why?"

61

"Why what?"

"Why do you write them? Is it for the compulsory arts curriculum?" Aubin's poems sounded more interesting than the book I was currently reading to fill my mandatory art hour each evening.

Aubin sighed, but it sounded content. "No, this is just for me."

I had no idea what he meant by that, but I was entranced in spite of myself. "Where do you find them?"

Aubin smiled just a bit. "Books, mostly. Old ones in the scanned records. And language documents. Sometimes I'll find journals people wrote."

"Journals? Like research publications?"

"No, a personal journal. Someone might write their thoughts or experiences in a book or something."

None of what he said made sense. "Why would they do that?"

Aubin was silent for a moment, and then he shrugged. "Lots of reasons. I do."

His answer seemed too personal, as if it was an admission I shouldn't be privy to. I didn't want to intrude, didn't want to ask more about him. "I didn't know those things still existed," I said.

Aubin's gaze was steady. "There's a lot to find if you look for it." His riddles were daunting and made me feel I was off balance with nothing to hold on to, like the room had tilted just a bit and I was in danger of falling if I didn't concentrate and hold on.

"Tell me another word."

"Cafune..." he said just above a whisper, his smile gone, his look was intense.

"*Cafune.* That's beautiful. What does it mean?"

Before he could answer, the still around us shifted by the sliding of the door and the noisy entrance of three hulking and arguing Athletics teachers. They carried with them the smell of sweat, and my nose wrinkled involuntarily. "Another time." He smiled as he stood and cleared his area. He tossed his garbage in the incinerator and walked out of the open door before it could slide closed.

"Cafune." It played on my lips.

Osiem

Gallie – The Proofs are ranked by percentile. One doesn't need to be a Quantifier to know not everyone can do so well. Was your class competitive?

Finch – What is the relevance of her class's scores?

Gallie – I believe this information is relative to Ms. Black's intentions.

Finch – I don't see how.

Gallie – You will find my questions to be objective, Council Finch. Ms. Black? Was your class competitive?

Hessa – I don't know what you mean.

Gallie – I think you do.

Hessa – Our class had high scores.

Gallie – What was the Second Stat cutoff score in your year?

Hessa – I don't know.

Gallie – Again, I think you do.

Hessa – I scored ninety-four percent.

Gallie – And Toan?

Hessa – He scored ninety-seven.

Gallie – So the cutoff of ninetieth percentile for the First Stat was higher than ninety-four and lower than the ninety-seven percent, and the cutoff of eightieth percentile for Second Stat was lower than ninety-four percent. Am I right?

Hessa – It appears so.

Gallie – That is a competitive score. Did all of your comrades do as well?

Hessa – By definition, at least seventy-nine percent did not.

Gallie – I'm asking specifically about your friends, Ms. Black. How did they do?

Hessa – Some did well, some did not.

Finch – What does this have to do with the matter of the court?

Gallie – Alright, I'll be more specific. How do you know Keene Sourret?

Hessa – She was a friend. We studied together.

Gallie – Did Ms. Sourret perform well in her classes?

Hessa – Yes. She worked hard and received good grades.

Gallie – How did Keene Sourret score on her Proofs?

Hessa – I don't know, scores are confidential.

Gallie – Ms. Black, don't waste our time. Did Keene Sourret obtain classification?

Hessa – No.

Gallie – No what?

Hessa – No. Keene did not obtain classification.

Gallie – But you said she studied well, worked hard. How did she miss classification?

Hessa – Only thirty percent obtain classification. That leaves many who don't. Sometimes working hard is not enough.

Gallie – Is that the explanation for why Keene did not obtain classification?

Hessa – (shrug)

Gallie – Answer aloud, please, Ms. Black. The transcriber cannot hear gestures.

Hessa – I don't know.

Gallie – I think you do. Didn't Keene Sourret disclose to you that she forfeited her Proofs deliberately?

Hessa – (shrug)

Gallie – Aloud, Ms. Black. And the truth, please.

Hessa – I don't remember.

I hadn't expected to see her that afternoon, four days after our

Proofs, but I raced to let her in when the home security announced "Keene Sourette at the front door."

Keene was already smiling and waving when the door slid
open on my command. She was strangely dressed in a skirt and
blouse, her long hair that was usually down around her shoulders tied back tightly in a knot at the top of her neck. She was
carrying her screen clutched to her chest by her left arm. It
might have been her strange outfit, or the way her smile flickered as if she was nervous, but something made my mouth go
dry with her sudden appearance at my home. "Hi, Keene," I
said, but it sounded like a question.

"Hess! Hi! How are you?" The light flashed against her dark
eyes. I was taken aback by her question; every other interaction
I'd had over the past four days had started with *How did you do?*
"Hessa? Everything okay?"

"Yes, of course!" I forced myself to smile, happy to follow
her lead away from the topic of Proofs. "I'm good, Keene,
good. Do you want to come in?" She nodded, and her smile
slipped as she frowned and looked behind her. I looked past her
too, but there was nothing there but the empty street and rows
of plastic turf in front of identical houses.

The door swept closed behind us, pushing a puff of warm
air at my back as I followed Keene down the hall. She had been
there enough times to know where my room was and didn't hes-
itate to climb the stairs and walk the hall until we were in my
room with the door closed. She sat at my desk, her screen laid
across her knees and her hands tied tightly together so that her
knuckles were white. Her jaw clenched, and she bit her lower lip.

"Why didn't you text to tell me you were coming?" I sat on
the bed facing her.

"Yeah, sorry, I didn't want a record of us meeting, in
case…" Her whisper was breathless, hurried. Uncertain.

I squinted, my brows pulling in as I tried to understand. I
shook my head. "A record? In case of what? Keene? What's going on?"

Her eyes shifted just a bit before her forced grin grew. Her
painted lips pressed together. "I look silly, don't I?" I shook my
head, but she rushed on. "I'm looking for a job." She shrugged

as if that explanation was enough.

"Looking for a job?" My voice cracked. I could feel my face tighten, knit in confusion. "What do you mean?"

Keene's face settled into a more sincere smile. It seemed sympathetic. Apologetic. She reached out and her fingertips lit on my lower arm, just a brush as if she was afraid I'd break, or she'd burn. "A job," she repeated with a shrug. "I didn't obtain classification. I. Didn't. Stat." She recited that last sentence as if trying to practice a memorized line, or to convince herself.

I don't know what I expected as her answer, but that wasn't it. Keene had always been quick and confident with solutions in class and scored higher than me on every test. If there was ever a time that Toan couldn't help me with class work, I asked Keene. Of course, that rarely happened.

I cursed my lack of composure as I felt my eyes widen and instructed my mouth to stop gaping. "You ... didn't?" I wished I had something more intelligible to say right then. I wrapped my arms around myself, suddenly cold. What was the appropriate way to express condolences for a future lost? I couldn't stop the words from falling out. "What happened?"

Keene shrugged again and then smiled insincerely. "Doesn't matter now, does it? I'll make the most of it."

"What did your parents say?" Apparently I couldn't make myself shut up.

Keene's smile fell, she lowered her eyes, blinking fast, and looked away. When they returned to meet mine, her brows were furrowed with determination. "It doesn't matter." Her voice was flippant and did not match the scowl on her face. "I don't want to talk about them. I came here because I need to tell you a secret. I wanted you to know. I've been seeing someone. Do you remember James?" I frowned for a minute, searching through my memory for anything that would make her words make sense. *James.* I remembered a night we had gone to a restaurant Keene suggested on a break from a study group, Keene, Toan and I with a few other friends. A tall man with dark, curly hair, a limp and an oddout band on the sleeve of his one arm had stopped by our table and chatted. He was friendly to all of us, but I remember how he looked at Keene when she introduced him to us. James. I remembered wondering if it was more daring or dangerous for him to be looking at her like that in front of us all. He obviously wasn't intimidated. It was if he didn't know or didn't care of the consequences he could face as an oddout being too familiar with a Lineage student. I remembered looking around, relieved no Protector was in the restaurant to see.

"That odd — that *guy* at the restaurant," I said, and she nodded.

"That was his father's restaurant." As she spoke, Keene glowed: a huge smile and reddened cheeks. Her eyes were even glistening. I hadn't seen anyone smile like that before.

"He only had one arm..." I shouldn't have said that out loud.

"One leg too. Oddout medical experimentation when he was four. What's that matter?" Keene's eyes widened and flashed with anger.

"It doesn't. I, uh, of course it doesn't, but how does he work?"

Keene's face relaxed a bit and her voice lowered to a natural tone. "He works with his father at the restaurant. It's okay, he has a job. And I'll find one too." Keene touched my arm again, with more substance this time. "We're getting matched this weekend, by an oddout official. It's a secret because my parents can't know. They're all worked up about my Proof scores, trying to find a way to appeal so I can rewrite. I don't care about that, though, and before they say anything about it, James and I will be matched and there won't be anything they can do." She smiled again, but I couldn't force myself to smile back.

"What ... I mean ... are you sure?" I felt sick for her, my stomach churning heavy and cold.

"Of course I'm sure! I love him, Hessa!"

"But you'll be a Band oddout! Is he even Band? Or is he a Chosen?"

"His family is Chosen, but it doesn't matter. They don't care if I'm Band or Chosen."

How could it not matter? Band and Chosen oddouts were disparate by definition; Band failed their Proofs and were ex-

68

cluded as inadequate. The Chosen rebuked the system and all
the progress science had given us in using natural selection to
maximize cognitive skill. To them Band oddouts were no better
than us Lineage families, just ones that had failed out of their
own evil society.

A memory flashed in my mind of the eccentric Chosen
oddout arrested on the street for shouting condemnation for the
Deciders. The Protectors had knocked him down and subdued
him with their stun lasers, so that his sign fell forgotten on the
sidewalk. It read: *Certification is Unnatural*, which confused me.
Genetics unnatural? What was more natural than 'natural selection'? My father had pulled me away from the scene, grumbling
and warning me about the irresponsible way Chosen oddouts
believed in primitive unseen powers instead of trusting in
known science.

How could Keene choose to be with someone who misun-
derstood her whole life of studies?

"What will you do?" I wished I could just stop talking. Each
question seemed more offensive than the last, and I wondered
why Keene didn't get up and leave. But I couldn't stop asking. I
couldn't understand how she had come to her decision to give
up — everything. Everything. No certification meant no job
placement or career, no housing allotment, no grocery rations,
no procreation permit, no health care… Everything she had
worked for was gone. "You'll lose everything."

I didn't realize I had whispered aloud until she said,
"Everything but James." And she was still *smiling*. "Hessa, you
know what I mean. You have Toan, right? The rest we can figure out. He has a job, I'll find one. We'll find a way to rent a
place. It doesn't have to be big or fancy. And kids? Who knows.
He didn't have access to education, and he's doing okay. Maybe
I can teach them. It'll work out so long as I have him. See?"

I didn't see, at all. My middle felt cold and sick at the idea of
her predicament. But she was so happy. She smiled at me the
way I'd seen teachers smile at simple children with pity that
they'd never understand the complicated answers.

"Enough about me. How did *you* do on your Proofs?"

I wished I could get out of that moment without answering.

I mumbled, "Second Stat."

"Oh, congratulations! And Toan?"

"First."

Keene nodded. "I knew you two would do well. That's great! Have you set a date for your Matching Appointment yet?"

I felt foolish and simple to be so predictable when she had just shared a revelation I still couldn't believe. I wanted to deny her assumption that our Matching was inevitable, but as I opened my mouth I realized it was just that. I had always known. Like everyone else. As long as we scored high enough on our Proofs, we were meant to be matched. I shook my head instead. "Next week."

She laughed at that and said, "Who'd have thought that *I'd* be matched before Toan and Hessa!" And it sounded strange, her comparing her oddout pairing with our approved Match. Finally, I managed to keep that thought to myself.

After Keene left with her secret, I tried to focus on a math puzzle at my desk, but a conversation I had had with Keene a few months earlier crept back into my memory and interrupted my work.

We were studying in a common room at school. The room was wide and lit brightly through the ceiling of windows. The hushed whispers of students working together created just enough of a low buzz to block individual conversations. It was easy to focus there. Keene sat across the narrow table from me so that her screen bumped into mine every few minutes. I'd look up and she'd smile apologetically, her whispered "sorry" would float to me on a whiff of her fruity smelling gum. Once she bumped, but when I looked up she wasn't looking at me. Her eyes were trained across the room. I turned to see her watching two guys standing by the door they had just entered through, seemingly looking for a place to sit.

"They could sit here," she whispered to me with a suggestive laugh and raised eyebrows. "I wouldn't mind being distracted by *him*."

"He's a Medic." I shrugged. He was handsome, but not handsome enough that she should miss the red slashed across his arm.

"So?" When I looked away from the Medic friends, I was startled to see Keene looking at me. "So?" she asked again in a low, even voice.

Her stare on me was heavy, as if she had a question she didn't want to ask. It was uncomfortable, even on her familiar face, so I looked away. "I dunno, so I guess he's not worth the distraction if he's not even a Quantifier."

"We're not Quantifiers, *yet*." The sharpness of her voice forced me to look back at her. She was staring at her hands, her fingers twisting around one another, the skin shifting white to pink with the moving pressure. I figured she must be nervous about our upcoming Proofs.

"You'll do fine, you'll obtain certification no problem." I hoped I sounded confident.

"And what if I don't want to?" Her voice was defiant, but so low that I wasn't sure I heard her right over the hum of the voices blurred around us. Didn't want to? Who wouldn't? I had no idea what to say, so I didn't say anything at all. Light flashed in her eyes as if they were wet. "It's easy for you, Hess, your love fits into *their* plans, mine..." She looked away, but her lips kept moving. Even though I strained, I couldn't hear what she whispered after that.

"What, Keene? I didn't hear you."

Keene looked back at me, and the haunted look in her eyes was gone. She raised her shoulders and shook her head as if brushing away a flying irritant. "It's nothing. Just sometimes ... I wonder what the deal is anyway, why do they even *have* Matching rules?"

"You know it's because..."

"Oh, I know what they say about maximizing genetic tendency, building an efficient and effective society, blah blah blah. But why is that so important anyway?"

I looked around to see if any of the instructors were close enough to hear our conversation. I didn't have time to be assigned to a justification lecture if they heard her dissident questions. "High competency and specialization strengthens each sector of the community and make us all..." I stopped reciting because Keene was giving me a look with her eyebrows cocked

71

and her eyes rolling. She made a sound that was somewhere between a grunt and a snort, surprisingly full of disdain.

"See? You should be a Judician, the way you can recite the
rules." I huffed ungracefully at that, but her comment confused
me. I knew I was meant to be a Quantifier. All I had to do was
pass my Proofs.

"Are we going to study or not?" I tried to sound flippant,
but Keene looked at me a moment longer than necessary before
nodding and sitting back up to her screen, and I knew she wasn't
focusing on the problem on the display when she turned her
glassy eyes back to it.

Knowing her secret about James, her strange comments
from that day made more sense. I felt sick that I hadn't said
more to dissuade her then. It was my responsibility as her
friend, as her classmate, to help keep her ambitions aligned with
her classification. Now? I doubt my argument would have had
any impact.

Nigon

Gallie – So your friend Keene failed her Proofs and became a registered Band oddout.

Hessa – As far as I know, yes.

Gallie – Have you seen her since your Proofs?

Hessa – No.

Gallie – I thought you were good friends.

Hessa – We were, yes.

Gallie – So why haven't you been in touch?

Hessa – You know why.

Gallie – Please answer the question.

Hessa – Certified professionals aren't supposed to socialize with oddouts.

Gallie – There's no law against it.

Finch – The court is aware of the rules, Counsel Gallie. Inefficient use of time can result in de-certification.

Gallie – So you feel comfortable associating with people outside your certification, but draw a line at consorting with oddouts.

Finch – You are summarizing your subjective opinion. What is your question?

Gallie – Never mind, I'll move on. Ms. Black, did you know that your friend, Keene Sourette, is dead?

Hessa – (silence)

Gallie – Hessa, did you hear me? Keene is dead. She jumped in front of a hover last Four. Does that surprise you?

Hessa – I — I'm sorry to hear that.

Natalie Corbett Sampson

It was true that I hadn't seen Keene since the morning she told me her plan to marry James and said goodbye. There were no laws about oddouts and certified employees socializing, but everyone knew that that kind of a relationship would bring unwanted attention and suspicion. Time is precious, and wasting time is a crime. If the Authority looked close enough, they could always find a reason to strip away one's certification. Visiting with oddouts was considered the most inefficient use, there was no opportunity to learn, no skill development, no collaboration with oddouts, so no reason to interact with them at all. I missed her, of course, but there wasn't anything I could do about it.

That's why I was so happy to run into her on the hover one night on my way home from work. Chance encounters happen, and sharing a quick, spontaneous chat wouldn't hurt anyone. I was happy to see her, that is, until she looked up at me and I could see her eyes. They were flat, haunted, sad and scared, rimmed red and surrounded by pale, swollen lids. My mind swirled, trying to guess what could have caused her to look so tortured, and my stomach started to churn. Her gaze locked meaningfully with mine and she tipped her head toward the door then stood up as the hover slowed at the next stop, not bothering to look back to see if followed her. I did.

I struggled to keep her in my sight as she moved quickly through the crowd on the hover platform to a bathroom at the back of the station. When I entered a few minutes after her, out of breath and full of questions, she stood waiting for me and threw her arms around me. I stood startled and unsure before awkwardly slipping my arms around her and patting her gingerly on the shoulder blade. I could feel her shaking, and my fingers started to tingle with her fear. I pushed her back gently to see her face.

"What is it, Keene?" I whispered, wondering if the bathroom was free of monitors. This was more than a chance meeting on the hover. I'd followed her here. Why hadn't she gone to the Protectors if she was so scared of … of what? Maybe she was scared of *them*. Her wristcomm was missing from her arm. I covered my communicator with my hand, as if that would block it from recording our location or conversation. It wouldn't, of course, but the chances of them finding the data on a random

74

inspection were low enough we should have been safe. I didn't feel safe, though. If the Authority caught us here, if Keene was hiding from the Protectors and I was here meeting her? Helping her? I pushed the thought away, leaving a cold, empty feeling in my middle.

"James ... is dead." Which explained the empty look in her eyes. My chest clenched painfully and my breath stopped.

"What happened?" I gasped and wished, as the words escaped, that I had taken a moment longer to respond with more tact.

Keene's whispered words fell over each other. I had to lean in close to hear and catch each one to grasp the meaning. "He was sick. I thought it was just something he'd get over. But I didn't know they —— they took his kidney too, when he was three. Organ Donation Program. He, he never told me. And he just kept getting worse. We couldn't afford a Medic's fee, and his parents couldn't either. I asked my parents for money, but they said I'd chosen that life, so I had to live with the consequences. A neighbor told me about an oddout who said he was a Shaman. He said he knew what he was doing. James's parents said not to trust him, but he was so sick, I had to do something. So the Shaman came and gave him some medicine, but he got worse so fast and ... he died. He was gone, so cold, the next morning." Keene's voice was flat and even, and the way the words echoed on the tiled walls of the bathroom only made them sound hollower. My friend wasn't there, just her face and her body and the familiar berry scent of her shampoo. Her eyes and her voice were foreign and empty. Keene didn't cry, but my eyes burned with tears and her face blurred before me. I swatted at my cheek with a shaking hand.

"What... What do you need? What can I do?" I asked, even though I wasn't sure I'd be able to help with anything she requested.

"They say it's my fault."

"Who does, Keene?" My voice cracked painfully through my dry throat.

"James's parents. They said I poisoned him. They called the Protectors. My neighbor said I should go ... somewhere ... she

said the Shaman was taken away last night, and no one knows where they took him. They're coming for me." Even as she spoke, her eyes darted from mine around the small room and back, as if she expected Protectors to come through the walls.

"But how can it be your fault? You did what you could..." Keene's desperation was contagious. I could feel my skin crawl from the fingertips that touched her arm to my shoulder and then my chest, setting my heart racing.

She shook off my hands and my words. "I didn't poison him, but it *is* my fault. I didn't find a Medic in time. I ... I couldn't save him. I hired the Shaman, and he killed him. *I* killed him." The words were broken, but her voice was neutral, and some- how the lack of emotion in her tone was more disturbing than if she had been wailing.

If the Protectors were indeed looking for her, they'd find her soon, and then what? I had heard rumours of oddout con- tainment, but I didn't know what was true and what was urban myth. Despite my effort to shut them out, images of experi- ments, torture, forced organ donation flooded my brain. Words spoken to my father that I wasn't meant to overhear echoed in my memory: *"Those oddouts, worth so much more dead than alive and pitiful."*

"Come home with me, Keene, we'll figure this out." I tried to keep my voice reassuring, but the truth was I couldn't imag- ine a way to make things right for her.

"I can't lead them there, to you and Toan. They'll make you an oddout, they'll charge you too!"

"We'll think of something," I pushed. For a second there was a spark, a light that might have been hopeful in her eyes. She sighed and her shoulders relaxed just a bit, and I wondered if all she needed was someone to tell her what to do. "Come home with me," I repeated, trying to steady my quaking voice.

She nodded curtly, once, and I turned to leave the wash- room. She followed, keeping so close I could feel her breath on the back of my neck. I was pleased that I had convinced her so easily but felt sick to my stomach when I thought about the trouble I was bringing to our home. Toan would understand. He'd have to. But Keene was right — if the Protectors found her hiding with us, we'd loose our certification, become oddouts, be charged with abetting and face containment as if we'd been oddouts all our lives. No reprieve because of our past successes. I tried to shutter the images of oddout medical patients out of my mind again.

The noise of the station hit me as soon as the bathroom door swept open. The noise and chaos of people moving, the smells of work and sweat and smoke and food gathering off each and building a shield that affronted my senses. My stomach lurched, and I swallowed my lunch back down. I changed my mind — we couldn't go home. We would figure out another plan, but just as I turned to face her, I felt Keene push past me. She shoved my left shoulder with enough force that, taken off guard, I stumbled to the right into an oddout cleaner who stank of sewer. He swore and I righted myself, looking to see where she'd gone. I couldn't see her but could follow her trail in the parting and closing of the mob, a zigzagged path leading from me to the hover track.

For a second I glimpsed a blue hat break free of the mass, rising above the tracks at the same second the hover pulled into the station and then disintegrating in a cloud of red. Someone screamed. I turned away and threw up on the floor in front of the bathroom. My heart was knocking against my chest bone, and I tried to suck air into my stopped lungs. The hover platform spun, and my eyes blurred as dark started to creep in.

That's when I saw them on the stairs, not ten feet from where I stood: two Protectors, with dark glasses and angry, pinched mouths. They stared toward the place where she had been. One leaned toward the other and spoke near his ear. The second shrugged and put his wristcomm to his flapping mouth. They turned and ascended the stairs out of the station.

I shook behind the oddout's cleaning cart, even though they had left without once glancing in my direction, until the intercom came on, announcing the interruption in hover service. "At this time, the hover will adjourn for a regular ten-minute maintenance procedure. Please observe patience and efficient use of time until the route resumes."

I forced my feet, one over the other, to climb the stairs and walk to the next station. It took too long, and by the time I caught the hover at the next stop, it was already dark and Toan had texted me three times asking where I was. I'd replied each time with vague responses, too nervous to say more.

Toan met me at the door when it slid open, and I fell into his arms and cried. He brushed my hair from my face and made soft shushing noises in my ear, whispering words I didn't register. When I was able to stop, he took my hand and pulled me into the kitchen, where he made me sit while he ordered hot green tea from the synth.

"Can you tell me now?" he asked when he was seated across from me. I knew I had to.

"I saw Keene." I looked at him, but his face stayed still with a concerned, open look in his dark eyes. "James is … dead. He got sick and she couldn't call a Medic, so a Shaman came and gave him medicine, and he died. And his family, his family blamed Keene and called the Protectors. They were chasing her and they found her there…" My voice crackled to a stop, and he put his hand over mine on the hot mug. He waited. "She saw them and she, she just…" I couldn't say more.

"It was her," Toan whispered, and I looked up to meet his familiar eyes. "The central panel, the news, said there was an interruption at the station. They didn't say what it was, and I turned the channel looking for a game. The Gossip Site had the scene posted and said someone jumped. I just kept going. I figured it wasn't true." I started nodding as he spoke, and tears leaked out of my eyes. Toan's long fingers were wrapped around mine on my mug, so I couldn't wipe my wet face. "Why were you there? At the stop?" His eyebrows knitted in the middle.

"Keene was on the hover when we met, and she asked me to follow her when she got off. I did, and we talked in the bathroom. She told me what happened, and I told her to come here, I tried to help her…"

"You told her to come *here?* What were you thinking, Hessa?"

I pulled my hands back away from Toan's, stung by his reprimand. "I was thinking she's our friend, and she was terrified and in trouble!"

Toan reached for my hand again, but I pulled it closer and

gripped one hand with the other at my chest. He sighed, sounding like he was trying to reason with an obstinate child. "Hessa, I know, but what could we have done? If the Protectors were looking for her, surely they'd find her here, and if we were helping her?" His voice grew shaky and trailed off.

"I know," I whispered.

"Hessa, at best we'd lose everything: certification, our jobs, our house. At worst? I don't even know! We'd probably be charged and detained." His face had turned white, with blotches of red on his neck. His eyes were wide and his lips narrow and gray. He looked nearly as scared as Keene had before she ... before.

"I *know*." I took my mug and dumped it in the incinerator. I took a new cloth from the drawer, ran hot water over it and wrung it in the sink while the hot water burned my clenched fists, until my heart slowed and my breathing came on its own. I wiped the clean counter, watching the water leave streaks and smears on the fabristone. "Toan, it was Keene."

The chair scraped the floor, and I heard his feet pad across the kitchen. "I know," he whispered, echoing my words and all there was to say. He put his arms around me, and I curled into the crook of his shoulder. "I know," he whispered once more. I matched my breath with the rhythm of his chest moving in and out against me.

10

Iota

Gallie – So you had friends who were oddouts, you had friends from different classifications. It appears you consorted with a diverse group of people.

Finch – I don't know what Ms. Black's friends have to do with this.

Gallie – Well, one of them is dead. I would like to delineate for the court what value Ms. Black found in relationships with people that had nothing in common with her.

Finch – She is not charged with inefficient use of time.

Gallie – No, she's not, she's charged with murder. But I am establishing a pattern of disregard for rules and societal expectations.

Finch – Stay relevant to the charges before the court today, Counsel Gallie.

Finch – Of course, Counsel Finch. Ms. Black, what value did you see in pursuing a friendship with a Creator who had no common interests?

Hessa – Just because I'm a Quantifier doesn't mean I'm only interested in maths.

Gallie – Oh? What else are you interested in?

Hessa – Well, I like to watch baseball, and I usually enjoy reading for my compulsory arts hour each day.

Gallie – Baseball? Did you ever play a game?

Hessa – No.

Gallie – And arts, have you played an instrument? Did you write a book?

Hessa – No.

Gallie – Why not?

Hessa – Because I

Gallie – Because you're a Quantifier.

Finch – Counsel Gallie, permit the accused to answer your questions herself!

Gallie – What kind of relationship could you have with these people? Did your friendship with Aubin extend beyond being colleagues?

Hessa – We were colleagues and friends.

Gallie – Did you visit with Aubin away from the Education Department?

Hessa – He came to dinner at our place once.

Gallie – Was Toan home?

Hessa – Of course.

Gallie – Did it not go well?

Hessa – It was fine.

Gallie – Then why did he only come once in the several months you were friends?

Hessa – He was busy, we were busy, and it only happened to work out once that he could come.

Gallie – So you invited him again, but he couldn't make it?

Hessa – We talked about it, but there wasn't a good time.

Gallie – I see. Tell us about the dinner you did share.

Hessa – He came over, we chatted over a bottle of wine, had a nice dinner and he went home.

Gallie – I'm sure there's more to it than that.

Finch – Is that a question or an opinion?

Gallie – Was there more to it than that?

Hessa – Not really, no.

Gallie – Tell us more about your dinner with Aubin Wallace.

Hessa – I think we had seared chicken and green beans. Chocolate cake for dessert.

Gallie – Ms. Black.

Finch – She has answered your question. What specifically is it that you want to know?

Gallie – What did you discuss?

Hessa – Our jobs. Funny stories.

Gallie – Was the conversation friendly?

Hessa – Of course.

Gallie – Did it become confrontational?

Hessa – No, why would it?

Gallie – As a Creator, Mr. Wallace had very different interests and ideas than two Quantifiers such as yourself and Mr. Whitley.

Hessa – So? We were friends. We could talk as friends even with different interests.

Gallie – You and Aubin were friends. Would Toan consider Aubin a friend?

Hessa – Yes, because he was my friend.

Gallie – That's very kind of him to share you like that.

Hessa – We were just friends and colleagues. Toan knew that.

Gallie – I'm sure.

Toan asked me why I was nervous, but I denied it. "I'm fine, Toan."

"You're biting your nails and you've checked your wrist-comm four times in the last five minutes." Truth was I *was* nervous, but I didn't know why. I shrugged instead of answering, so he said with a laugh, "It'll be fine, Hessa."

"Thanks," I said and added, "I know," because I believed everything he told me.

We were sitting in the media room, having run out of tasks in preparation for Aubin's arrival. Toan's fingers flew over the sensor on the arm of his chair as he flickered through screens on the central panel. I had tidied the house and hidden away our clutter in drawers. Toan chose a special dinner from the market, one that was well out of our typical budget per serving. He even caved and bought fresh vegetables at an extraordinary price. My mouth watered at the thought. It had been a long time since I'd had natural instead of the engineered frozen vegetables included in our ration.

I think the fresh vegetables were his apology for his reaction when I told him I'd invited Aubin over. He'd sighed and frowned and argued, "What are we going to talk about?" and "We don't have the time for that," and "Our rations will be

nearly out, what will we serve?" I'd answered each question, trying to keep frustration out of my voice, until I finally snapped
and said, "He's my friend, Toan. You're never there for lunches
anymore, so I eat with him. Forgive me for having a life when
you're too busy to be around," and stormed up the stairs to my
room.

Twenty minutes later I was completing my compulsory arts
hour by reading on my bed when there was a knock at the door.
"Open," I commanded the door, and it slid to the side to reveal
Toan standing there with his hands wringing and his head down.

"Can I come in?" he asked. I nodded, and he stepped
through and paced in front of me. "I know you want dinner to
go well. I know it's important to you." I waited for a 'but', but
he stopped talking and looked at me. I nodded. "I'm sorry I
have been so busy, Hessa. I wish I could get away more but the
work … it's just so…" He stopped and dropped his hands at his
sides, defeated.

"I miss you," I heard myself whisper. I hadn't planned to say
it. I didn't want to make him feel guilty for doing his job.

"I miss you too," he said, taking a step closer. "I know he's
your friend, Hessa. Of course we can have him for dinner if you
want." I smiled, and he stepped forward again. "And…" Another step.

"And?" I could feel my heart start to beat faster in response
to the way he looked at me from under his brows.

"And us. I'll come more often for lunch. I'll make sure to
keep a day free each week. Wednesday? Would that work?" I
nodded. "Wednesday then. I'll come each Wednesday." I stood
up and hugged him, relieved he understood. He tipped his face
down into my neck and kissed me behind the ear.

He came the next two Wednesdays before meetings were
called that he couldn't reschedule.

Aubin was my friend, so why was I so nervous about dinner? Our house system flashed on the screen on the wall and
spoke, making me jump: *Aubin Wallace is at the front entrance.*
Toan laughed at me and stood, stepping down the stairs to the
front door and calling "Admit" to the house system. I heard the
door slide open as he shouted a welcome. I heard Aubin's voice,

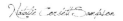

too low to make out his words. My head felt light as I slipped down the stairs to the entryway.

Toan turned as I came into the room. "Look, Hessa, he brought a bottle of that Iranian wine you love. Must be good Creator intuition, eh?" Aubin's eyes were on me, and I saw him blush just a bit. His hair was brushed back, the ends at the nape of his neck curled against the collar of his shirt. I nodded.

"Thank you, Aubin, let's open it now," I said as Aubin showed me the deep blue glass bottle.

Aubin smiled and looked at his feet. "One ration bottle a month is a lot for one person to drink alone."

"Here, Hess, you dilute the wine while I heat the supper." Toan handed me a flask of water and three glasses he must have grabbed on his way and turned into the kitchen. I led Aubin up to the media room, where Toan had pushed aside the or-thochairs and set up a table and three chairs for dining. I poured a shot of wine concentrate in each glass then topped it up with the dilution water, handing one glass to Aubin. We stood facing each other with the short table between us. I felt frozen, awk-ward, exposed, guilty, as if caught. I sipped the wine, and it burned a path through my middle, cold with nerves. I wondered why his presence played such mean tricks on my mind.

"Thank you for the invitation," Aubin said, breaking the spell.

"I'm glad you could come." Our polite formality sounded ridiculous, and I laughed. Then he laughed. And I felt the cold seep out and my shoulders relax. Toan was right, as always. It was foolish to be nervous.

Dinner was ready shortly after that, and we sat at the table sipping the wine and taking courteously small bites of the beans and chicken. The meal was delicious and conversation sputtered as we ate.

Aubin's fork clinked as he lay it down on his empty plate. "That was scrumptious, thank you, guys."

I smiled. "Toan did it. He got the chicken servings from the new market."

"I haven't been in there. Is it a good place to shop?" Aubin looked from me to Toan for an answer, then back to his administrations as he diluted another glass of wine.

Toan nodded. "We don't go often since we're on weekly ration delivery, but it has everything we need for extras."

"Does it have ingredients?"

Toan's eyebrows tipped in. "What do you mean?"

"Ingredients. You know, unprepared meat, spices, flour and salt — to make a meal yourself."

"Why would you want to do that? They have a good selection of pre-made meals that only need to be heated. More choices than the old market."

I watched their words bounce back and forth, feeling a knot start to grow in my full stomach.

"I think it would be fun."

"Fun?"

"Sure, why not?"

"Cooking a meal isn't a very productive use of your skills. You must have writing tasks that are, um, *fun*, but that also provide a greater contribution, don't you?" Toan leaned forward in his chair, resting his elbows on the table so that I could see him mirrored upside-down, his tidy cropped hair shiny in the silver reflection, his eyes serious and dark. I knew he was unsettled by Aubin. He seemed ready for a debate.

"I love writing, of course, but I like to try new things too." Aubin's smile was casual, as if his statement was a given truth anyone would understand. "Wouldn't you?" He looked from Toan to me. The question was for both of us.

I shrugged. Toan's answer was more definitive. "My priority is to develop my Lineage-given skills as a Quantifier. If I have extra time, I do more to advance those skills and contribute to the community in the way only I can. There are oddouts who are trained to make meals and need the occupation. Why take their jobs from them?"

"I suppose, but I'm only one person making meals for myself and maybe a friend or two. That's hardly competition for the factories making meal servings."

"But you could be spending that time contributing your Creator skills."

85

Aubin nodded. "I could, yes, and I do. I'm on a couple of community boards. But I think trying new things, exploring new skills and new ideas, makes me a better writer. It helps me develop my creative skills too."

Toan pulled his eyebrows down and turned up the corner of his lips to make a face that wasn't entirely polite. "I guess that must be a Creator thing, then. Making a meal wouldn't contribute anything to my work as a Quantifier."

"Toan," I groaned.

"No, it's alright, Hessa, he's got a point. What do you think? Are you interested in learning new skills that are not related to math?"

I detected the burn from both of their stares on me and felt expectation from each of them to agree with his own argument. Aubin's handwritten note flashed in my mind, and I remembered my intrigue as he deciphered the marks into words.

"I guess it depends on what it is," I hedged and wondered if the scowl that flickered on Toan's face was real or born from my guilty imagination.

Toan leaned back in his chair and tossed his palms up. "I just think you were given the privilege of your classification for a reason, and yours is a position most oddouts, a lot of your classmates, would love to have. You are classed as a Creator. You can do that job better than most others. Not using your time to do that is failing to develop and contribute that skill. It could be considered ungracious of you. Illegally inefficient, even."

"Toan." My warning was sharper the second time.

Toan whipped his look to me. "What?"

"Hessa, really, it's fine! I'm interested to hear his perspective." Aubin had a laugh in his voice. "I'm worried that our system of sorting and classification limits and ignores other skills individuals may have. I enjoy a good debate. It doesn't make me a Decider, but I can still enjoy it. I'm not a Preserver or an Interpreter, but I like to study history and learn new words in different languages. I still enjoy cooking or planting a garden, even — why should only oddouts be able to take pleasure in that?"

"You have a garden?" I asked, but they both ignored me.

"You just said it yourself. You're not a Decider. Or a Preserver or an Interpreter. Time spent studying those skills is time lost that you could be developing the skills you have, the ones you've been trained with so that you can contribute. There are Deciders and Preservers and Interpreters who can do those skills so much better than you ever will be able to, so why waste your time?"

"But I don't think it's a waste of time if I enjoy it and grow from the experience."

Toan leaned forward again, diving back into the debate. He seemed to be enjoying it more than his Quantifier self would ever admit. "Grow how? You can't use it for your work. Certainly, time spent within your skill set would yield greater gains, greater growth, and it would be growth you could contribute!"

"Yes, but time spent on my interests will always allow me to grow as an individual."

"Ah-*ha*! There is your mistake! '*As an* individual'." Toan slammed his hand on the table, rattling the glasses and rippling the wine; he had caught Aubin in his argument. "You are a Creator. You have an obligation to contribute because you have been given the opportunities that come with being a Creator: further education, work placements, housing and medical and food rations. Rejecting that obligation in an effort to seek personal gratification? That's a theft of resources, inefficient and illegal. Not to mention selfish."

"Toan!"

They were too deep in their argument to acknowledge my presence, let alone my interruption. Aubin's smile had grown tight; his lips lightened as they pressed together and up. His wrists rested against the edge of the table, but his hands were fisted with white knuckles. "But Toan, don't you see? Personal gratification, being happy and engaged and interested, those all make my contributions within my classification stronger."

"I'm sure there's a way to find that gratification within your skill."

"But why limit it to that?" Aubin matched Toan's glare evenly.

I couldn't reach to kick him under the table, so I stared hard at Toan, willing him to feel my eyes on him, pulling him back. He turned and saw me. At least he had the grace to blush. "Aubin, on this I think we'll have to agree to disagree. Perhaps it *is* a Creator trait that I'll just never understand."

Aubin's smile was genuine again as he nodded at Toan and said, "Perhaps." But as the 's' blew off his tongue, he turned to me and raised his eyebrows in a silent question. His dancing scrawl flashed in front of my eyes again. I sensed he could feel my answer, or at least that my answer might betray Toan's conviction. I had to look away.

11

Odinnadtsat

Gallie – So the lounge at work and one dinner at your place. Where else did you meet with Mr. Wallace?

Hessa – I ran into him once at the CDB.

Gallie – The Central Database? Why were you there?

Hessa – I needed to check a reference.

Gallie – Couldn't you do that with your own access from home?

Hessa – I found conflicting records. I wanted to verify the source to determine which was right.

Gallie – What reference was it, specifically?

Hessa – I don't remember.

Gallie – Why was Mr. Wallace there?

Hessa – I don't know.

Gallie – You don't know or you don't remember?

Hessa – I don't know.

Gallie – You didn't ask him?

Hessa – It wasn't my business to ask him.

Gallie – Do you remember the date?

Hessa – No, sometime in Eight, I think.

Gallie – Did you talk with him when you saw him?

Hessa – Of course.

Gallie – For how long?

Hessa – I don't remember, a few minutes.

Gallie – What did you speak with him about?

Hessa – I don't remember. It was months ago.

Finch – Is this line of questioning relevant to the charges of the accused?

Gallie – I'm trying to establish the specific

nature of Ms. Black's relationship with Aubin Wallace.

Finch – Ms. Black has testified to being friends with Mr. Wallace.

Gallie – None of his other friends have been charged with his death. Did you plan to meet Aubin Wallace at the CDB that afternoon?

Hessa – No.

Gallie – Are you sure?

Hessa – Of course I'm sure. I ran into him by chance.

Gallie – And you spoke with him for only a few minutes and can't remember what about?

Finch – These questions have all been asked and answered.

I had to consciously make my right foot shift past my left, and vice versa, for the entire five blocks from the hover station to the Central Database. Many times I almost turned back. I felt sick for lying to Toan. When he had asked about my plans for my day off, I hoped he wouldn't ask why I wanted to go by the CDB, but of course he did.

"Is your computer not working? Can't you find the information you need from here?" He frowned at me over his glass of water paused halfway to his lips.

"It's working fine, but I have a reference that has conflicting records. I want to make sure I have the accurate source." I couldn't look at him and took a big gulp of water to busy my mind and my mouth.

"Hm. I haven't heard of that happening before. Good luck, then." He turned to the incinerator, so I let out my breath. "I'll be late, Hess, so don't wait for me to eat."

"How late?" I tried hard to keep my voice neutral and free of disappointment. Toan turned to me with a small smile and a smaller shrug of his shoulders. "Okay," I sighed and took another gulp of water to keep my face from scrunching up.

The truth was I wanted to find a reference on handwriting. I hadn't been able to forget Aubin's fluid script, the way my eyes tripped to follow it across the page. I wanted to see more of it and see if there was a way to learn how to read it. Maybe even how to write it. Maybe I could craft something for Toan as a present; I could write out our names to decorate the wall, or a fancy nameplate for his desk. To keep that a surprise, I'd have to keep my research a secret. Maybe then he wouldn't be upset about me wasting time pursuing such a frivolous skill. Maybe he'd see some value and interest in it if I produced something meaningful for him. Maybe. But if I searched for references on my computer, he'd see it on the network and then he'd ask questions I just didn't want to answer. Not yet, anyway. A surprise to be revealed was different than a secret hidden. *Right*. So as I walked, my mind spun my thoughts into justification, and I felt sick from it. It was the first time I lied to Toan.

The CDB was only five streets from the hover station, but my hesitance made it a longer walk than it should have been. I knew the building was tall and thin like the buildings around it, a narrow rectangle, balanced on its small end to maximize space over a minimal footprint, but I couldn't look up to see it because the light bouncing off the sky blue glass was blinding even through my mandated sunglasses. When the door slid open, I took a deep breath, as if I was about to step over a threshold from which there was no return and glanced around to see the audience I felt staring at me. There was no one, of course. I felt ridiculous for the drama. My cheeks burned and I shook my head, forcing my left foot forward.

I had been to the Central Database many times, originally with my parents and later with Toan for school assignments. We spent hours studying there together when the school was closed. It was quiet and still, good for concentration. The unseen fans whirled with white noise and kept the temperature even and comfortable. There was a crisp freshness and lemon scent in the air that made me feel alert. Toan once said it was the dust cleaners they used. The familiarity of the CDB had always been reassuring. But that time when I walked into the lobby, a vision of Aubin's library museum flashed in my mind. I could almost see rows and rows of shelves lined against the opposite security wall. Spines of books in varied colours, heights, thicknesses stood as sentries on guard, waiting, though I don't know for what. I wrinkled my nose, remembering his description of the

91

dusty paper smell. I blinked, fast, and focused on seeing reality instead: the long work tables with wedges of table screens lifting out of the surface in front of each stiff chair. Opposite the entrance, a long, translucent but protective wall shielded the drives and network equipment.

I approached a screen and activated the holoboard. The iridescent qwerty rectangle glowed above the desk. Without logging in — to save time and convenience, I told myself — I entered 'handwriting' into the search field. With a flicker the screen filled with references that had 'handwriting' in the title. I scanned through the results, overwhelmed by the number of choices. I glanced over my shoulder, pulled my screen from my bag and laid it beside the computer to transfer files. I chose two that looked like instructional manuals with 'reading' and 'writing' in the titles and slid them to my screen with a flick of my finger. I erased the search and brought the computer back to the initial page.

I turned from the computer to find a less central place to sit. The tables in the large room seemed open, vulnerable and too visible. I walked toward the corner of the room where I remembered there were smaller tables tucked away.

I found an empty workspace in the first corner, slid into the seat and laid my screen on the table, my bag on the floor. I brought my screen to life with my fingertip, selected one of the references and told my heart to slow down; there was no reason to be nervous. The title, *Reading and Writing Handwritten Text*, spread across the screen in typical black type, but crossing through it was a strip of red loops and lines that I presumed was the title displayed again in script. I squinted, as if that would improve the intelligibility of the lines. The 'R' at the beginning of the title was similar to the typeface 'R', although it was tipped significantly to the right. The straight line was no longer vertical. A loop hung on the top right side, and a line stuck out from the bottom of the loop, completing the letter. As the line slid away from the 'R', it underlined the following letters. The next little loop looked nothing like the 'e' it replaced, and the 'a' seemed to have been simplified to a small circle, missing the hood that covered the circular 'a' in the type font. The 'd' and 'i' were easily recognizable, but I wouldn't have known the bumps, circle and loops to be 'n' and 'g' without knowing the word that was written. As I looked, my heart slowed and my eyes focused on the screen, blocking out the sounds and sights of the CDB behind me. I was fascinated.

With my finger, I slid the pages forward to the first of the illustrations. The top of the page displayed the capital and lower-case typed 'Aa' side by side in a large font. Underneath there were rows and rows of alternating triangles and circles, some more recognizable as an A than others.

I reached down and rummaged in my bag until my fingers found the envelope Aubin left on my desk. I pulled it out and flipped it over to see the small blue word on the front, and then slid the pages forward to a page lined with 'Hh'. Aubin's 'H' stood almost vertical. The straight lines were connected by a swirly line that looped from the bottom of the right line, through the middle of the left line, before curling on the left of the letter. There were no 'H's like his on the page, though some were similar. I slid the pages forward until I found rows of 'Ss'. The variance on the page was daunting. A few were comparable to the typed 'S' snake shape, but the lines fluctuated from nearly circular in their twists to nearly vertical, with two opposite bumps. Others showed a small loop balancing tip-to-tip on a bigger triangular one. Aubin's small 's's were shaped like teardrops.

I traced Aubin's letters of my name on the envelope with my finger and then repeated the movement on the table. I slid the pages back to the beginning of the book to study all of the letters from the beginning.

"Hessa?"

I jumped, said "SHIT!" and my screen bounced out of my fingers onto the floor. I turned, heart racing, to see blue eyes. Aubin stepped forward to retrieve the screen, but I was closer and bent from the chair to pick it up first. "Sorry, Hessa, I didn't mean to startle you."

"You didn't."

He laughed and tipped his head to the side as he slid into the chair beside me. "I didn't? That was a strange way to say hello then."

"Hello. Better?"

"Yes, hello."

"What are you doing here?" I was surprised by the edge of demand in my voice.

"I like to write here. I come here on my days off. It's quiet, no distractions, and I have the opportunity to look up words if I need to. What about you?"

I opened my mouth and then closed it again, unable to remember my excuse on the spot. In my hesitation I saw his eyes fall on my screen. I covered it with my hands but was too late. "Just checking a reference," I finally said, which made him smile again.

"Are you looking at handwriting? Why didn't you ask me? I can show you."

I shrugged. "You're busy."

"Don't be stupid. Besides, you need my help. You're doing it wrong."

"I'm just reading. I can do that, you know, even if I'm only a Quantifier."

"You can't learn to write by looking at it. You need to actually *do* it, which means you need a pen and paper."

"I know that." My face felt warm, and I wished I was anywhere else.

"Do you have some then?" I could hear a laugh in Aubin's voice that I did not like.

"No." I had no idea where to get blank paper or a pen anyway.

"It's your lucky day. I have some." He pulled his bag into his lap and reached in with both hands. He pulled out a small stack of loose papers lined in light blue, and laid it on the table. The edges were misaligned; the corners poked out at uneven angles.

"Where'd you get that paper?" I hadn't seen so many sheets of paper other than in a locked drawer in Uncle G's study.

"I get a ration of it each month," Aubin said as he touched the top sheet almost lovingly with the tip of his finger. "I like writing on it better than a screen."

94

He reached in his bag again and drew out his hand, fisting a long, thin metal cylinder with a point at one end. He opened his fingers, the pen resting on the palm. "Here," he said when I just looked at it.

I remembered Uncle G showing us a pen, but we weren't allowed to touch it — it was too old, and we were too little. He said his grandfather had used it a long time ago. He had shown us how he held it and Toan and I laughed, thinking it looked like a silly horn, like the rhinoceros or the generated ceratops we had seen in the holozoo. "Where'd you get that?" I don't know why I whispered.

"Certification gift, after my Proofs," Aubin said, then, "It won't bite." he lifted it closer to me. I took the pen. It was cold and smooth and surprisingly heavy. I rolled it between my thumb and fingers and then pulled it into my fist and curled my fingers around it. It felt awkward.

"Let me show you." This time there was no hint of a laugh. His voice was serious and gentle. He took the pen back and pinched it between his thumb and first two fingers. "Like this, like you're picking up something small." He laid it on top of the table and I picked it up again, this time trying to imitate his hand with my thumb and fingers. It tipped back and forth as my digits struggled to find a balance of power in the grip. "Here," he said, laying his hand over mine and pulling the pen through my fingers until they were closer to the point, "that might be easier. Give it a try."

I looked from my cramping fingers to his face. "Try what?"

"Write something."

"What should I write?" The words sounded foreign.

His eyebrows rose with his shoulders. "Why don't you start with your name? Here, copy this." He put the envelope with my name above the papers on the table so I could see it and pointed to the top left of the 'H'. "Start here."

My hand shook as I put the point to the paper. First I pressed too hard, and the pen wouldn't move. I let up a bit and moved my hand downward, leaving a thin, wiggly line behind. When I got to the pale blue line, I lifted up the pen and repeated the downward stroke just to the right. I lifted it again and drew a

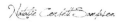

line from the middle of the left side to the bottom of the right. I had written an ugly, shaky 'H'.

"Ugh, that's awful!" I laughed.

Aubin turned the page and scrutinized my letter. "It's great, Hessa. It takes practice, you know. Go on with the 'e'."

With Aubin's direction, I imitated his example. After a few minutes, my paper displayed my name in large, shaky letters, so messy it was almost illegible. I couldn't stop the grin from spreading across my face.

"Well, look at that!" I said, more to myself than to Aubin. He made a pleased hum beside me, and I smiled at him. "I'm going to write 'Toan'." I turned to my screen and skipped through screens until I came to the page with 'Tt' at the top. The examples were instantly disheartening. Some were similar to the horizontal and vertical lines I was familiar with, but others looked nothing like a 'T'. Some were circular, some not, some with single lines, others with loops and tails turning to the right or the left. I sighed. "How do I know which one is right?"

"There's no one right letter — it's not a math problem. Everyone writes differently; that's why there's so many. These are just examples. Pick one that looks right to you, and as you practice, it'll become your own."

"But that's what makes it so hard to read. If everyone's handwriting is different, how do you learn all the letters to be able to read them?"

Aubin tipped his head. "Some are easier than others, but usually it's pretty close, and the context helps you figure out ones that aren't very clear. C'mon, start with a 'T'."

I looked over the page and settled on one that looked like a typed 'T'. I drew the line across, and then the line down. I slid pages to the 'Oo' and drew a small circle next to the 'T' with a tail that linked it to the 'a' I remembered from my name, and finally to the two bumps I remembered from the cover. Toan's name lay in front of me.

Aubin laughed.

"What?" I turned on him, frustrated with my face burning. "What's wrong with that? It's not that bad."

He held up his hands, palms facing me. "It's great, Hessa, really."

"Then what are you laughing at?" I glared at him, daring him to deny his mirth.

"You stick out your tongue when you write and bite on the end of it."

"I do not!" My voice raised and my face flushed hotter. I realized I probably did.

"Shhh!" Aubin laughed. "I'm sorry, but you do."

I turned back to my page with 'Hessa' and 'Toan' scrawled in large, wobbly letters. I had the letters I needed to write a project for Toan, but they looked horrible. Obviously I had more work to do first.

"Now write the alphabet. Start with A and go through to the end. Then you'll have all of the letters the way you want to write them in one place and can make up words from that."

I started scrolling through the screens of examples, but it was too much to look at. "Can you write them out for me?" I slid the paper across the table to Aubin. "Then I don't have to look through all of those every time."

"Sure." He took the pen from my hand and held it in his, his fingers automatically finding the right places to pinch and balance the weight of it. With deftness and speed and a faint brushing sound, Aubin's hand glided across the page, leaving a line of isolated letters in its wake. He wrote both the capital and the small letter, starting with 'A' and ending with 'z' across the top of the page over my 'Hessa' and 'Toan'. He pushed the paper back toward me. "There."

I put my finger on the 'A' and stepped through the letters, mentally comparing each to the letters I knew from type. "How is *that* an 'E'?" I laughed. In the place between the 'd' and the small loop I knew from my name to be 'e' was a larger letter that looked like a heart had been turned on its side and the point cut off.

Aubin laughed and said, "Well, that's *my* 'E'. Find your own — just write what you think an 'E' looks like." I took the pen back and thought of a typed 'E' in my mind. I put the pen to paper and drew one vertical line and three horizontal ones. It looked childish under his truncated heart. I sighed in frustration.

I felt Aubin's hand on my shoulder and caught my flinch just in time to stop it. His palm was warm through my shirt, the weight of it soothing. "Don't stress about it, Hessa, just have fun with it. It's not worth doing if it's going to frustrate you. Remember, I learned to write when I was little, you've never done it — of course it's going to take time." I nodded, surprised to feel the threat of tears in my eyes.

I kept my gaze down. "I guess I'm not used to not being able to do something. I mean, I can't do *everything*, obviously, but I usually only do what I *can* do." I laughed and shook my head. "Sorry, that doesn't even make sense."

"It does." Aubin took his hand back, and I looked up at him, startled by his retreat. "Write me a note," he said with a shrug.

"Why? What would I say?"

"Just for practice. For fun. You can say anything you want."

"You won't be able to read it."

"I promise you I will." He emphasized his assurance with a nod, and I felt myself smiling. "I've got to go, Hessa, but it was good to see you here." He stood and gathered his bag, I collected the paper and pen and held it toward him, but he stepped back away from my offer. "No, you keep it to write me a note. I have more. I'll see you tomorrow at work."

The space was empty in Aubin's departure, the air too still and the CDB too quiet. I gave him a moment to be gone and then collected my own belongings. I dropped his pen into my bag with my screen.

I collected the papers in front of me. The pages were in a messy pile. I picked them up and tapped them on the table to make them fall into order. I turned the pile and tapped the adjacent edge. A smaller sheet fell out of the pile and floated down to the floor. I picked it up and noticed the reverse was marked with Aubin's writing. I flipped it over and studied it.

I could recognize a few of the individual letters, but the whole words were still illegible to me. I put my finger to the page and started to figure out the letters and words, referencing Aubin's alphabet as I went. I couldn't retain the meaning of the

earlier words as I deciphered the ones that followed, so I
opened a document on the screen and transcribed the letters as
I decoded them. When I got to the last letter, I sat back, pleased
with myself, and turned my attention to read the words I had
typed.

Smile. I see you.

Anew. Cuor contento as naught before.

Laugh. I hear you.

I breathe your breath. Sweet and shared.

Tangled, fisselig, confused, bewildered.

The words strung together were beautiful. They touched me
so that my eyes stung with tears, but even in type I could not
discern their meaning. At first I thought I had gotten the letters
wrong or made an error in transcribing them, but when I
checked again it was accurate. Then I remembered Aubin's ancient words from lost languages. The context around it was no
help in determining what they meant. The serenity of the words
slipped away as my frustration with my limitations grew. I
stuffed the papers and screen back into my bag and hoisted it to
my shoulder, making a mental note to hide the pages before
Toan came home that night.

12

Tinikarua

Gallie – Was that the only time, or did you meet Aubin by chance at the CDB again?

Hessa – No.

Gallie – No what?

Hessa – No, I did not run into him again.

Gallie – But you continued to meet with him at work.

Hessa – Yes, we saw each other at work. We were colleagues.

Gallie – So you've said. And how frequently did you share your lunch break?

Hessa – Most days.

Gallie – More often than you spent lunch with Mr. Whitley?

Hessa – Toan was very busy.

Gallie – No one is judging you for your choice of lunch date, Hessa.

Hessa – No, just for his death.

Finch – Ms. Black, please refrain from derisive comments; they won't help your cause. I will maintain operative and forward moving questioning.

Gallie – We are narrating the truth in these circumstances, Ms. Black. Your cooperation is appreciated.

Finch – She is cooperating.

Gallie – Good. I will repeat my question. Did you spend more lunches with Aubin Wallace than with Toan Whitley.

Hessa – I suppose.

The next day after I saw Aubin in the CDB, I was held back

from my lunch break by a student needing help. By the time I reached the lounge, Aubin was standing at the table, collecting his garbage. He turned upon my entrance and flashed me a bright smile. I smiled back.

"Hessa, I figured you were busy, and I wasn't going to get to see you this lunch."

My snort in response was less than ladylike. "A student had some questions about my lesson today. I guess it wasn't one of my better lectures."

Aubin's eyes were trained on me and seemed to slip to a deeper blue as he said, "I can see how some would be bewildered."

I didn't know what he meant, but the casual lift of his shoulder did not match the intensity of his stare, and the discrepancy made my middle flutter just a bit. I looked away to put my lunch and papers on the desk, pull out the chair and slide into the seat. "I find it difficult to teach integrals to complete mastery in the half hour allotted by the curriculum."

"If I knew what integrals were, I'm sure I'd understand why." Aubin's voice was light again, with a laugh. "Hey, do you have a note for me?"

I didn't know why my face felt warm but hoped it didn't show. "Um, no, not yet. But I do have this." His eyebrows rose with intrigue as I slipped my hand into my pocket to find the paper he had left behind. I laid it on the table in front of him, and his face paled. The smile that seemed always on the ready sunk to a glower, and his eyes frowned. "What's wrong?" I asked.

Aubin snatched the sheet from the table and stuffed it into his pants pocket. "Nothing." He muttered a question that I couldn't make out as he turned away.

"Pardon?"

"Could you read it?" His voice was sharp and impatient.

I was confused by his reaction. I had been pleased with myself for deciphering the words on my own, but he wasn't acting like the proud teacher I expected him to be. "It took some work, but I figured it out." I thought he shook his head just slightly. He gulped his water. "Why? What's wrong?" I asked again.

101

"Nothing."

"You seem pretty upset over 'nothing'." For a minute we didn't speak, and the quiet was heavy and tense. "I didn't understand what it meant, if that helps."

He looked up at me. "What do you mean?"

"I mean I didn't understand it. I could read the words, and they sounded beautiful, but I couldn't work out what they all meant together. What is it about?"

"Nothing," he said again, but without the sharp tone that time. He laughed then, a short chuckle that sounded almost as relieved as it did sarcastic. "I guess that's just the way poetry works." He stood and removed his garbage. From the distance of the incinerator he said, "I'll catch you later, Hessa," and turned and left the room before I could say goodbye.

With his departure, I had a heavy, sinking feeling in my stomach that I couldn't justify. Too late I realized the note was not mine to read. But his response seemed extreme, even with that truth. He was the one who had shown me how to read the letters; he was the one who had left the note behind, even if by accident — how was I supposed to know it wasn't meant to be read? My silent defense didn't make me feel any better. I decided to give him some time and apologize when I saw him next.

But that became my next problem. Aubin did not come into the lounge for the rest of the week. I saw him in the halls from time to time, but he was always busy or moving away, and I didn't get the chance to say anything to him. By Sunday I was no longer surprised when he didn't appear, leaving me to spend my lunch hour pretending to follow the Quantifiers' complaints about their classes or eat alone. What did surprise me was the loneliness I felt in his absence, the way my chest felt tighter each time the door opened and it was not Aubin on the other side.

Monday morning I woke up resolved without even realizing I had considered my options. I was impatient waiting for the grocery delivery and was on my way to the hover station moments after I had shoved the food into the cupboards and cooling system. It was hot and muggy, and the rain that threatened to fall was hanging invisible in the sky. It smelled of worms. My pace was fast enough to make my breath short, and I struggled

to suck in enough of the soggy air. On the hover I sat sandwiched between a fat man in a suit who was working on his
communicator and a woman who stank like an Athletic. I made
myself as small as I could, pulling in away from them on both
sides, and stared at my folded hands until the hover slowed and
stopped at the CDB station. I rushed from the hover station to
the CDB and arrived out of breath. I stopped under the vent
just inside to feel the push of cool processed air, catch my
breath and collect my thoughts. That's when I first let myself
think about it long enough to realize why I was there. My heart
continued to race long after my breathing slowed.

I felt like I was sneaking around the Database, looking for
his shock of blond hair. He was huddled in the third corner I
checked, opposite where we met the week before. His head
hung over a notebook, causing his curls to fall and block his
face from me. His hand floated back and forth, swaying as if
dancing to music only he could hear. I stopped in my tracks as a
sickening quiver in my stomach sent chills up my neck to tingle
under my scalp. I turned to leave but he looked up just then, his
blue eyes trained on me. He put down his pen and gave a small
smile. His silence willed me forward.

"Hi," I said when I was close enough.

"Shit," he said with a forced laugh.

I felt my lips pull up without my direction. I had found him
but had no idea what I needed to say once I was there. I had no
idea how to express what I felt standing there with him after his
week of absence. Not angry, though I wanted to be. Relieved,
maybe? And definitely confused.

"Are you going to sit?" Aubin was watching me. His words
triggered my feet, which moved me to the table. I sat. "Well?"

"You haven't been to lunch." I felt stupid for my blurted
words. My cheeks felt hot, my stomach felt tight, twisting tighter.

"No, I haven't. I thought it was better if I didn't."

"Just because I read your note? I'm sorry. I didn't realize it
was private." I sat up a little straighter since my words were
making more sense. Of course, that was why I was there, to
apologize so he would come back.

Aubin shrugged and looked away. "Don't worry about that."

"You're not angry that I read it?" He looked back at me and shook his head, keeping his icy eyes steady on mine. "But I thought... Then why —"

"It was meant for you, Hessa, I just didn't mean for you to *read* it. And when you did, well, I just didn't know what to do then."

I must have frowned. My confusion must have been apparent to him, because it was too palpable for me to hide. He reached into his pocket and drew out a wrinkled, folded sheet. He put it in front of me on the table, leaving it covered by his flat hand for just a second too long.

When I looked up from the sheet, his face was pale. His mouth was twisted to the side, his teeth chewing on the inside of his lips. His blue eyes were wet, and he blinked then swallowed with a force that moved the muscles in his jaw and then his neck. His voice was a broken whisper. "It's meant for you, Hessa. You might as well keep it."

Before I could reply, he was standing with his notebook clutched to his chest, two pens fisted in his hand. His empty hand reached toward me and then hung in the air between us, hesitating, as if he had forgotten what he meant to do with it. After a moment it fell to his side. He turned and started to walk away.

"Aubin!" I hadn't realized I was going to call out until I heard my voice. He turned but stood silent, waiting for me to continue. "Are you going to come to lunch again?"

"Read that. If you still want me to, I will," he said, with a nod toward the paper on the desk. I couldn't figure what one had to do with the other. When I looked back up from the desk, he was gone.

I retrieved my screen from my bag, turned it on to an empty screen and pulled up the keyboard. Aubin's alphabet was folded hidden inside the case. My fingers shook as I unfolded both papers and lay them side by side on the table, rubbing them flat with my palm. It was easier to transcribe the second time, and within a few moments I could read his poem in text on my screen:

Smile. I see you.

Anew. Cuor contento as naught before.

Laugh. I hear you.

I breathe your breath. Sweet and shared.

Tangled, fisselig, confused, bewildered.

Our conversation twisted with the words I read on the screen. "*Meant for you, Hessa,*" he had said. I read the poem again. If meant for me, then the 'you' in the poem was ... me? He sees me, he hears me? 'Confused and bewildered' I understood — that's how I felt too. The rest of it I still couldn't make out. It just didn't compute in my analytical mind. For a moment I considered showing it to Toan; he understood things much better than I, so maybe he could work it out. But my visceral response to that idea was immediate. My face grew hot, my throat tightened over my churning stomach. This note was not for Toan to see. It was private, just for me from Aubin.

Just for me. From Aubin. Just. For me.

I see you, I hear you ... sweet and shared ... Confused. Bewildered.

I started to feel the pieces fall into place. As if a light went on, I could see what the poem meant, not the individual words lined together but the feelings behind them. My head spun and I smiled behind the hand pressed to my mouth to hide it.

Just for me, from Aubin.

But I was with Toan. I loved Toan. I had loved him all my life.

Then I felt like I was going to be sick.

I knew I should throw the note away. Rip it up into unsalvageable pieces and discard them, clear it from my possession. I closed my eyes to build my resolve to do just that, but I saw his written words, legible in my mind, seared into white lines floating on my darkened lids. I couldn't clear them from my mind.

Sweet and shared. Tangled. Bewildered.

I opened my eyes and swallowed my stomach back down to its rightful position. With shaking hands I refolded the paper along the creases and tucked it into my pocket, pushing it against the seam to make sure it would not fall out. I wished I had brought my secret stash of Aubin's paper and his pen in my bag. I checked my wristcomm; there was enough time left in the

day before Toan arrived home — I could still get there first and work on a note.

I don't remember much of my trip from the CDB to the house. I must have caught the hover just as it was leaving the station, because I don't remember waiting there. I checked the time as I kicked my shoes off at the front door and remember knowing I had a little over two hours before Toan would be home. If he didn't leave early, which he never did.

I considered typing a note to Aubin. It would have been easier. I knew I could get the words to come more easily, to say the right things. But somehow it felt like cheating. The gift, and the quandary of Aubin's poem burned in my pocket. With those words he had let me in to feel his thoughts in a way that a typed note wouldn't allow. I owed him the same effort, even though I knew I couldn't return his feelings. "I love Toan," I heard myself whisper.

The paper and pen Aubin had given me were hidden in a box in my closet behind a storage tote of old mementos we couldn't be bothered with or bear to throw away. I pushed the plastic tote aside and reached back, feeling for the box in the space too high above my head to see. When my fingers found it, I hooked them under the lid and pulled it out of its hiding spot. I sat at the desk in my office and laid the paper flat in front of me. I positioned the paper with Aubin's alphabet to my left so I could reference it as I wrote. I started with the capital 'A'.

It took me more than an hour and several crumpled pages. When I was finished, I leaned back in the chair and held up my note to scrutinize it. My letters were various sizes of large, while Aubin's were uniform and compact. My lines were jagged and uncertain, tipping up away from the blue guides, while Aubin's were straight and smooth. My ink ebbed from dark and indented to so light it almost wasn't visible, whereas Aubin's was even and consistent. But my words were there, my thoughts were transcribed from my mind through my hand into a tangible, legible existence.

Aubin, Thank you for your beautiful words. I understand them better now. I am sorry I did not see it before. I am matched with Toan, but I hope we can still be friends. I would like it if you would come to lunch again.

Hessa.

I felt guilty as I read it over. I had spent over an hour on four short sentences. Looking at the proof of my idleness, I realized that Toan would never justify such a waste of time, even if I used this new skill to make a gift for him. He wouldn't see the spirit in the lines, the sentiment in the process, just time spent unwisely and lost opportunity. I knew I couldn't share my new interest with him, just as I knew I couldn't stop learning how to write. It would have to stay a secret, and that realization burned in my chest. But some secrets are harmless, I reasoned, and what he didn't know…

I dumped my crumpled failed attempts into the incinerator and slipped the good folded note into my workbag. By the time Toan came home I was able to surprise him with the table set and dinner ready to be heated. I even remembered to have his music playing. He kissed me on the cheek and thanked me in a way that made me feel guilty again for the time I had wasted and then asked me about my day.

"Good, uneventful." I shrugged, watching the food fill my fork. Without revealing the handwriting, I couldn't explain my afternoon spent on the trip to the CDB and then writing the note. I forced his focus onto his day by asking questions about the research he couldn't share and the stories he could. After we ate, we moved to the couch and watched a show on the central panel. I let him pull me to his side, snuggling up against him. I smiled at him when he kissed me. I loved Toan.

The next day I knocked on Aubin's classroom door and went in upon his invitation. His room was smaller than mine, and the lighting was set lower so it felt cozy, and close. Posters and pictures covered the walls so that color had taken over the white — landscapes of big skies, rolling hills bursting with splotches of colorful plants, animal close-ups, detailed to show texture of fur, scales, skin. Larger-than-life portraits with unfamiliar names typed underneath; Emerson, Whitman, Thoreau, Muir, Fuller. I hadn't heard of any of them, of course, and I wondered if they were real or characters in the stories he had read.

I felt him watching me and asked, "How are the students not distracted by all the pictures?"

He looked around the room and said, "I prefer 'inspired' to 'distracted'."

He looked back at me, waiting. I knew he knew why I was there. He didn't mask his impatience with small talk, so I held my breath and stepped closer to his desk, heart racing. I laid the folded paper on his desk in front of him and let out a breath. When his eyes moved from the paper to meet mine standing over him, I couldn't hold his lit gaze. I looked away with an attempted smile and muttered, "I'll see you at lunch?" I hadn't meant for it to be a question, but my voice rose in uncertainty. I wanted out and was moving to the door before he could answer, but I could hear the paper flutter as he opened the folds just before door slid shut behind me.

When I reached the lounge at lunch, Aubin sat at our regular table and gave me a hesitant smile. I felt lighter when I sighed, and couldn't contain my giddy grin. He was there every lunch from then on. Until he requested his transfer.

13

Tragedasa

Gallie – Until your own match, what was your experience with matched partnerships?

Hessa – I don't know what you mean.

Gallie – For example, what was the nature of your parents' relationships?

Hessa – In what way?

Gallie – Was your parents' match arranged or self-chosen?

Hessa – Their match was arranged by their parents, who were research partners.

Gallie – I see. And Toan's parents? Was their match arranged or self-chosen?

Hessa – They were matched through an agency.

Finch – Does this line of questioning have an objective purpose?

Gallie – Yes, you will see the purpose in another question or two. Would you say your parents' match, and Toan's parents' match, were successful?

Hessa – I guess, but —

Gallie – Are your parents still together?

Finch – That's two questions, Counsel Gallie.

Gallie – Answer the question, Ms. Black. Are your parents still together?

Hessa – Yes.

Gallie – And Toan's?

Hessa – They were until Uncle G died.

Gallie – So would you say you were taught, by their example, to respect your match?

Hessa – I love Toan.

Gallie – Yes, that's very nice, but not the answer to my question.

Hessa —Yes, I respected our partnership. I was thankful to be matched with Toan.

Uncle G died the month that Toan was fifteen and I was still fourteen. I remember waking up in the darkness of my small bedroom when the central panel indicated an incoming emergency call. I heard my parents' quickened steps on the stairs and felt urgency in their wake. I snuck down and hid on the stairs behind the wall, where I could see the call but they couldn't see me.

Aunt Maryne was on the central panel screen, talking in an unfamiliarly frantic tone. I could see a hospital room behind her — the harsh lights bounced off her dark hair and made me squint. Her words were scattered, her dry eyes so wide that the dark irises were surrounded by white instead of lids. I heard the words 'accident' and 'dead'. I heard my father cry out, a wail that shook its way deep to the middle of me. I had never heard a sound like that before. Or since. It was a terrible, guttural cry that echoed in my head long after the night was over. I wanted to run from it, to go back to my room and back to sleep where the call and his cry might prove to be a nightmare if I could wake myself up, but the very next second I saw Toan. Not on the central panel screen, but in my mind. I stumbled into the room where my mother had wrapped herself around my sunken father on the couch. She had tears in her eyes as well. My father's face was hidden in his hands, but a low moan still escaped from his shaking form.

I looked from my parents on the couch to the wall screen, where Aunt Maryne's pale, shocked face was larger than me. "Toan?"

I wasn't confident I had spoken the word out loud until Aunt Maryne shook her head fast and blinked, and then rushed to say, "He's fine, sweetheart, he's still at home."

My father shook off my mother's arms and his sobs and dragged his sleeve across his face. "I'll go get him, Maryne. We'll be right there."

"Thank you, Nimran," Aunt Maryne said, and the screen went black.

"Hessa." I jumped at my mother's voice behind me and turned to face her as my father stalked past me out of the room. "There was an accident, and Gauss has died."

My eyes filled with tears at the same time as I my stomach churned with relief and guilt that Toan was safe. "I want to go with you."

I expected a refusal, so I started to line up my reasoning, but my mother just nodded. "Get dressed," she said softly, and I hurried to my room before she could change her mind.

I had always wanted to ride in a car, but I shuddered when the long black one pulled up in front of our house. I held my breath from the tangy-sharp scent as we approached. It reminded me of thunder and lightning storms. Everything about the car was dark — the cavernous space I climbed into with my parents, the windows, the leather seats, the short, rough carpet on the floor. It smelled bad inside too, like something left wet until it deteriorated into pieces. And somehow it was cold, even though it was hot outside. My mother slipped her arm around me as I watched my father without looking directly at him. He stared out the dark window, turned away from us, but I could see his face reflected back. His eyes were wide, like Aunt Maryne's had been, but his were wet and jittery, as if searching. But I couldn't see anything he could be looking for outside.

I was told to wait in the car with the driver while my parents woke Toan and brought him out. I was relieved I wouldn't have to be there to witness them telling Toan about the accident, but being trapped in the car with the silent oddout made my legs twitch and my mind jittery. My head hurt. Just when I decided to ignore my parents' instructions and go in, the door to the house slid open and three shadows came out. The car door lifted open and Toan fell in against the seat. When the door swung shut again, he leaned against it, away from me. He wouldn't look at me, which hurt almost as much as the chest pain that stabbed when I studied his tight, turned-down lips and wet cheeks. Without thinking about it, I reached across the space between us and laid my hand over his on the seat. He startled and glanced my way. His eyes flashed the reflected streetlights as they filled again with tears. He turned his hand over and squeezed mine. It

111

was the first time we held hands.

At the hospital we were ushered into a small room, just big enough for a plastic couch along one wall and matching plastic chairs facing it. We were only there a minute or so before Aunt Maryne slipped into the room. I hung back with my parents as Toan hugged his mother. Toan cried, and I started to cry too. Aunt Maryne held him, whispered in his ear and rubbed his back in a way she had not done since we were four or five. When Aunt Maryne approached my parents, she held my father the same way. I sat silent beside Toan in the small room while our parents came and went with adults we didn't know. We whispered a bit and cried, but mostly we just sat, silently holding hands. My throat hurt and my head pounded. Toan's face stayed white and wet. As the sun started to creep through the window, my parents and his mother returned alone, together, and announced it was time to go home.

The car that took us home was brighter with the light coming in the shaded windows and smelled as if it had just been cleaned, but I still didn't enjoy the drive. It was too smooth, like we weren't moving at all, and I missed the rocking of the hover. We dropped Toan and Aunt Maryne off at their home. I remember wondering, as they walked up to the door, how their house could look exactly the same when their world was irreversibly changed. I imagined Uncle G's shoes at the door, his tie hanging over the kitchen chair, and wondered who Aunt Maryne would hand it to when she said, "This doesn't go here." Once home, I took my mother's suggestion to go back to bed, more because I wanted to be alone than because I felt like sleeping.

The next few days were a blur of activity contrasted with long periods of sitting around. My mother took me to the store, where we bought a month's worth of meal servings and stashed them in Aunt Maryne's cooling system. Toan and I sat silently studying or watching shows on his central panel (sitting on the floor, even though Uncle G's orthochair was empty) while my mother and Aunt Maryne discussed everything from the cleaners' schedule to the arrival dates of Uncle G's brothers. My mother spent a lot of time sitting and nodding at the table while Aunt Maryne talked on the communicator in the kitchen. All the time we were together, studying, watching shows, there was very little talking. I remember not knowing what to say to Toan. It was like he was locked away from me.

We were all sad. Toan was distant, my mother was short-tempered and Aunt Maryne organized with a focus and efficiency I didn't know was possible. I wavered between distracted and teary with a queasy feeling in my stomach that would not go away. But my father was devastated. At night I could hear him talking to my mother in his room. Sometimes his words were halted by a wail that was a muffled, broken version of the first one I heard the night of the accident. Most mornings he went to work early before I was up and ready for school and came home late after the sun had set. When he was home, he spent his time in his office with his numbers. My mother asked me to take his dinner up to him one night. I knocked on the door so softly, I wasn't sure he heard me on the other side. I was about to knock again when I heard him say, "Come in."

The door slid open, and I met his eyes over his desk. They were dull. His face was flat, without the lines that usually creased the sides of his eyes, his mouth and his cheeks when he smiled. His thinned hair still stood in all directions, but it didn't look funny anymore. "Mom sent up your supper," I said, though it was obvious because I held it in my hand.

My father tipped his head to his desk and looked away from me, back to the computer screen. I was suddenly fearful to enter farther into the room, to move closer to him, which seemed ridiculous. I knew he'd never hurt me, but the pain he was fighting emanated from his slouch, radiating from him with a physicality that seemed infectious. I tiptoed toward him and laid the plate where he indicated, turned and fled the room. I felt safer when I heard the door slide shut behind me.

Uncle G's funeral assembly was a week after the accident. I wore my best school uniform that matched the gray bands my parents had stitched on their sleeves. The community hall was filled with Uncle G's colleagues from the bank. The chairs were filled with somber dark suits, and I made a game of tilting my head so that the shiny gray bands on most of the left arms would line up just so. One of Uncle G's brothers couldn't come because of his sensitive work schedule, or so he said. The other was able to work remotely, so he arrived the night before and worked from the hotel then took his lunch hour over the service time and planned to leave right after the service to finish his workday on the flight home.

I sat between my mother, stoic with her straight-backed posture, lips pressed together, and my father, who stared at his folded hands. While I listened, a Judician announced the details of Uncle G's death; the date and time, the manner (unchallenged accidental cause) and his heirs of record (Aunt Maryne and Toan). The Judician declared his work placement to be vacant, and his employer signed papers requesting his replacement. Finally, the Judician asked the audience "Who will be responsible, in partnership with Maryne Sloane, for the advancement of Toan Whitley's education and match?"

That was the only time my father raised his eyes from his hands. He pressed himself to standing and said, "I will." His voice caught.

The Judician scanned the audience for the source of my father's answer and nodded. "Your name and classification, sir?"

"Nimran Black, Quantifier." Aunt Maryne smiled at my father from the desk in front of the Judician as the Judician banged the antique gavel on the top of the desk and declared the assembly concluded.

My parents convinced Aunt Maryne that she and Toan should spend the night. Toan was in the spare room beside mine. I could hear him turning in the bed. I missed the times when we were small enough to share a room when our parents visited. Late into the night I could hear my parents and Aunt Maryne in our living room. My mother and Aunt Maryne talked and laughed a little, but their voices were hushed and heavy. When I heard my father, his voice was still hollow. He stopped talking and started to wail again, and I thought I heard Aunt Maryne consoling him. That was the last time I heard him cry.

On her way to bed, my mother stopped in my room, as she used to when I was little. I was still awake, which shouldn't have surprised her. She crossed the floor and perched on the side of my bed, brushing the hair back off my face. "You okay?" she whispered.

114

I nodded and said, "I don't like hearing Dad cry," though I didn't mean to say anything at all.

"I don't either, Hessa. He is very sad. Uncle G was very important to him, his ... his closest friend. He has lost a great deal."

"He's sadder than Aunt Maryne, even."

My mother hesitated and then nodded. "Yes I suppose he is."

"Why? Did he love Uncle G more than Aunt Maryne did?"

My mother brushed back my hair again. In the light coming in from the door, I could see by her furrowed brows and pinched lips that she was thinking. "I think he probably did."

For some reason that answer scared me. "Did he love Uncle G more than he loves you?"

She smiled softly and stopped stroking my hair to lay her hand on my head. "He loved him very much, Hessa. Very much. There are different ways to love, and people can love more than one person. His love for Gauss does not limit his love for me or for you. Your father and I were lucky to be matched with each other. With your father's Proof scores, well, and Uncle G's, of course, they were expected to apply for Lineage Progression. And your father truly wanted a family — we both did. We are a good match, and we are so lucky and happy to have you. And then your Uncle G and Aunt Maryne were arranged, but they grew to love each other in their own way, I think."

"But not as much as Dad and Uncle G." I could tell even then that my understanding was shallow and limited.

"No, probably not. Not in the same way. Aunt Maryne is sad, of course, but she has Toan and she has her work and she has us."

"Dad still has us."

My mother smiled and nodded again. "Yes, Hessa. He'll need us very much."

14

Quattuordecim

Gallie –Was there anything special about the summer months of Seven and Eight?

Hessa –No.

Gallie –You can think of nothing new or unusual
that happened during that time?

Hessa –No. Nothing.

My lunches with Aubin became routine again, and I felt better
for it. I was convinced it was better for everyone involved if I
kept my learning to write between Aubin and I. It was a harmless omission of fact, really; handwriting was only a lazy, selfish
pastime that served no purpose beyond being something I enjoyed. When I was studying Aubin's notes or writing my own, I
felt a calm that was new and divergently invigorating. Math and
numbers were easy for me; they were my history and my calling.
But if I could learn to *write*, a skill that was so far from quantifi-
cation that there was no intersection with my encoded aptitude,
maybe I could do more than I imagined.

I didn't have to lie to Toan. I worked time into my schedule
when I knew he would be occupied at work. At first I wrote lists
— of tasks, menus for the week, my students' names, numbers
and dates. When I ran out of lists, I wrote out lyrics to the
counting songs I remembered from my childhood. I saved the
papers, stashed in a folder that had kept some old photos in my
desk, for the infrequent lunch I found myself alone in the
lounge with Aubin. I slipped him the folder for his review, enjoying the smile he'd hold on his face as he skimmed through
my scratchings and nodded.

"What's this?" he asked when he came to a song I had written out.

"It's a song, can't you read it?"

He checked over his shoulder as if out of habit and looked closer at the paper. "Of course I can read it. Did you write it?" I didn't know what he meant. I had written all of the notes, but he knew that — why else would I show him? I frowned at him, and he looked up from the paper with his eyes narrowed. "Did you make it up?"

"No, stupid," I laughed. "It's 'The Fifty Little Monkeys Jumping on the Beds'. Uncle G taught it to us to help us learn division when we were little. Haven't you heard it before?"

Aubin shook his head just twice. "No, I haven't." He studied the page as if he could glean wisdom from the juvenile lyric.

"Never?"

He laughed and closed the folder, leaving it in his lap under the table. "No, never. My parents didn't sing me number songs."

"What did they sing you?"

He shrugged. "They made stuff up. My favorite was one my father sang about a whale stuck in a puddle and a worm who tried to save him."

Before I could stop myself I snorted. "That sounds foolish!" As soon as the words were out of my mouth, I felt my face flush.

Aubin must have seen my embarrassment because he laughed. "It was supposed to be. It was funny." His eyes were unfocused in a distracted gaze. His laugh softened to a light, thoughtful smile. "It was funny," he whispered, but he wasn't talking to me.

I felt like I was intruding, so I stared at my sandwich and picked at the crust, waiting for him to come back. A bubble of mustard clung to the side, so I wiped it with my finger and put the tart glob on my tongue.

"Hessa, you have to stop writing lists." I looked up, startled. My argument was ready, but he prevented it with his continuation. "You're missing the point. Writing isn't about the mechanical process — it's about the creation of your own thoughts,

117

about making your ideas concrete for other people to see, to feel."

I laughed at him. "Huh? Now you're not making any sense."

He checked over his shoulder again and lowered his voice, which increased its intensity. "Hessa. Your handwriting is beautiful, but that's just the method. You need to *write* something, write down your own words."

I found my arms crossed tightly and instructed them to unfold. I laced my fingers together and forced my shoulders down, off guard. "I can't." My voice was smaller than I meant it to be.

"Why not? You did once."

"When?"

"You wrote me my note, when you first started writing." He dug into his pocket and pulled out a folded paper that I knew was my initial attempt at writing. I didn't know he still had it, or why. He stuffed it back away.

"That note was stupid."

"Far from it. It was honest, concise. Explicit." I thought I saw a wash of pain douse the familiar flash in his eyes. He worked his jaw and blinked, and the expression was gone. He smiled. "You can."

And then I felt trapped, backed into a corner. "I'm a Quantifier, Aubin. I'm not like you."

"Yes, you're certified a Quantifier. You're a great math teacher. But that's what you do. It's not who you are."

"What's the difference?" The words spat from my mouth with a force that surprised me more than it seemed to surprise him.

"Everything."

I rolled my eyes, frustrated by another of his cryptic declarations. I busied my eyes and my hands, gathering the refuse from my lunch, and stood to take it to the incinerator. His hand lit on my arm, and a static spark zapped between us. I flinched. He laughed. But his palm stayed, warm and solid.

"Sorry," he said, but I didn't know what for. I sat back down and he took his hand back, leaving that spot on my arm cool. "Prove me wrong," he said lightly. "I'll give you a word, and you write something about it. Three sentences tops."

"I can't."

"So prove it."

We sat still in our chairs with our eyes locked. He dared me, and I challenged him back. In hindsight, I think I realized in some deep, hidden part of me that we stalled in that moment on a brink, a precipice from which a fall would change everything. Or maybe by then I was already falling.

"It'll be terrible, and you'll laugh."

His smile was quick, but I was too stubborn to return it. "There's nothing wrong with laughing, Hessa." He waited.

"Fine. What word?" I tried to sound defiant, audacious, but I'm sure he saw right through it.

"Dharma."

"What?"

"Dharma."

"What does that even mean?"

"You have to find out for yourself." His smile turned obnoxious and I restrained the urge to punch him. His ever-present pen started flying over a page in his notebook even before he turned from me to watch his hand. He tore the corner of the page.

"Is that one of your ancient words?"

He nodded, his insufferable grin spreading to his eyes. I wanted to storm out, to stomp my feet like an insolent child, but he stood before I could make my move. He held out his hand with the small scrap of paper he had torn from the corner pinched between his first two fingers. My own hand lifted in response, in betrayal. Our fingers touched when I took the paper. The spark was not static. He winked at me, which only made me angrier, and then turned and left the room.

My hand was fisted around the paper. I had to will my fingers open so that it lay flat on my palm. In Aubin's familiar script, I could easily read: '*dharma. You can do it, A.*'

I shoved the scrap into my pocket, threw my garbage in the incinerator and stomped out of the room. Without his audience, my behavior was less satisfying.

I didn't know where to look to find the definition of Aubin's word. My Quantifier access to resources did not define current words other than mathematical terms, let alone a word long lost in an ancient language. The only place I could search was the Central Database. And I needed a legitimate reason to go back so Toan wouldn't know I was wasting so much time. In my head I developed and rehearsed a story about meeting a colleague to help him develop some lesson plans. Some of it was true.

Toan nodded as I recounted my prepared explanation Sunday night during dinner. "Will you need to reschedule the grocery delivery? I can be available on Saturday if it you can't work around it."

"No, thanks, he can meet me in the afternoon." I couldn't meet his eyes. The pasty carrots stuck to the roof of my mouth. It was hard to swallow them down.

"That's great, Hessa. He's lucky to have you helping him. I'm sure he'll have it worked out in no time."

"It's my job," I said with a shrug and a mouthful. I lined up the carrots on my plate into perfectly even stripes.

"It's more than that. You're a great teacher, you know? You really care about those kids." I heard his movement a second before his hand found mine on the table. He squeezed it twice. "You okay?"

"Uh-huh." I swallowed hard to keep my food down. My explanation had not seemed so malevolent in my mind. Now that it was out of my mind and shared with Toan, my throat felt tight and my chest burned. I wanted to take it back, but I couldn't. It was too late.

Even though I was looking at my food, I knew he was watching me. I forced my eyes up to meet his. "You don't look great, Hessa. Do you want to take a sick claim from your compulsory run? I can run alone, or I could take one too and we could stay home and play a game or watch a show and get our arts compulsory done early." He touched my face and I bit my lip to keep a confession from spilling out.

I nodded, and when I trusted myself, I added, "I'd like that."

Toan cleared our dishes to the incinerator and made us tea while giving a monologue about his work with a vagueness that

120

kept confidentiality intact and made it difficult for me to understand. In an effort to make up for my deception, I listened intently long past the point that he usually lost my attention. He was laughing as he recounted a misunderstanding that had reduced days of work to a nonsensical collection of numbers. "Just by dumb luck, Hessa, the result was as expected, but the supporting proofs just didn't align. He spent hours trying to find some small mistake near the end, when in fact he had it wrong days before. I've never seen anything like it. He was so mad, and then they fined him for the wasted time."

He brought the tea over to our table and sat across from me, smiling. "What?" I asked and wiped the corner of my mouth to see if a piece of rice or sauce remained.

"Nothing. I just … I love your smile." So I smiled again, to make his own smile widen. From the corner of his eyes small wrinkles were starting to crease. They were new, a sign of adulthood that looked good on him. It was strange how his eyes could change with age and at the same time still stay the same ones I had known all my life. If I squinted just a bit, I could see his wide, round, five-year-old eyes in place of the shining ones before me.

The next morning I smiled when Toan kissed me on his way out of the door then busied myself while I waited for the groceries to arrive. I watched the clock tick slowly on, willing time to pass and the grocery oddout to arrive so I could leave. To keep the queasy turning in my stomach away, I tried not to think about my trip to the CDB. By the time the oddout finished bringing our groceries into the kitchen, I had Aubin's pen and papers, including the scrap with my assigned word, in my bag with my screen, all sitting by the door, and my shoes on my feet. I hurried to stash the groceries away in their right places, swung my bag onto my back and called "Lock door" as it slid shut behind me.

The hover station was almost empty in the middle of the day. Without a crowd the platform was spacious and bright. I paced beside the clear barrier that separated the platform from the track and watched the digital schedule on the glass of the barrier counting down to the hover's arrival until the swoosh of

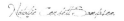

air was pushed out of the tunnel ahead of the hover.

When the doors opened, I stepped in and sat against the cool window. I opened my bag. I had my own seat, but I still didn't feel safe bringing Aubin's note into view. Instead, I pulled out my screen and turned it on, trying to look attentive to a screen of numbers in front of me. My eyes tracked over the rows of symbols from the lesson plan for the next day, but my mind was circling around the note in my bag. 'Dharma'. D-H-A-R-M-A. It sounded sort of like a curse word my father liked to use, though softer. It didn't sound like an action, I couldn't imagine what I'd be doing to say 'I am dharmaing'. That sounded ridiculous. *I dharmaed last night*, I thought and laughed to myself. Perhaps it was a toy? A food? It could be a fancy dessert they serve at a high-class restaurant.

At the CDB station I disembarked and walked down the street, my gait awkward and clumsy at a pace stuck between a fast walk and a slow run. My breath was short and my heart beat in my ears. The sun was up there somewhere, baking the city in heat, but the forest of buildings blocked the brightest light. I walked through one shadow into another of varying darkness and color, depending on the shades of glass blocking the sun. I shivered as the trickle of sweat that traced its way from the base of my skull down my neck and spine turned cold in the treated cool air inside the CDB doors. Once there, I had no idea which way to turn.

The CDB was always busy but spacious enough that people were spread out. I sat at a desk screen and opened a search under the public access. I didn't want a trail on my account; my Quantifier status would not provide access to translations and definitions anyway. I touched the field on the screen to bring the cursor alive. I didn't want to speak the word aloud, so I activated the holoboard and typed the word — 'dharma' — out on the glowing holographic keys. I touched the screen again to send the word into the database search process. I gazed at the spinning indicator showing the progress. My eyes fixed and froze. My attention turned inward, closing close around me and the whirling lights on the screen.

A hand on my shoulder startled me out of my trance. I

jumped and turned and swallowed the curse, leaving a withered "shhh" sound escaping in its place.

Aubin laughed. "Shit?"

"No, I was going to say 'hello'."

Aubin smiled and nodded. "Sure. What are you looking for?"

"You already know that," I grumbled, turning back to the screen, where text had appeared. The top line read, '*Term dharma unknown*' and was followed by suggestions of closely spelled words. My eyes fell on my father's curse word, included in the list. I was sure I could use *that* word in a sentence just then.

"You won't find it there," Aubin said, stepping up to the computer and crowding my space so I had to take a step back. His fingers flew over the holoboard as the screen changed in response to his typing. "Here, use my account."

The entrance to his account looked like mine, with the same blue screen, white text and Authority crest in the top left corner. The welcoming line greeted Aubin instead of showing my name, and the personal details were his, of course, his classification, address, work appointment. He backed up to give me space in front of the computer and waved in invitation. I typed 'dharma' into the search field, and the screen flashed to a list of results. Aubin pointed to the top one. "Here's your definitions," and moving his hand down the screen, "these are literary references in which the word is used, and those are variations of the word."

"That's a lot of information," I said, daunted.

"Start with the definition. Forget the rest of this for now. Did you bring your screen?" I hesitated, not sure I wanted proof of this project on my system. He waited with his hand out, so I conceded and handed him my screen from my bag. He tapped the side to transfer the search file and then handed it back to me.

"Thanks, I think."

"You're welcome. I'm sure."

"Are you staying?" I had known he would be there, but I didn't realize until just then how much I had been hoping to see

123

him.

"I wish I could, but I can't stay. I've been here since early this morning, and I have to do my compulsory run and some errands. But I'll see you at lunch tomorrow?"

I nodded, pushing my mouth into a smile so the disappointment didn't show on my face. "Yeah, sure. See you then."

Aubin smiled and touched my shoulder again. My breath caught and stopped until his hand lifted away. He turned and strode through the sliding doors while I kept my head bowed over my screen, watching him from under my eyebrows. He didn't turn back, and I felt my stomach sink.

I headed to a corner desk and slid into a chair. From my bag I pulled Aubin's blank sheets and his pen, smoothed flat the scrap of paper and lay them beside the screen. I took a deep breath and placed the pen in my right hand, careful to set my fingers just in the right positions. From Aubin's scrap note I copied 'dharma' onto the top of the page. I looked at the file on my screen. There were several definitions. Some had other words I couldn't understand, like 'Buddha' and 'cosmic'. I sighed and rubbed my hand over my jaw to direct it to unclench. How would I know which was right? Which one had he meant? I pointed my finger and closed my eyes. I spun my finger, tracing a circle in the air and placed it gently on the screen. Opening my eyes, I saw one definition entry highlighted and read the text. The words trailed one after the other, building in confusion instead of clarifying the meaning. At least I knew each individual word. I copied it out slowly on the page:

dharma (Sanskrit): The unique and ideal path in life of each individual person, and the ability and inner knowledge of how to find it.

I read the definition in my own writing, and it started to transform. The words, convoluted in type, linked together like the letters in my writing, building into a concept that I could understand beyond the confusing words. Aubin wanted three sentences about the word, and I was sure the definition didn't count since it wasn't mine. Where from there? I underlined the words in the definition that seemed to mean more: *ideal, path, individual, knowledge, find*. I thought of Aubin's poem that I shouldn't have read and my reply to it, his surprise revelation and my apologetic denial. I felt a warm flush of something rise from my chest into my face at the memory. Guilt? I felt badly that he gave me access to his secrets, even if it was by accident, and I had rebuffed him. But what else could I do? Matched to Toan, my choices were made. I was on my path already. Maybe I could let Aubin see that and make him understand. That idea spurred me on, and I scratched frantic scribbles on the papers for long enough that I lost track of time. When I had something good enough through the crossed out attempts, I rewrote it on a clean sheet:

Numbers itemize and count my responsibilities. My dharma is found in my match, my job, my duty of Aptitude. I know limits and confines and laws. My path is precise, the rules definite and reliable and safe.

I almost crumpled it up, but Aubin's challenge forced me to line up the corners and fold it in half, tuck it in my bag and keep it for him to read. Then I slumped, spent, as if I had doubled my compulsory run on a humid day. I took a deep breath and forced myself to stand up. I packed the rest of my belongings in my bag and went back to the hover station, hoping to arrive home with enough time to catch a nap before Toan returned from work. I didn't feel any different.

The next morning, I didn't want to wait until lunch. Instead I stood outside of Aubin's classroom door in the morning until I saw his familiar shape sauntering down the hall. He smiled and wished me a good morning as he pressed his palm to the panel and walked through the opening door. I followed.

"I hope you're here for the reason I think you're here, and not for the reason I fear you're here," he said with a laugh in his voice.

"What does that even mean?" I tried to sound annoyed but was truly perplexed. "Can't you ever just say something straight?"

"I hope you're here to show me something, not to tell me you can't do it."

"I wrote something." I wanted to sound irritated and impatient, but my throat was tight and made my voice crack at the end of the sentence.

"Good. Let's see it." He kept his right hand stuffed into the

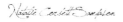

pocket of his slacks and held out the other. Light shimmered off the red band around his arm as it moved toward me.

"It's not any good." I didn't move. He didn't either. His hand remained floating between us.

"Well then, it's as you expected. You have nothing to lose by showing it to me."

I wanted to growl at him. A real growl, like an angry dog. I didn't. Instead I pulled the folded paper from my bag. I had refused to let myself read it again since I had folded it in the CDB — the urge to crumple and incinerate it would prove too great. My hand shook as I held it out to him, my heart was racing and my throat tightly sore.

He held my gaze instead of watching his hands unfold the paper and winked at me with a smile just before he looked down at my writing. His eyes flickered back and forth and then up to the top of the page and back and forth again. His smile faltered, but he pushed his lips back up. His eyes stayed dark.

"See? It's awful." I made an effort to snatch it back out of his hands, but he stepped back as I stepped forward.

"It's beautiful, Hessa."

"You're lying."

"I'm not. I can ... I know how you feel." His voice was low, just more than a whisper, and even, controlled. It was if he had used the note to see right into me and seemed hurt by what he had seen. My chest burned and my stomach twitched. "And *that's* the purpose of writing." He folded the paper along the set crease and held it out to me.

"You wanted it, it's for you." I held up my hand in refusal, but it trembled, so I pulled it back to my side.

"Even better," is what I think he muttered as the paper disappeared into his pocket. He started moving things around on his desk. After a discomforted moment, he met my eyes and said, "I should get ready..."

I nodded and took a deep breath, feeling my heart slow to normal, but my stomach still churning. "Me too. Thanks for reading it."

He finally smiled again. "Thanks for writing it. It really is lovely. I think you should write some more."

"Give me a word," someone said. It was me. I wanted to try again, try for a happier reaction that showed he was proud of the work I'd done to learn and the work he had done to teach me. Happy about the effort we made together.

His natural smile returned. "Okay, I'll find one and give it to you tomorrow."

"Great!" I said, my stomach settling a bit. I took a step toward the door. "I'll see you at lunch?"

"See you then," he said as the door slid open and I stepped into the hall.

15

Fünfzehn

Gallie – So your testimony is that you met Aubin Wallace in Seven, spent time with him as a colleague and a friend, but that nothing else changed in your life or in his that summer?

Hessa – I was only talking about me. I can't speak for Aubin or his life.

Gallie – Unfortunately, neither can he.

Finch – That is an inflammatory comment, Counsel Gallie.

Gallie – My sincere apologies. Was he pursuing a match?

Hessa – Not that I know of.

Gallie – How close was he to his mandatory match date?

Hessa – I don't know.

Gallie – He wrote his Proofs four years ago.

Finch – The court knows he was a year from his mandatory date. This line of questioning is unnecessary.

Gallie – I am establishing intent. Was Aubin actively looking for a match?

Hessa – I don't know.

Gallie – Why don't you know? He was coming within a year of the mandated matching or Hazard deployment. This seems like an important concern for someone you have identified as your friend.

Hessa – We didn't talk about it.

Gallie – At the time of his death, there were no active accounts in any Matching Agencies for Mr. Wallace, which suggests he wasn't looking for a match.

Hessa – He wouldn't go through an agency.

Gallie – No?

Hessa – No.

Gallie – And why not? Agency Matches work well. You've said yourself Mr. Whitley's parents had a successful match through an agency.

Hessa – Aubin wouldn't have been interested in that.

Gallie – And why not?

Hessa – Aubin wanted to find someone he loved.

Gallie – But I thought you said you didn't talk about it with him?

A sealed yellow envelope with Aubin's 'HESSA' written on the front was on my desk the next morning. I didn't even wonder at the time how he had gained access to my classroom; likely he'd charmed the oddout who cleaned the rooms after the students left for the day. I commanded the door locked then sat at the desk and lifted the envelope. I traced the 'H' with my finger.

I pulled the flap open with my thumb and glanced at the closed door before sliding the paper out of its tight cocoon. It was folded precisely in thirds, corners to corners, with the creases pressed clean. I opened it slowly, savoring the reveal. I was becoming better trained in reading handwriting, especially Aubin's familiar tidy script. It took me longer than reading text, but I didn't need a reference anymore to decode the varied letters.

Hessa, Thank you, again, for your poem. You have a way with words that is a wonderful surprise. But I'm afraid you missed part of the definition — the word 'inner' is of utmost importance to the concept of 'dharma'. The rules and confines you identify in your poem are 'outer' ones. I find myself repeating, being a Quantifier is what you do, not who you are. Inside. I'm afraid you have a poet's heart, whether you believe me or not. As you requested, here is another word for your study and muse: 'jayus'. A.

I read it twice and then a third time before folding it along Aubin's creases and slipping it back in the envelope, then the envelope into my bag. My head buzzed and my fingers were twitchy. I felt my lips pulled wide in a silly grin. The whole week before I could go back to the CDB was impossible. *Jayus*. It sounded funny, happy and light, but 'dharma' had fallen far from the fancy dessert I first imagined it could be. I hoped we'd have an opportunity to talk about it at lunchtime, but by the time I made it to the lounge Aubin was surrounded by several of our colleagues and involved in a lively but good-natured debate about a sporting event I hadn't heard of. He smiled at me as he listened to the history teacher argue some detail of the match. When I smiled back, he winked at me. I felt my face flush warm and looked around to see if any of the other teachers might have seen. Most of them were intent on claiming their turn the moment the Preserver stopped speaking, and the few who weren't were looking at their screens. I sighed, and the queasiness in my stomach settled with their disinterest leaving a hollow feeling that I had to share Aubin's time.

It wasn't until Friday that I was alone in the lounge when Aubin came in. I rushed to speak before our moment of privacy was lost. "You have to tell me what it means."

"Hello to you too." He pulled his brows together and laid his lunch on the table. "Tell you what *what* means?"

"'*Jayus*', the word you gave me. What does it mean?"

He shook his head slightly. "That's part of the process, Hessa. You have to find out for yourself." There was a laugh in his voice that made me clench my teeth.

"I can't! I can't get to the CDB until Monday." The whine in *my* voice annoyed me more than his smothered laugh.

He laughed outright at that. "Gimme your screen. I'll put my account access on your search program, and you can use it to find definitions whenever you want."

"I can't. What if Toan sees it?" The words blurted out unbidden.

Aubin frowned, his eyes narrowed in a steady stare. "So what if he does?" The laugh was gone. His voice was low and even.

"He doesn't know I've been writing. He wouldn't understand. He'd just think it was a waste of time."

Aubin looked at me for a moment with an intensity that made me fidget. I shifted in my seat. "Hessa, secrets are never good to keep. You shouldn't keep one from your match."

I felt chided and spat out defensively, "It's not like that, it's not a *secret*. It's just not worth upsetting him. And what do you know about matches anyway?" His glare turned dark and he kept his eyes trained on mine. In an effort to demonstrate confidence and cover for the churning in my middle, I thrust my hand into my bag and pulled out the screen, shoving it in front of him on the table. "Fine, put it on." He raised his left eyebrow so I added a faint, "Please."

It wasn't like Toan ever used my screen anyway.

Aubin still frowned as he passed the screen back to me after entering his account information. I muttered, "Thank you," and he nodded, and everything felt more settled.

"I guess you won't need to go to the CDB anymore," Aubin said around the bite of sandwich in his mouth.

"Guess not," I said, and then thought about the words. I liked working at the CDB, a world that seemed a better fit for my new interest than my tidy desk at home. I liked meeting Aubin there, away from our colleagues. Away from Toan. "It's quiet, though. Maybe I'll still go to work there sometimes." My voice was high and shaky, which made my cheeks warm.

"Maybe I'll still see you there, then." Aubin's voice was strange, low and husky, and so I looked up at him from my lunch. He finally smiled, so I smiled back.

"Maybe you will."

That night I was glad Toan was working later than me. And then I felt sick at the idea that I was happy to have the time without him. Still, I hurried to catch the earliest hover so I could be home with as much time as possible before he arrived. I negotiated with my guilt by taking the servings out of the freezer and putting them in the heater, ready to cook when he sent me a note to say he was on his way. I sat at the kitchen table with my screen and Aubin's paper and pen and accessed his search account. Enter: *'jayus'*. The screen flickered and then flashed a list of holographic definitions in the air in front of me. Without thinking, I closed my eyes and set my finger in the middle of the glowing letters, highlighting one entry:

jayus (Indonesian): A moment of awkward humor, as when a joke is delivered so poorly, one feels the irresistible urge to laugh.

I laughed as a memory of Toan standing in my childhood

131

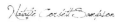

kitchen, trying to tell our parents a joke he couldn't quite remember, came to mind. Even my father laughed at his attempt,
and it had been a long time since my father laughed. Toan
turned red and refused to continue, despite their pestering. He
finally slipped a defeated smile at me when my parents and Aunt
Maryne segued into a story of their own about my father and
Uncle G and a failed attempt at a compulsory arts hour.

I copied the definition from the screen onto a piece of paper
and tried to remember the feeling in the small kitchen with our
parents and Toan and his joke. Toan was embarrassed, that was
easy enough to see by his red face and hunched shoulders. Our
parents laughed and teased him and then fell into their own
memories, leaving Toan and I to our silent communication. I
could read his gentle smile and shining eyes and knew just what
he felt. In that instant, excluded from our parents' reminiscing,
we were a team, Toan and I. In memory that moment epito-
mized my bond with Toan. We had been partners since we were
babies. Partners in play, in making and cleaning up our messes,
in causing trouble and trying to keep that trouble from our parents. After Uncle G died, we spent even more time together as
my father tried to support Aunt Maryne in raising Toan through
his adolescent years. We were partners in school projects and in
jobs, in math competitions and studying. And then we were
partners in everything else, from keeping our house to our compulsory runs. We shared everything: our time, our resources, our
stories, our memories, our plans for the future. Ourselves. He
was my best friend. I wanted to capture that safety, comfort,
familiarity in my writing about 'jayus'.

Head down, I scratched out words, scribbled over my attempts and scrawled new ones. My wristcomm buzzed on the
table beside me, making me jump. A message from Toan; he
was on his way home from the hover station, which didn't leave
me much time to clear away the evidence of my wasted hour. I
separated out the failed attempts and tossed them into the incinerator. I carried the couple of good sheets to the hall, where I
stuffed them into my work bag. I turned on the heater for supper and double-checked that the files and search program on my
screen were closed. When Toan walked through the door, I was
sitting at the table watching the news and trying to slow my rac-

ing heart with deep, catching breaths.

"What smells so good?" Toan smiled as he bowed to peck the top of my head with a kiss. "You should have eaten. You didn't have to wait for me."

"I thought you might want some pasta." I hoped my effort to sound casual didn't have the opposite effect.

"Mmm, I'll eat pasta anytime." Toan peeked in the heater at the servings I had chosen.

"I know." And I did. Pasta was his favorite. I wondered what Aubin's favorite food was and then wondered why that question came to mind. I shook my head to clear it as guilt fluttered in my stomach. I stood to retrieve the cutlery.

"Thank you, Hessa." He stepped behind me, put his arms around my waist and kissed my neck. I squirmed because it tickled and turned around to nestle against his chest, where I felt safe and warm and his lips couldn't reach me. The heater sounded when dinner was ready, and I stepped back out of his arms to fetch our supper. Toan sighed and let me go.

On Monday morning I waited for the grocery delivery with an impatience that was becoming familiar. I reached the CDB just before noon and walked the perimeter of the large room before settling into a comfortable chair in one corner, from which I could see the approaching aisles. I tried to swallow my disappointment; it wasn't as if we had *planned* to meet. I pulled the papers from the bag in my lap, set them on the table and then flipped through to find my most recent attempt. I forced my attention to the page in front of me and tried not to be distracted by his absence. I wanted my note done and ready to show him the next day.

I don't know how long I sat there working before I sensed movement and lifted my eyes to see Aubin walking toward me. He smiled when our eyes met. "Shit," he laughed as he sat beside me.

"Hi yourself. I didn't know if you were coming today." I hated the way my voice sounded, uncertain and weak.

"I did my errands first this time."

I nodded, not knowing how to respond to that, and returned to the page on the table. Aubin shuffled beside me, retrieving his notebook and pen from his bag, and settled into his own work. I glanced up and he paused in his movements to smile at me, I smiled back, relaxed.

We worked on our silent words for a while, side by side. My handwriting had gotten faster by then. I was able to get an idea written down before losing the concept in the rambling commotion of my thoughts. I had trouble organizing my ideas, though, and finding the right order in which to write them. I could see the whole, the scene or concept, but I struggled to find a way in to delineate the details and present them in a comprehensible composition. In short, I didn't know where to start.

"How is it going?" Aubin asked after I let out an audible sigh.

"Meh."

"Meh? What's that? Is that a technical Quantifier term?"

I laughed. "Yes, it means 'Terrible, but I don't want to admit it'."

"I see. I'll have to use that one someday. Quite poetic, actually ... 'meh'." I swatted his arm with the back of my hand.

"How come I haven't seen any of your work?" I was surprised that I asked it out loud.

He frowned and looked away, the smile falling from his face. "You have." His voice was soft.

"Only by accident. I show you what I do, you should show me what you've written."

He looked back and studied me for a moment, and then a moment more, just long enough for me to become uncomfortable. "Give me a word," he whispered.

I shook my head and pulled my eyes away, scrunching up my nose to make a face. "Don't be foolish. I don't know any secret ancient words." Aubin shrugged as if something had been settled and turned back to the papers in front of him. I reached across and snatched his notebook. His reflexive grab at it was a moment too slow.

"Hessa—"

134

"I'm just finding you a word." I had seen him flip through the notebook before and knew he kept a list on the back pages. I hurried to turn past the pages that were weighted with his handwriting to demonstrate that it wasn't my intention to intrude.

When I reached the pages where the list started, he relaxed back into his chair. "Okay, gimme a word then."

"It's hardly fair, you know. You know what they all mean."

"So find me a new one." He paired his challenge with a daring raise of his eyebrows.

I tried to glare at him. "I'll give you two."

"Two. What if they don't go together?"

"You'll make them go together. That's *your* challenge."

I closed my eyes and raised my finger. He laughed beside me. "What are you doing?"

I opened one eye. "Shush, I'm concentrating."

"Sorry," he said and pressed his lips together.

I closed my eye again. My finger spun its circle in the air and then fell to the fated place on his page. I opened my eyes slowly, as if fearful of what might be revealed. "Here's the first: '*kilig*'. K-i-l-i-g."

"Got it." Aubin sat with a cocky smile, not moving to write down the word as I dictated the spelling. It annoyed me. "And the second?"

Glaring at him I flipped over a couple of pages, raised my finger again and let it fall a second time. I turned to see what was underneath. "'*Morbo*'. M-o-r-"

"Got it," he interrupted.

I slapped his notebook shut and thrust it across the table at him. "Fine. Let me get back to work then. We'll reveal our results tomorrow morning."

"Tomorrow morning? You've had all week!"

"You're the Creator, Aubin."

He didn't say anything in response to that, just held my gaze steadily and tilted his head. In my mind I heard his insistence that my classification was only my job. I suddenly felt vulnerable, as if he could see more of me than I wanted anyone to. I

135

looked away to break his spell.

By the time the reminder alarm on my wristcomm buzzed, I had one page of handwriting that had slightly fewer words crossed out than not and a small pile of discarded efforts. I wasn't ready to be finished but I was worried that if I didn't leave then Toan would beat me home. Aubin paused in his writing to watch me gather my things. I scrunched up the papers destined for the incinerator and he asked, "Do you want me to get rid of those for you?"

"No, you'll cheat," I said without looking up from packing away my paper, pens and screen.

"Cheat how?"

"These are garbage. You'll read them. You'll see how much worse it is when I'm working on it." When he didn't reply, I stopped moving and looked at him. I couldn't read his face; a smirk played on his lips, but his eyes were pensive. "What?"

"Nothing."

"What?" My voice was irritated by my hurry.

"As a math teacher, don't you put as much emphasis on the process as on the end result? I've seen the work you grade at lunch — screens of numbers with one small answer at the end."

"That's different," I said, though to be honest I wasn't sure how. I suspected Aubin didn't buy my rebuttal, because he leered as he nodded and then went back to his own work. With my packed bag clutched in one hand and the stack of garbage papers in my other, I was ready to go. "I'll see you tomorrow morning for our trade?" I looked down at Aubin in his chair, and a tress of hair fell from its place behind my ear in front of my face. I blew a puff of air at it to shift it away, but it fluttered out, just to fall in the same place over my eyes. Aubin laughed. He stood and stepped closer to me. I wanted to step back, but my legs didn't respond.

"Lemme." He gently reached up and brushed my forehead with the tip of his middle finger, catching the hair and sweeping it away to the side of my face. His tickling touch froze me, rooted where I stood, my tongue dry and useless pasted to the roof of my mouth. "Better?" And then I knew as clearly as if he had spoken aloud that he wanted to kiss me. And knowing that

136

tightened my chest and caught my breath. But as sure as I was that he wanted to, I knew he wouldn't.

"Thanks," my mouth finally said. My voice cracked, and I wished I hadn't spoken at all. I turned away and hurried across the CDB to the incinerators near the exit and then through the doors. I didn't slow my pace until I reached the hover station, where I had to wait for its arrival. My heart and breath raced. As I paced the station platform, I realized I couldn't go back to the CDB. I couldn't meet with Aubin anymore, even if it was just to work or talk together. I probably shouldn't even see him at work. With his light touch, what was innocent and benign had turned dangerous. I was edgy as I waited on the platform. My senses were heightened as if on alert of an imminent attack; I could hear the mechanical clicking of hidden machines, the disjointed words of clashing conversations. I could smell the endeavors of the day on the people walking past me — gym sweat, stale office air, cleaning solutions, baking ingredients.

My stomach churned and my mind raced. I knew that I shouldn't waste my time with the writing. Who was I to question my role? Who was I to forsake the gifts and talents I had been given, and the ones I had worked to achieve and master my whole life. My parents had sacrificed their time and money to give me the best education, the best opportunities, and I had obtained Second Stat classification. As a *Quantifier*, I repaid their support with this? If the employment department found out I was wasting time I could be contributing, they would have grounds to fire me, to take away our grocery ration, our housing, and where would that leave me and Toan? Toan. Toan! My partner and best friend, and I was lying to him. Why? He was right. He was always right. If I had time to waste on a stupid, frivolous hobby that accomplished nothing, *contributed nothing*, I should be spending more time on giving back what had been provided to me by my family, my employer, my colleagues. My match. I was a Quantifier; the rest was useless folly.

I was done with writing. With that resolution, the guilt and fear ebbed and my heart slowed to a regular, less painful beat. I took a deep breath, held it and let go. I started toward the wall incinerator, but the hover arrived with a push of air and a whistle. I couldn't chance missing the hover, so I stuffed my papers

back in my bag and decided to destroy them at home. I felt better with my decision, calm inside and out, and ready to relax on
the ride home.

I met Toan at the door when he arrived and gave him a kiss.
It surprised him, I think, because he laughed and asked, "What's
gotten into you?"

"Just happy to see you." I brushed it off. I was moving forward from then on. There was no reason to upset him by telling
him what I had done, only to share what I had decided to do.
The past didn't matter as long as I learned from it to improve
the future. I knew where I belonged and was happy again to be
there. I was a Quantifier, and a good one at that. And I was
Toan's match.

That night my sleep was disrupted by incomplete images. I
could feel more — hot, shaky, pulsing in my head and deep in
my chest — than I could see as colors and ideas swirled around
me and made me toss about in my bed. In the dark I heard
Toan enter my room, and my eyelids turned red with the light
flashing on outside them. I blinked my eyes open to find Toan
kneeling beside my bed. He looked concerned but smiled. "Are
you alright, Hessa?" His hand hovered over my head as if he
was waiting for permission to touch me.

I swallowed a couple times, my eyes darting around the
room and searching the corners for shadows left over from my
dream. Then I pushed myself up on my elbows. "Yeah, I'm fine."
It was a lie. I was shaken by the remnants of the dream that
were clinging to my consciousness, just out of sight of my
memory.

"You were calling out in your sleep."

I felt a pit of dread settle in my stomach when I wondered
what I had said. I was afraid to ask him. I shook my head instead
and tried to assure him, "Just a silly dream, I think. I'm fine."

"Do you want me to stay?"

I was awake enough by then to focus on his eyes and see the
hope they showed as they widened just a bit. But I was tired and
anxious and unnerved by the feelings left from the dream I
couldn't remember. Talking in my sleep sounded dangerous.
What would it tell him? I shook my head again and put my hand

on his. "No, I need to get some sleep. I'm fine, really, Toan. Go back to bed, and I'll see you in the morning."

Toan smiled and kissed me on the forehead as he rose. He wished me good night at the door after a tentative moment of hesitation and turned into the hall. I heard his feet pad down the stairs to his room until the door slid shut between us.

I couldn't sleep for some time, but then I did, solidly and without dreams so that when my communicator buzzed at my wake time, my eyes were heavy and my head felt somnolent. I stumbled through my morning routine and rested my head on Toan's shoulder on the hover as he worked. When we parted ways in the lobby of the Education Department, I smiled up at him.

"Are you coming over for lunch?" I asked. I knew his answer already.

"I wish I could, but I can't today. Maybe later this week." He was distracted by a colleague coming in the door behind us and nodded to him as he finished talking to me. "I've gotta go, Hessa. I'll see you later then?"

"Bye," I called after him, though I don't think he heard me as he fell into step with his colleague. Leaving me without his kiss. He turned just as they reached their security door and smiled and waved to me before disappearing through.

I walked to my classroom. There I found a yellow envelope taped to the door, where anyone could have seen it. I removed it, placed my palm on the panel and then walked through the door as it slid open. I dropped my bag on my desk and fell into my chair, studying the envelope in my hand. I considered not opening it, but even as I did I slit the seal. The edge of the envelope sliced quickly into the flesh of my thumb, and I cursed. A thin red line appeared, and I put my thumb to my mouth to clean the blood away.

Inside was a paper folded in three. I gently tugged to release it and opened the folds. As expected, Aubin's handwriting covered the page.

Challenge words: kilig, morbo
You challenge me with words and yet
the greater challenge is within me. A strong kilig. Irresistible.

like nothing felt or seen or known or believed before now. A light.

Morbo tastes in my mouth, flutters in my middle and squeezes my heart.

Dichotic and impossible, they clash and cut me. Pain.

But like a tongue fondles a metallic wound, I can't resist. And so I persist against my will. And against yours. Until ... I can't see where it ends. If it ends, or not.

The end of his words was punctuated by his lovely, sweeping 'A'. I should have incinerated it. My body reacted to the words my mind did not understand. I was holding my breath, and something in my abdomen fluttered. My heart pounded against my ribs, knocking as if to break out. I blinked and found my eyes were wet. I put the paper down to press my fingers against my eyes and push back the tears, determined to regain control. It was irrational, my reaction to those words. I wasn't even sure what they meant all strung together, and yet the result was stronger than me. I thought of the assignments submitted by my students. Screens of number trails that moved from the question, step by step to the answer. That was rational. That was logical and exact and complete. And just as I salvaged control, the door slid open and I heard him clear his throat.

"Hessa?" Aubin asked when I turned at the sound of his ahem. "Are you alright?" He stood there with a look of concern.

I laughed, and it sounded a little wild and hysterical to me. "I'm good, Aubin, just fine."

He hesitated, as if unsure, and then stepped closer. "You found my note. I've come for yours."

I had forgotten the paper that I owed him in my bag. The same one I would have destroyed on the hover platform had the hover not arrived just when it did. I should have told him I didn't have it. I still don't know why, or even how, I reached into my bag with my blind fingers and found the folded paper. My hand shook when I passed him the page without looking at it. He smiled, said, "Thank you," then tucked it into his pocket.

"Aren't you going to read it?"

"I was going to read it later, but I guess I can read it now if you want?"

"Sure." I shrugged as if it didn't matter, but suddenly it did. It mattered very much, because I had written about Toan and how comfortable and safe and familiar he was. Rational. How I was with him. I wanted Aubin to know that, and I wanted to *see* him know that.

He hesitated and looked at me then opened the paper and started to read. I studied his face. His eyes stalked back and forth, his lids dropped lower. His usual friendly smile stayed, but it became painted in an unnatural pull. His face seemed to pale while the skin on his neck reddened. Together the growing contrast made each shift more profound.

"Has Toan read this?" he asked. I shook my head, not wanting to let out the air I held. "You should show it to him. He might like to read it. To know…" His voice was casual, as if he was suggesting I try a new snack, but his eyes were trained on mine. Our eyes locked for a moment of indiscernible length; it was probably only seconds, but it felt much longer. He blinked first and broke the spell by looking away. "You should tell him, Hessa."

Tell him what? About the writing? About how I felt? About Aubin? "I can't," I whispered and it seemed to answer it all.

Aubin nodded, a quick short bob of his head, his lips pressed together. "I've got to go get ready for class. I'll see you at lunch." It was an assumption, not a question. My decision to distance myself from him and from writing echoed in my mind as I watched him disappear around the corner into the hall. I didn't take that chance to tell him I wouldn't be there.

By lunchtime I convinced myself that I owed him an explanation for my planned absence from the lounge, so I went to find him there. We sat and talked with our colleagues, and an opening never arose for me to explain it to him. Not the next day either, or the next. By the end of the week, I couldn't remember what had frightened me at the CDB. I decided it was foolish of me to think he might complicate our friendship. He *knew* I was matched with Toan. And the writing. Even after a few days, I missed writing. I missed the calming effect it had on my anxiety, the way it forced me to slow my thoughts, my actions and concentrate on just one task. At lunch on Friday he stood and cleared his place at the table but left behind a piece of paper with a list of words and instructions that read: *Chose one for yourself and two for me.* I could feel a wide smile spreading as I heard the door slide shut behind him and I tucked the paper into my bag.

I should have my stuck to my resolution. It would have changed everything. I know that now. But I don't regret that I didn't, *because* it would have changed everything. I convinced myself I was foolish to be fearful. How I chose to spend my own time was my concern alone, and what Toan didn't know wouldn't hurt him. If I were smart, my employers wouldn't know. I could keep my new interests and experimentation with writing and words to myself, to my available time. I knew I was in control.

But I wasn't. Words have a power that cannot be suppressed. It was just a matter of time.

16

Seize

Gallie – Records from your wristcomm locator demonstrate that you were at the Central Database most Mondays in months Eight and Nine of last year. Is this true?

Finch – Have you presented Ms. Black with those records so that she may comment on what they show?

Gallie – I'll rephrase the question. Is it true that you went to the CDB most Mondays in Eight and Nine of last year.

Hessa – Yes.

Gallie – What was your purpose for going?

Hessa – I went there to work.

Gallie – To work?

Hessa – Yes.

Gallie – Why would you waste time traveling all the way to the CDB to work instead of working at your own office at home?

Hessa – I found it easier to concentrate at the CDB. There were fewer distractions.

Gallie – Did Mr. Whitley know you were going to the CDB?

Hessa – Yes.

Gallie – What reason did you give him for your trips there?

Hessa – I told him the truth. I went there to work.

Gallie – Did you meet with anyone while you were there?

Hessa – No.

Gallie – Are you aware that records indicate Aubin Wallace also spent time at the CDB almost every Monday in Eight and Nine?

Hessa – No, I have not seen his records.

Gallie – Did you see Mr. Wallace at the CDB on Mondays?

Hessa – No.

Gallie – No?

Hessa – No.

Finch – The question has been asked and answered, Council Gallie, please move on.

Gallie – I just find it surprizing. The CDB isn't a terribly large space. You would think two colleagues, friends by Ms. Black's account, would notice each other if they were repeatedly in the same building.

Hessa – I went there to work, not to socialize. I was concentrating. I would guess Aubin was as well.

Gallie – That is your explanation? That you were both so focused on your own work that you never saw each other at the CDB?

Hessa – Yes.

Gallie – It doesn't seem to be the most probable of accounts, does it?

Hessa – I don't know, I haven't studied the statistical probability of the situation.

Gallie – I'll ask again to be certain for the court. Did you meet with Mr. Wallace at the CDB on Mondays?

Hessa – No.

Mondays became the most essential day of my week. I would hurry through my household responsibilities timed perfectly to end with putting away the grocery ration once the delivery oddout left. I was able to catch the ten thirty hover and arrived at the CDB before eleven. I packed a lunch, though not a complete lunch. It was two halves of a lunch that I'd share with Aubin, who brought two halves to share with me. Our table in the corner of the CDB with our lunch and papers spread out between us became an isolated retreat from the rest of my life. I took on more projects at work and joined a community board to remedy my guilt over wasting my time with writing. And keeping it from Toan. My new responsibilities kept me busy late into every night. The only free time I had remaining to commit to writing was a small hour on the days Toan stayed at work later than I did. And my Mondays at the CDB with Aubin.

I didn't realize how vital my writing time had become. I was happier when I had that time as an outlet. The calm and the focus I found while I was writing buoyed me through my hectic days at work and my evenings full of meetings and tasks. The buoyancy slowly depleted day by day until I could renew my resources with another dose of writing time. It was the week that Toan and I were quarantined that I really appreciated my need for it.

Toan appeared in my classroom door just after classes ended on a Friday.

"Hey there." I smiled first, before I noticed his frown. "What's wrong?"

He held up his wristcomm that displaced a red cross on the screen. "Quarantine."

"What? Why?" I was already turning my wrist over to touch my own display, which glowed to reveal a red cross as well.

As if in answer, Toan coughed then offered an apologetic but weak smile. "The Medic heard me cough in a meeting and called me into his office. He ran a blood test and found a virus, so he put me out for three days. You too."

"But I'm not sick!"

Toan shrugged.

"Is anyone else in your department sick?"

He shook his head. "I haven't heard of anyone, no, but I think they're all being tested before they go home because of me." I plucked away at the holoboard, organizing work to complete from home, keeping my eyes from the desk drawer in which I kept the folder full of handwritten papers. Toan slumped into my office chair and watched me. "It wouldn't be so bad, actually. I'd love a few days home with you. I don't even feel sick! But it's the worst time for the project. We're so close to discovering what the——" I looked up from my busy hands, which was probably what reminded him of his audience, and he

145

changed his words. "—to finding a solution. I hate to miss the time right now." I nodded at him so he would know I understood his frustration.

Monday. The word flashed in my mind. "How long is the quarantine for again?" I braced myself for his answer, determined to keep my face neutral.

"Three days. We're back on Tuesday."

I nodded, not trusting my voice.

"We'll have to reschedule the grocery delivery too."

"Right." I was glad for the distraction of slipping my screen into my bag. "How much time do we have?"

"We can use the hover until five, then our access to public services is terminated until Tuesday morning."

"I'm almost done."

"Don't rush, Hessa, we have time." He stood and paced to the door. I hurried to add my folder of handwritten pages to my bag while his back was turned.

With a cautionary four days of work transferred to my screen, I followed Toan out of the room and down the hall. I allowed him to take my hand as we walked from the Education Department building to the hover station. He was quiet as the hover took us home. I could tell he was stewing over something at work and knew better than to ask what he was thinking. I didn't mind. It gave me time to think as well. Aubin would know from the staff notices that I had been quarantined, so he wouldn't expect me at the CDB on Monday. I wondered if he'd miss me.

Toan and I spent Saturday, Sunday and Monday together but separated by the walls of our home. Toan squirrelled himself away in his secure office. I wrote lesson plans for the week and marked assignments, distracted by the proximity of my papers and pen in my bag. Several times each day I approached his door and stood outside listening to him talking to his colleagues, waiting for a quiet moment to interrupt him and steal back some time between us. An hour after suppertime Sunday night, I tip-toed to Toan's door and heard silence, so I touched the intercom button. After a moment the door whooshed open and he greeted me with a foul face and an annoyed grunt. "What is it?"

I took a step back and my eyes pricked with tears. "It's past supper time, Toan, are you hungry?"

He sighed and squeezed his eyes shut, then rubbed them with his hand. When he opened them again, they were less pinched and narrow. He reached out his hand and closed the distance I had created between us then took a deep breath. "I'm sorry, Hessa. I'm just working on an equation that is so frustrating. I didn't mean to growl at you."

"I know."

"Go ahead and eat. I'll be a while yet." He was already turning back to his desk before finishing his sentence.

I didn't eat. I always waited for him. By the time he emerged from his office it was dark out and I was yawning in the media room. We made a cold supper of cereal and ate watching the late news on the central panel. I stood at the end of the show and stretched my arms over my head. "I'm headed to bed," I said, but Toan just started at the screen. His eyes were rimmed red and tired. "Do you want to come?"

Toan shook his head without looking up at me. "Actually, I should go back to work. I've got to do a bit more tonight." He pushed himself out of the chair and squeezed my hand as he walked past and up the stairs to his office, leaving me alone.

The next morning was Monday, of course, and I was lost without my routine. I heard Toan up and back in his office before the sun rose. I was too restless to go back to sleep. I showered and puttered about the house, doing the tasks that I usually rushed through on Mondays. There was no grocery delivery, no deadline to finish. I fought the feeling that I was forgetting something important, missing something I needed to do. I considered going to the CDB, even though I knew it was ridiculous. Even if I could walk the distance, it would take me most of the day and I'd be denied access when I got there because of the quarantine.

Finally, when I could stand the edge no longer, I went back into my office and turned my computer on to a screen of student results. I laid a single sheet of paper with Aubin's ancient word written on top. After considering both options, I left the door open, hoping that hearing Toan's footfalls would give me

more time to react than the sound of the door opening behind me.

Mamihlapinatapai. Aubin's search resources on my screen told me the word meant 'a look shared by two people in which each wished the other would start something they both want but that neither can begin'. The definition didn't make much more sense than the word itself. Begin what? *A look shared by two people.* I suspected the relationship between the two people determined the type of look and the *something* they wanted to start. I wrote down pairs of people: Toan and myself, my mother and father, Aunt Maryne and Uncle G, then my father and Uncle G. I didn't write 'Aubin and me'.

I was about nine when Uncle G and my father took Toan and me to the holozoo. I don't remember where our mothers were or why they weren't with us. Toan and I ran from display to display, pointing out the lifelike animals.

"How many spots does that leopard have?" I remember Uncle G asking. The leopard lounged on a rock by his watering hole.

Toan started muttering numbers, but I turned to our fathers with my arms crossed. "That's impossible to count!"

"How's that, little? Just start at one." Uncle G always looked right at me when he talked to me, which was less unsettling than my father's averted gaze.

"If she moves, we can't count them. If she doesn't move, we can't see all the spots."

My father laughed. He laughed more back then. "She makes a smart argument, Gauss."

Uncle G smiled over my head at my father. "She is her father's daughter, Nim," I remember him saying, and I knew somehow it was meant as a compliment, not a tease. I could hear Toan's whispered numbers behind me, but I was gripped by the sight of our fathers looking at each other. My father looked different, his features slackened in a gentle smile, his eyes still. Uncle G's face mirrored my father's, and his eyelids drooped to meet my father's shorter stance. His lips barely touched each other at rest. I remember feeling excluded, but not in a way that made me feel badly for it. And I remember feeling

148

sad when their contact was broken by Toan's frustrated growl as the leopard stood up and stretched.

"That's alright, son," Uncle G laughed. "Let's go find the zebras. Their stripes are easier to see."

At my desk so many years later, I wondered if the look I saw them share would have been called 'mamihlapinatapai' by someone, somewhere, sometime. I briefly considered writing about that look in the zoo, but somehow it felt too private. I closed my eyes and summoned the image of Toan's dark eyes. I tried to find the energy I remembered from our fathers' gaze in a moment I shared with him. Any moment. Memories of Toan and me in different places, different times flickered behind my eyelids, but I couldn't retain the vision of his coffee-brown color. The eyes kept lightening to blue and I was left seeing Aubin, standing in front of me at the CDB, his look intent and my forehead tingling from the brushing touch his finger left when he swept back my hair. *Mamihlapinatapai.*

I shook my head and muttered, "What a stupid word." I decided I was hungry, and if I was hungry I was sure Toan was too; he had skipped breakfast. I didn't want to eat alone. I hid my papers away and went to the kitchen to fix sandwiches for both of us and then carried them to his office door. When he met me at the door as it slid open, I could tell he was trying to keep exasperation from his face with a tense smile that didn't reach his eyes. He might have hidden it from someone else, but I knew him too well.

"Lunch," I said, raising one hand with a plate an inch higher in explanation.

He took the plate, still blocking the door. "Thanks."

"Can I come in? I thought we could eat together."

He looked over his shoulder at the computer lit on his desk and said, "Just a minute." The door slid shut when he stepped away from the threshold. I waited, feeling foolish standing in the hall with my sandwich on a plate in both hands. A moment later the door slid open again and Toan said, "Come in," from behind his desk.

As I entered he turned his screen over so that it was face down on his desk. His computers were blank. I tried to swallow

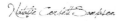

the resentment that heaved in my middle. He wasn't keeping secrets from me willingly; they weren't his to tell. And he wasn't the only one keeping secrets. I settled into the armchair beside his desk.

He must have sensed my feelings because his smile was apologetic. "Thanks for bringing up lunch." He picked up the sandwich and held it toward me. "Cheers."

I smiled and tapped my sandwich against his, echoing, "Cheers." We hadn't done that in years, and I was surprised he still remembered. "Are you getting much done?"

He shrugged. "Some. I'll be glad to get back to the office tomorrow, though. What about you?"

"Some." I don't know why I lied. Maybe it was just easier.

I had hoped having lunch with Toan would cure my restlessness and my loneliness, but he was anxious to have me leave so he could return to work. He wouldn't say it, but his attempts at conversation were unusually awkward, and he alternated glancing at the time on his wristcomm and the blank screens on his desk. When he looked from his communicator to me, I raised my eyebrows in question, and he knew. "I'm sorry, Hessa, I'm just in the middle of this. It's hard to switch gears."

"I know," I said, and it felt familiar.

I put his empty plate on mine and stood to leave. He blocked my way and put his hands on my shoulders. "I really am sorry, Hessa. I know I could have made these few days better if it had happened at a better time for work. We finally get a chance to spend some time together and, well, I *had* to get this done."

I forced a smile and nodded, not sure why my eyes were wet. "I know." He pressed his lips against my forehead. When he stepped to the side, I left him in his office and took the plates to the kitchen. I stood watching the incinerator dispose of the plates. Their edges glowed red then disappeared until there was nothing left but a sweet, burned smell. I wondered what to do next. I was anxious. My legs ached for a run, my mind raced with incomplete thoughts that jumbled and tangled. I felt hungry but wasn't. I felt bored but impatient and fidgety, needing to do something but not sure how or what. And then I caught movement out of our kitchen window and my eyes fixed on the sight of Aubin walking up to our door.

I met him on the step before he could reach the sensor that would announce his presence throughout the house.

"What are you doing here?"

His eyes widened, and he looked all around us. "Hi, Hessa, it's nice to see you too. Why are you whispering?"

I had no idea why so I ignored his question and repeated my own, my voice only a little louder. "We're in quarantine," I added.

"I know. That's why I came here. How are you feeling?"

"Fine, why?"

"You're in quarantine."

"Oh, right. Toan was identified with a viral infection. My quarantine is associative. I feel fine."

"Good, I'm glad to hear it." He paused and silence grew between us that felt a bit dangerous in my front yard, but Toan's office window was on the other side of the house. "I knew you couldn't make it to the CDB, and I wanted to give you this." From his jacket pocket he withdrew a folded piece of paper. My heart sped up as I took the paper and put it in my pocket. "And this." He had opened his bag and handed me his journal. I hesitated then took it, being careful not to open it and reveal his private writing. "Open it," he challenged.

I looked at him a moment more and then opened the book. The pages were blank, his script missing from the light blue lines. It wasn't his, just one identical to it. He stepped toward me and flipped the pages back to the front. Inside the front cover were two lines of his letters that read, *For your exploration, Hessa. I hope this helps you find your dharma, A.*

"Aubin, it's beautiful. How did you find it?"

Aubin's laugh surprised me. "I have my secret Creator ways. It's for your work, you know, all the mistakes you make. You should be keeping them, not burning them." I nodded.

I slid my hand across the soft, textured cover —— cool and bumpy. "Thank you," I whispered. The folded paper in my pocket felt like a hot, heavy stone. He stood on our walk, waiting for something more. "I'm glad you came, it's good to see

151

you," I said at first, just to say something but realizing its truth when I heard the words aloud.

His smile widened. "Do you have something for me to read?"

I winced. "No. I didn't write it today."

"No? Why not?"

"The word was too hard. I couldn't find anything to write about it," I said instead of '*I couldn't use the memories it provoked*'.

"Oh." And suddenly the disappointment carried in that syllable was more than I could handle.

"I'll try again," I rushed to say, and Aubin nodded, which made me feel better. "I'll bring something tomorrow."

"Okay, well, I'll see you then."

"Yes, I'll see you then. Thanks for coming." He turned and walked back to the sidewalk, turning to the left and away from our home. I wondered if he'd look back, but he didn't. He kept a quick gait, his hands deep in his pockets and his head high and forward. At the end of the road he turned and disappeared behind the buildings.

Suddenly the journal in my hands made me feel exposed. I turned and entered the house, bounded up the stairs two at a time to my office and shut the door. I opened my locked drawer and put the journal under some files there, closed it and double-checked the lock. Only then did I relax. I pulled the folded paper from my pocked and spread it out on my desk with two flat hands.

Hessa — A note instead of a poem today as we have missed our weekly chance to prattle. There was a word in German, yes another ancient language, that is a label for the space between things: 'zwishenraum'. I like the way that by giving a label to a space, an absence, a nothing, that nothing becomes something. A word makes it become tangible. See the power of words? To create and define. Magic, don't you think? A.

I smiled and read Aubin's note a second and then a third time before slipping it into the folder in which I kept his scraps of paper. I think I knew I shouldn't keep them; they were a dangerous opportunity for someone to stumble upon and ask questions, but I couldn't bear to part with them either, which became my deliverance.

I retrieved my new journal and wrote the funny German word at the top of the page. I pictured the space between my desk and the wall that regularly claimed wires, pictures and small tools, once even Aubin's pen. By the time my stomach requested supper, I had a page long story of a ferocious creature called the Zwishenraum who survived on the sustenance of stolen items and the frustration of people who lost them. I locked away my journal and folded the copy I wrote out for Aubin and then put it in my work bag. I breathed contentedly and went out to heat Toan's meal.

17

Zeventien

Gallie – Did Mr. Wallace ever give you any indication that he might have feelings for you beyond being your colleague and friend, as you have testified?

Hessa – No.

Gallie – No?

Finch – This question has been answered, several times. Move on, please.

Gallie – I question the truth of the answer.

Finch – Ms. Black has sworn the truth. You must have facts to challenge that.

Gallie – Did you ever give Mr. Wallace reason to believe that your match status would not be an impediment to a deeper relationship with him?

Hessa – I don't know what that means.

Finch – Neither do I, Council Gallie, please clarify.

Gallie – Did you ever give Mr. Wallace reason to believe that you would consider a relationship with him in spite of your match with Toan Whitley?

Hessa – No.

Gallie – Is it possible that Mr. Wallace could have misinterpreted your friendship in a way that was not your intention?

Hessa – He knew we were friends and knew I was matched to Toan. What more was there to interpret?

Gallie – That's what we're trying to determine, Hessa. Unfortunately, Aubin isn't available to tell us what he considered your relationship to be.

Finch – That comment is uncalled for, Gallie. Please adhere to the facts.

Everything changed again one Monday a few weeks later. I don't remember anything about the day before that moment; I'm sure it was filled with my usual mundane routine around the house, grocery delivery, rushed trip to catch the hover and impatient ride to the CDB station. Aubin and I were sitting at the table we usually shared. The garbage from our communal lunch was piled in the middle, waiting to be removed to the incinerator across the room. We had a light-hearted argument about who should deliver the refuse to be disposed of, and neither had backed down to do it, leaving the mess as a reminder that we were equally stubborn. The sun was warm through the window behind us, pressing a blanket of heat against my back. I had my hair pulled up and back, off my neck and out of my face. My hand was cramping from my concentration to write my letters well. I laid my pen in the seam of my journal and wiggled my fingers to free them from the cramp.

"What are you working on?" I asked Aubin.

He didn't respond right away but kept writing. By then I knew enough to wait him out. He ended his thought with a sharp poke to the page — a period — and smiled up at me. "Nothing," had become his typical response.

I rolled my eyes at his evasion. "What word are you writing about?"

He hesitated just long enough for me to see uncertainty in his eyes and wonder why he was reluctant to share. It was if he was weighing his options of avoiding or admitting a truth. Then he said, "*Cafune.*"

"*Cafune,*" I repeated. "You told me that word before but not what it means." He was looking at me but didn't answer. His jaw worked as if there was an internal struggle to speak or stay silent. "Well?"

"Well what?" He looked away.

"What does it mean?"

He shrugged, looking down at his paper. "It's just a beautiful word."

"Liar."

He looked up, startled, and asked, "What?"

"You know what they all mean! Why won't you tell me?"

He shrugged again. I guessed he wanted to suggest it meant nothing, but his shrug said the word meant more than he wanted me to know. "It's just an action, something someone does, like tie a shoe or open a door. But it's more, um, personal than those — it is hard to explain."

"So show me." My voice cracked into a whisper. My fault. I was the one who said that. It was my idea, my suggestion.

He looked up from his paper at me for a moment and swallowed hard enough for me to see his jaw tighten. He whispered, "Let down your hair."

"What?"

"Take out the hair tie, let down your hair." He said that louder, with more determination.

My hand was already raised to the tie in my hair, but I asked, "Why?"

"*Cafune*. You want me to show you what it means."

I hooked my finger through the elastic and pulled. I shook my head to release the strands that remained clumped where the tie had pressed them together. My hair fell thick and hot over my shoulders. I thought Aubin's eyes widened.

"Well?" I asked, because he hadn't moved.

He swallowed again, and his hand rose by inches off the desk, where it floated, still, in the space between us. His German word, 'zwishenraum', echoed in my mind, and I wondered if the 'zwishenraum' would keep his hand away. His hesitation was momentary, his hand suspended in indecision, but it felt like a lifetime. I could see thoughts working through his eyes. My own mind raced, willing his hand both forward and away in the contradiction that can exist only in theories and thoughts. I held my breath, heard my heartbeat in my ears. Our world stopped in that moment, with the possible outcomes differentiated by Aubin's decision and mine. That's how both of us were culpable, not one or the other. In that moment, and from the instant that his hand moved forward instead of back, we were united in responsibility.

Aubin's hand reached my hair, and the shock of his touch paralyzed me. His fingertips grazed my scalp. I didn't want them anywhere else. Each individual hair gave a tingling pull as a current ran to my core from each finger's glance. I could hear the high-pitched whisper of each hair sliding against his fingers. The sensations pooled and filled me with *something* I hadn't even realized I needed, while at the same time they left me instantly needing more. I sucked in a breath, my eyes locked with his. His hand slid slowly through my hair, away from my head. At the end he twisted his wrist and twirled a lock around his fingers then gave a gentle tug that stormed right through me.

"That's *cafune*," he whispered. I couldn't say anything back.

Then he was closer, we were just a breath apart, but I don't know who moved forward. There was a moment in which his eyes asked permission and mine assented, because in the next moment my eyes closed and his mouth lit upon my lips. His initial touch was light, fluttering, soft, but then the anticipation I hadn't even known was there took over — I don't think I should say any more than that.

And then I hated him. Really, I hated myself but it was easier to hate him. My breath roared back, heaving my chest up and down. My ears roared. I pulled away, but my hair was still twisted around his hand. The window light behind him caught on strands left hanging from his fingers yanked out of my scalp by my wrenched withdrawal. My hand slapped him, *so hard*, across the face, and we looked at each other in shock. My palm stung and his cheek reddened. He licked his lips and his eyes fluttered.

"Hessa—" he whispered.

"Shut up!" I hissed at him. "Just shut up!"

"Hessa." He shifted his hand as if to touch me again, and I jumped up and away from him, knocking my chair over behind me.

"Don't. *Don't.*"

And then I fled, without my bag or my papers or my screen. Without looking back. I couldn't see, my eyes were blurred and unfocused, but I knew the way. I ran from the CDB to the hover station, arriving as the hover pulled up to the platform and the barrier wall doors slid open. I paced in the hover as it pulled

157

away. I muttered until I caught a young girl looking at me with a frightened face. I sat down, crossed my feet at the ankles and wove my fingers together to keep my body still. My mind still raced. I realized I had left everything behind. But there was no going back.

I pressed my fingers to my lips, trying to rid them of his touch, but it didn't work. Even after I arrived home and left a note for Toan on his communicator that I was going to bed with a headache. Even after I had cleaned my teeth, washed my face. Even after I lay in bed for hours, chasing elusive sleep. Even then I could feel lingering tactile memories; his kiss fluttering then pressing on my lips, his minty breath on my tongue, his fingers tangling in my hair. Even then I could feel my head lean into his hand in my hair, my lips respond to his. I couldn't forget the way I had felt. When I finally realized I didn't *want* to, I was terrified.

18

Akhtin

Gallie – Did you and Mr. Wallace ever have disagreements?

Hessa – Sure, we disagreed about all sorts of things.

Gallie – What did you disagree about?

Hessa – I don't remember   small things, nothing important.

Gallie – If there were 'all sorts of things', can you give us an example?

Hessa – I don't know! Sports, sometimes, I guess, he liked a different baseball team than I did.

Gallie – Baseball? That hardly seems worth fighting about.

Hessa – That's what I said, nothing important. We disagreed, we didn't fight.

Gallie – Were you ever angry with Mr. Wallace?

Hessa – No. I could never be angry with Aubin.

I must have dozed for a bit before the alarm buzzed on my wristcomm. I know because for just a moment after I woke up enough to turn off the alarm, I couldn't remember why my stomach was twisted up in my throat. I felt like I was trying to shake off a bad dream I couldn't remember. The reason trickled back to me, but I didn't have time to do more than swallow down the bile that surged up my throat before my door slid open and Toan came in. He was dressed in his work slacks and collared shirt, smoothing down the bunches left in the sleeve where his gray armband pinched it.

"Hessa? Are you getting up?" He crossed the room and sat

159

on my bed. "Are you feeling better?" His palm lay on my forehead, cool and smooth. Soothing. Somehow it burned.

"No, I don't feel good at all." It wasn't a lie.

Toan turned his hand over to glance my cheek with the back
of his fingers. "You don't have a fever, Hessa, have you been
sick to your stomach?"

It would have been easier, but I couldn't stand to lie to him,
not then. I shook my head.

"No fever, not sick … it's really a terrible time for me to be
quarantined, Hessa. Do you think you could try? At least so I
can meet with the team this morning if I'm going to be out later."

The fire in my gut swelled and thrust me into a rage. I threw
back the covers, hitting Toan with them in the process. "Never
mind, Toan, I'll go. It's all about you, isn't it? Everything is
about your work." Toan winced at my outburst, and I had to
look away. Storming to the bathroom gave me a good reason to
ignore the pain blinking in his eyes.

"Hessa." He followed me into the bathroom. I pulled off
my nightclothes and turned on the shower. In the glass shower
door I could see his reflection. He stood in the doorway, looking timid, his mouth working as if he couldn't find the words.
"Hessa, if you're really sick, it's fine, I didn't mean that. I just
thought—"

I turned back to glare at him. "I said never *mind*!" I yelled,
because I needed him gone. His proximity with his familiar dark
eyes and bewildered look … hurt. It burned and squeezed in my
chest, making it hard for me to breathe, impossible to think.
"Just go and let me get ready."

His hands fell to his sides, and I turned away. I heard the
door slide shut behind him as I stepped into the hot water. It
scalded and pricked and cut into my shoulders and my back. My
face was already wet with searing, angry tears.

I hid in the bathroom, taking longer than I should to get
ready. Toan didn't come back in, but three times he used the
network screen to try to talk to me from the kitchen. Twice he
told me to go back to bed, the third time he said he had my
breakfast ready to take with us. I couldn't look him in the eye
when we met at the front door. He waited while I zipped my

feet into my street boots.

"Your bag?" he prompted when I stepped toward the door.

"It's at work." It made me feel worse to realize how easily the lie came to my lips.

He must have misinterpreted my sigh, because he gripped my upper arm to stop me at the door. "Hessa…"

I forced myself to look up at his face but couldn't quite manage a smile. "Let's go, Toan, we'll miss the hover."

We rocked out of the station, sitting side by side as always. Toan kept his gaze on his hands, his fingers twisted around one another. After a few minutes of uncomfortable silence he reached across my lap to lay his hand on mine. I turned my hand over and squeezed his and then rested my head on his shoulder, taking a deep breath of his clean soap smell. "I'm sorry, Toan. I had a horrible night's sleep, but that's not your fault. I'm sorry I was so nasty."

I felt the weight of his head as he tipped down to rest his lips on my crown. I could feel his kiss-pursed lips spread into a smile against my scalp. "You were pretty terrible."

"Sorry."

"Let's just start the day over from here. Are you feeling better now?"

"Mmhmm," I said, but I wasn't. If anything, his easy absolution twisted a sharp edge in my middle — but of course he didn't know exactly what he had absolved me of. I had no idea how I was going to face Aubin, but it was inevitable. I was glad then that Toan had pushed me to get up. Waiting to see Aubin wouldn't make it any easier, and there was no sense forcing an unnecessary associative quarantine on Toan. The thought of Aubin made my face hot with embarrassment.

"Is everything okay?"

It took me a moment to register Toan's question and determine to what he referred. "Huh?" bought me a moment more.

"You don't seem yourself today. Is everything alright? Are you sure it was just a bad sleep?" He squeezed my hand as he asked, and I felt the reassurance he conveyed. I remember thinking if that moment on the hover could be isolated from the past or the future, I would be just fine. Just us, together, with no secret job, no secret hobby, no Aubin. I would have stayed there forever. I nodded and squeezed his hand back.

I had to work to keep up with his hurried pace from the station to the Department building. Inside the doors he lingered a moment longer than usual and asked again if I was alright. I only had to smile for him to understand he had asked too many times. He kissed my cheek, wished me a good day and then rushed to the security check. I waited and watched while he was screened by the Protector and waved back before he disappeared down the hall. I turned my feet and forced one in front of the other through the hallways, eerily silent before the students' arrival, until I reached my classroom door. I pressed my palm to the panel, and the door slid open. From there I could see my work bag on my desk.

Aubin must have brought it in. I should have felt grateful, but the appearance of my bag on my desk made me feel uneasy, as if Aubin's presence lingered in the silent room, waiting for me, watching me. Which was silly. I cursed myself and stalked across the room to the desk.

My bag was closed. I had a strange feeling that opening it would release something as dangerous as a coiled snake or toxic fumes. With one finger and thumb I pulled the zipper gingerly across its track, leaving a dark, open gap. I peeked in. There was nothing ominous, just my screen, my writing journal and the folder with a few of my papers tucked away.

And a small yellow envelope with my name written on the front.

I picked it up as if it *was* a coiled snake, staring at Aubin's script. His 'H' was larger than the rest of the letters, though they were all capitals. His 'E' as a tipped heart, two 'S's swirling in synchrony and his 'A' with a traipsing tail that I touched with my finger. I checked to confirm the door was closed, took a deep breath and split the envelope open to pull out the folded paper. By the time I unfolded it, my hands were shaking enough to make it difficult to read the moving paper. I laid it on the desk and smoothed it under my hands.

Hessa,

I am sorry for so many things. I am sorry I upset you, to make you feel the way you must have to run away from me so quickly. I'm sorry if I've caused you doubt or guilt. I am most sorry if you have decided not to speak to me again. But I am not sorry I kissed you. Because you kissed me too, and that has to mean something. That makes the risk, the pain, the guilt all worth it. In English we use the word 'love' too much, I think. I love my brother, I love baseball, I love chocolate cake, I love writing and I love you. They can't possibly all be the same, can they? I hope to talk to you soon. Love A.

By the time I reached the last line, the letters blurred together through the tears I kept in my eyes. I blinked to keep them back, determined not to cry. My throat was tight and pained. I read the letter twice more before I folded it back up, slipped it in the envelope and into my pocket. It was a damning note with revelations that would ruin everything if someone else read it. I should have incinerated it right away, but I couldn't. It was his declaration, his words, his heart.

I had to hurry to get ready for my classes, and teaching kept me distracted all morning. I didn't allow myself to think about Aubin's letter in my pocket. I didn't take the time to think about what to do at lunch. I simply found myself walking to the lounge carrying the lunch Toan had made for me.

When the door slid open, I knew without looking up that the lounge was crowded with colleagues by the sounds of their chatter and the varied smells of their lunches. But my usual seat beside Aubin was empty. Aubin was there and looked up when I entered. For a moment our eyes met, and he smiled. His smile was nominal but not insignificant. It looked sad and relieved at the same time, and I felt my eyes threaten with tears. I looked away. When I approached our table, I managed to say, "Hi Aubin," without a broken voice.

He let out a big enough sigh that I could see his body relax. "Good morning, Hessa, it's good to see you."

I pretended to listen to the banter of our colleagues, but I couldn't follow their conversations. I tried to keep my eyes on my lunch, but they slipped a few times to steal a glance at Aubin. Each time I saw him, my breath caught painfully. I could tell he was forcefully attending to our colleagues as well. His

163

smile was polite but contrived. His voice was strong but flat. He
picked at his lunch. By ones or twos our colleagues packed away
their garbage and left the room, until Aubin and I were alone
with only moments until classes started.

"Hessa, I'm glad you're here."

I nodded because I didn't know what else to do then said, "I
read your note."

"Good." It seemed like he wanted to say more but was trying hard not to. He finally said, "We need to talk, but not here."

"I don't know what there is to say."

"Meet me at the CDB on Monday. We can talk there. That
gives you time to think, and if it's not enough time, we can meet
the next Monday."

"I'm matched with Toan."

"Or the Monday after that," he went on as if I hadn't spoken. "I'll wait as long as you need."

"Aubin, I don't know."

He moved, and I thought he meant to take my hand, so I
flinched, pulling it back behind my back. That made him wince
like I had slapped him again, and I was sorry for it. He folded
his hands together on the table, as if each held the other back
from impulse. "Just think about it, okay?" The desperation in
his voice scared me, so I nodded.

He gathered his things and stood to leave. He paused for a
minute and seemed to be waiting. I looked up at him and he
smiled. "Whatever happens, it'll be alright, Hessa. You'll be alright." And the look on his face made me believe him, even
though I had no idea how anything would be alright again. He
turned and tossed his garbage in the incinerator and then returned to the table, pulling a paper from his pocket. "I wasn't
sure about giving you this, because I don't mean to push, but
maybe it'll help you work through your thoughts." He laid the
folded paper beside my lunch mess and left without seeing if I'd
take it. He must have known I would. I sat and stared at it until
the communication screen on the wall started the two-minute
countdown to class. I gathered my garbage and incinerated it. I
admit I held the paper over the incinerator lid, trying to drop it
in with the remnants of my lunch, but in the end he guessed

164

right; I slipped the paper, unread, into the same pocket that hid his note.

Toan was in the lobby that afternoon when I left the education wing. He stood when I came closer and smiled, putting his screen in his bag. "Hey, Hessa, how are you feeling?"

"Alright," I lied. I felt horrible everywhere, burning in my chest, sickly churning in my stomach. My head ached and my eyes burned. My jaw was sore from clenching, my throat sore from holding back tears. "What are you doing?"

"Going home," Toan said with a smile, offering his hand for me to hold. I took it, expecting to be burned by his touch, but his hand was soft and cool. "I was able to move some appointments around so I could leave early. I'll have to do some work tonight, though."

"Toan, I'm fine, really. If you need to stay, it's okay, I'll be alright."

"Hessa, I want to help. I hate that I'm never there for you, and today I made it work. So just let me, okay?" I nodded and tried to smile, but a tear escaped and slid down my cheek. He wiped it gently with his finger. His eyes widened and he opened his mouth to say something. I knew if he breathed one more bit of kindness, I wouldn't be able to maintain control.

"Headache," I whispered, holding my palm to my forehead.

"Ah. Let's go home."

He squeezed my hand as we walked to the hover and read me interesting articles that appeared on the news stream of his screen as we rode. Once we were home he insisted I sit while he fixed our supper. He even dug around in the freezer until he found my favorite chicken and vegetable servings. "I wanted to get some fresh vegetables from the market at lunch. I'm sorry I didn't get a chance, but I couldn't get away." His apology was sincere and the disappointment in his voice was evident.

"This is great," I assured him as he placed the food on the table. "I really am okay, Toan, just a bad morning. You don't have to be so nice to me."

"Good, because I prefer to be mean." He laughed and I tried to join him. "Seriously though, Hessa, I know I've been too busy lately with work. I miss you. I miss working with you. I

165

miss being together."

"Me too." That wasn't a lie, though it felt like it.

"Hopefully soon I can apply to change my day off to Mondays. That would give us a lot more time together."

I should have felt happy about the idea. It should have made me lighter with relief, eased the queasiness in my middle, but for a moment I worried about how I'd get to the CDB. Then I remembered that everything had changed and I wouldn't be writing with Aubin on Mondays anymore. I should have been glad. If Toan was off with me, I wouldn't have time to miss writing. Or Aubin. But I wasn't.

"Do you ever wish we had scored differently on our Proofs?" Toan's question took me by surprise, and I gulped on the water I had sipped.

"What do you mean?"

Toan laid his fork down and looked at me. "I mean, what if I had scored Second Stat? We could be working together. Or if you had scored First, you could be in the secure department with me."

I shrugged. "What if one of us had failed? We wouldn't be matched, and everything would be different." I didn't mean for my voice to have the edge it carried.

His look at me grew severe with his eyes narrowed, his fork halted halfway to his mouth. "Is that what you'd rather?"

"Of course not," but in that moment I wasn't sure if that was the truth or not. I was so confused about what was real. "You were saying 'what if'. There are too many possibilities to wonder about. We should just be content with how things are without questioning it."

His face relaxed, and he nodded. "I suppose you're right. We are doing what we're meant to be doing, after all." I remembered believing that and wished it were still that simple for me. I hid behind a bite of food, hoping my confusion didn't show on my face.

In light of Toan's efforts to cheer me up and to convince him that I felt better, I didn't say no when he asked to come to bed with me. Instead of safe in his arms, I felt foreign, like I didn't belong. I didn't realize I was crying until he had pulled away and whispered, "Hessa, what is it? What's wrong?"

"I miss you," I managed to squeeze out. It was the truth. Not the whole truth, but the truth.

He held me tighter. "I miss you too, Hessa. It'll get better." I wasn't sure I believed him.

Afterward. He fell asleep and I watched him, studying the features I knew better than my own. He was still my Toan, and I loved him. It had never hurt to feel that way before.

I hadn't read the paper Aubin gave me, but I kept it in my pocket beside the yellow envelope. I didn't trust myself to read it. He had said I could use it to help me think things through, but I knew if it was something he had written, it wouldn't help me think at all. I didn't think when it came to him. I couldn't. I thought of the way my eyes teared at his poems, the way my breath held when he spoke, the way my heart raced when he kissed me. I didn't think, I *felt*. I reacted in ways that were illogical. I knew I couldn't meet him that Monday. It was too dangerous.

But over the following lunch hours in the lounge he acted nonchalant, casual with our colleagues and blasé toward me, and I started to change my mind. I wondered if I had misread him. I wondered if he thought I had initiated the kiss, and he had reacted. His quiet confidence in refusing to convince me started to seem smug. I wondered if he might be stringing me along, seeing how far I would go, and that made me angry. In the end, I did meet him that Monday, only to prove him wrong. I loved Toan. I was in control. I had nothing to fear.

When the grocery oddout left, I rushed to put away the food order. I picked up my bag from the front door and hurried out to catch the hover. I checked my pocket for the yellow envelope and the folded paper I hadn't read. It had become a habit over the past week to pat my pocket and feel them there. I tried to keep my mind blank during the hover ride, because I knew if I thought too much about where I was going, I would have turned back. I counted my breaths and concentrated on keeping them slow and even. I watched the world outside the window fly by too fast for me to focus on any one thing. Blurs of color that made me dizzy if I tried to focus. My feet carried me from the hover station to the CDB, and it seemed as if they moved of their own volition.

I stopped within sight of the table where Aubin waited. He wasn't bent over his journal as he usually was when we met. He alternated between pacing behind the table and stopping to stare out the long bright window. He didn't see me watching him. I could have turned away and left, but I didn't. After a halting moment and a deep breath, I found my feet moving forward toward Aubin's tall, lanky stance framed in the window. I blinked in the bright sun until his shadow covered my eyes and I could see easily again.

"Aubin," I said when I was close enough. I hadn't meant it to be a whisper, but my voice didn't turn on.

He turned, and I watched his face shift from surprised to relieved, then he forced a tight smile. "Hessa. I'm glad you came."

We stood looking at each other. I wasn't sure what I meant to do or say once I was there. I wondered if he knew. The moment grew uncomfortable, so I moved to sit at the table, just to break the contact with his blue eyes. He sat beside me and held one hand in the other. It reminded me of his wince when I pulled away from him the week before.

"I'm glad you came," he said again.

"You wanted to talk."

He nodded and swallowed, glanced away from me to the table in front of him, where his journal and two pens were laid out in perfect parallel alignment.

"I love Toan," came from my mouth unexpectedly. I didn't like the defensive way it sounded, as if I was bracing for an argument before one was raised.

His eyes came back to mine and he nodded again. "I know you do."

"Well then, what —"

But it was like I had loosened a restraint. He leaned forward in his chair, close enough that I could smell mint on his breath as his words rushed at me. "I know you do, I know you love

168

Toan. But you love me. I know that just as well. I can see it when you look at me and laugh at my stupid jokes. When you read what I write for you. When you look up and smile at me when I come into the lounge at work. You love me. I know it. And I think you know it too."

I was shaking my head as he spoke, but it felt like I was warding off his words instead of trying to deny them. "I love Toan," was all I could say in reply.

"I know."

"I love Toan." My whisper cracked and trailed off. I had nothing else to say.

"Did you read the paper I gave you?"

I pulled the folded paper from my pocket. As I did, the yellow envelope fell out and hit the ground. I tried to sweep it back up before he saw, but I was too late. His eyes followed the yellow envelope back into my pocket then moved up to meet mine. He didn't say anything. "I didn't read it," I said as I put the folded sheet on the table and pushed it in front of him.

"Why not?"

I didn't want to answer. I didn't want to tell him the truth, and I knew I couldn't lie. He took the paper and opened the folds then handed it back to me. His handwriting danced, beautiful and familiar. The sight of it made my eyes fill with tears. I looked away, blinking.

"Read it." His voice was gentle, whispered but firm.

I concentrated on his small, even letters. It was a list of words, their definitions growing from each to the right like branches.

ai - to love

chun — love or lust

aiqing — romantic love

lian — to feel attached to, to love

teng — to love dearly, sore and hurts

re'ai — to adore

xihao — to like or love, preference

bo'ai — universal, brotherhood love

169

zhen'ai — true love

chulian — first love

aihu — to love and protect

anlian — to be secretly in love

After his list, Aubin had written one line, ending, as always, with his signature 'A'.

All of these are Chinese words for 'love'. Can you find your definition here?

He was so quiet as I read that I remember wondering, in some small corner of my mind, if he was holding his breath. When I looked up, his eyes were shining and wet. He swiped his sleeve across his face and then took the paper from my hands, folded it and put it back on the table. He reached toward me, and I let him take my hand.

"I know you love Toan. You've loved him all your life. But are you *in love* with him? There are so many different ways to love." I heard my mother's voice echo in his, thought of my parents, Toan's parents, our fathers and the way I would sometimes see them looking at each other when they thought no one was watching. My eyes filled as I realized I was losing a lifetime of understanding. Aubin reached up and touched my cheek with his thumb, wiping away a stray tear. I reminded my body to breathe. "Can you say you are not in love with me?" he whispered.

I was shaking my head before I could think of my answer. "But I'm matched with Toan." The words fell out as a resignation, not an argument. My voice was bleak, as if my match with Toan was a snare. It hurt, everywhere. The conversation was not going as I had planned.

Aubin seemed to grab onto the despondency in my voice. He leaned closer. "There are ways out of that, Hessa. Maybe it was a mistake. It wasn't even your choice."

"We chose to match!"

"It was expected of you. I suspect you knew that was the expectation from the time you were small. You only chose what they wanted for you, not what you wanted yourself."

"I wanted to match with Toan."

"You wanted what you knew." I was shaking my head again, trying to keep his words out.

"Hessa. I'm going to kiss you." He leaned closer. I was still shaking my head, but when he moved his hands fell on either side of my face, I became still. I should have told him no, should have moved back, should have left, but I couldn't.

I didn't want to.

I moved forward to meet his mouth.

He kissed me, or I kissed him, I don't know which. My mind shut down and I sensed him, in the same way my heart reacted to his writing, even though my mind couldn't understand his ancient words. The confusion dissipated for a moment, and the truth he was trying to tell me was clear and right and so obvious, it hurt. And it all seemed so easy for a moment … until he pulled away.

He touched my lips with his thumb, his eyes heavy and soft on mine. "Hessa," he whispered so I leaned forward to hear him, "tell me you love him like that. If you love him like that, I'll walk away. I'll be gone tomorrow, and I won't bother you anymore. I promise. But it's killing me to be here without you."

I covered my face with my hands and cried. What had been so lucid just the moment before was tangled again. "I don't know, I don't know what to… " I moaned.

Aubin reached forward and gripped my wrists, pulling my hands from my wet face. His eyes were wide, bright blue against his pale face. "Then just tell me this: should I leave?"

His words collided in my mind, clashing with the thought of him vanishing from my life and pounding against my skull with devastating pain. I hadn't realized until that moment, but when he put it into words, I knew I couldn't stand to have him go. I put my fingertips on his lips, shushing him, then squeezed my other hand around his, as if holding him tightly enough would keep him there. I worked up the strength to speak. "No." The first time was a whisper. "No," I said with greater strength as I shook my head. "Don't go. Don't leave me."

"That's all I need to know for now." He reached up and put his hand on my head, his fingers combing into my hair. A memory of his voice whispered *cafune* in my mind. "As long as I know that, I'll wait. As long as you need me to, Hessa, I'll be here. We will figure this out." He sounded so sure, I remember sighing in relief and almost believing him that somehow everything would be okay. "Let's get out of here, go for a walk?" He spoke to me like a broken child, with reassurance and comfort that made me abide by his words and nod. I wiped my face and forced a smile and then shouldered my bag as I stood and followed him out of the door.

We walked for a long time, that Monday; through the city streets between the tall thin buildings that dwarfed us and threw the sun's reflection in our path, along the old waterfront boardwalk where the salt smell was soothing and fresh. We walked until the hover schedule demanded I return home to reach the house before Toan. We didn't talk about the future or working out our mess. He didn't kiss me again, or even try to take my hand. We talked about words and writing, and he made me laugh. And that might have been our best day.

12

Jis at ashar

Gallie – Hessa, are you alright?

Hessa – Alright? I've been detained, and I'm on trial for murder. No, I'm not alright.

Finch – Hessa, do you want to take a break?

Hessa – No. I want to get this finished.

Gallie – It is not wise to rush through a Court Summary. It's already past lunchtime, let's take a break now. With the court's approval I move that we take a twenty-minute meal recess.

I have always loved Toan. I still do. He was my best friend. I hated the thought of hurting him, but I had no idea how to move forward without doing just that. I couldn't stay the same. Each time my eyes met Aubin's, I was reminded of his kiss. Each time Toan smiled at me I thought of Aubin's list of Chinese translations for 'love'. And I knew things weren't right. I couldn't ignore the truth any more than I could stop writing once I started. The easiest solution would be to go back; go back to the time when Toan was the only man I could ever imagine loving, and I didn't know there was a part of me that wasn't fulfilled by numbers and logic and rules. It would have been easiest if it weren't impossible.

But it wasn't even what I wanted. I wanted to move forward.

It would be possible to break a match, of course, but the consequences would be severe. It was easier that we didn't have children. As the instigator of the break I would be given an employment transfer to move out of the district. To limit civil disputes, authorities do not allow detached couples to maintain contact, but I heard some people found ways around those rules. I hoped Toan would want to, if not right away, then maybe

173

someday. I hoped he could forgive me enough to let me stay in his life. It was a very selfish hope to have, but it was the only way I could consider moving forward. He had every right to hate me and want me gone for good, but I couldn't tolerate the thought.

Leaving the district would mean leaving my parents behind as well. It would break their hearts. Maybe they would feel differently if they had chosen to match for love, or even if they had been given the opportunity to choose. My father would never forgive me for betraying Toan, and by extension, Uncle Gauss. They had given up love for their commitment to community, for Lineage Progression, for Toan and myself. More than once I wondered if it was worth hurting everyone I loved. I never found that answer.

Finding a way to match with Aubin would be more difficult. Moving districts wouldn't change the fact that I was a Quantifier and he a Creator. When Aubin first suggested we move secretly to an oddout community, the thought of it made my head hurt and my lunch swell dangerously in my stomach. I saw Keene at the hover station, her frightened eyes, her empty voice. But Aubin was confident we could make it work. Being oddouts would allow us the freedom to be together. I grabbed on to his optimism and used it as a shield against my fears and doubts. For the first time in a long while I thought of Keene's happy smile the day she told me she had failed her Proofs.

I spent Ten going through the motions, acting out an identity I knew I was planning to shed. On Mondays we met at the CDB and shared ancient words and wrote. He wrote me beautiful poems, and I stumbled through attempts he assured me he loved. When we talked about when to leave, the conversation always grew stiff. He would have gone right away, I think, and I worry part of me will always regret that we didn't. I argued to wait a few days, a week, then just two more. Toan had deadlines looming at work — I didn't want to be responsible for disrupting his work as well as his home. Aubin was impatient but unwilling to force me along, and so he tolerated my hesitance and assured me he would wait as long as I needed. All of those reasons seem like excuses now. I don't remember why we waited; probably it was just that I was scared.

We often hiked in the park on Monday afternoons. Old habits were hard to break; I'd count the trees as we walked along a path. Aubin laughed at me, and I realized I was counting out loud.

"What? I can't help it." I laughed too, after I hit him on the arm. "I'm always counting, just like you're always writing."

He smiled at me and then said, "*Happiness, not in another place but this place ... not for another hour, but this hour.*"

"See? Did you just make that up?"

He laughed and shook his head. "No, I'm afraid not. An old poet named Walt Whitman wrote that."

I wrinkled my nose. "What is it supposed to mean?"

"Here and now, with you, I'm happy. Even if you count the trees."

His smile was easy. I envied his calm. I envied his assurance. "Easy for you to say," I muttered bitterly.

He looked bewildered. "Hessa?"

I felt the panic I could usually keep controlled rise up against my tight throat, and it exploded with a sob. "You're happy with here and now? This is a mess, Aubin. What are we doing? What am I doing?"

"Whatever you want to do, Hessa. I'm waiting for you to decide." His voice was even and strained. His words were patient, but his tone was not.

Our sudden argument had stopped us on the path. He took my hand and led me through the trees into a small clearing where the trees blocked most of the sun and the shade was cool. The breeze blew a scent of wet soil and some flower I couldn't recognize. He turned to face me, taking both of my hands in his, and waited.

"How am I supposed to know what I want? You have nothing to lose here, Aubin. Me? I'm going to lose everything."

"You can't lose me." His voice was quiet.

I opened my mouth to argue, but he kissed me before my voice could escape.

We hadn't kissed since that morning at the CDB. It was a mutual if undiscussed decision that respected my legal unavaila-

175

bility, a respect for Toan in an effort to make up for all of the other ways I was letting him down. But when he kissed me this time, the complications and indecision of our reality were swept away. His kiss made me sure and confident in who I was and who I was meant to be. When he kissed me, I wasn't Toan's match, a Quantifier and child of Nimran and Sarah Black; I was Hessa, a teacher who loved numbers and writing and Aubin Wallace. When he kissed me, I remembered why.

The kiss deepened and the energy moved from my mouth through my body, to my core and to the tips of my fingers and toes. When he moved away, I was frightened to have him out of my reach. I needed him close. I slipped my arms around him before he could step back and reached up to find his mouth again. There was a rush building that I had never felt before. The need scared me, but not as much as the thought of going without. My body took control, leaving my mind to wonder and worry. Aubin responded. His arms were tight around me, his lips wandering from mine to my neck and shoulders and back to my mouth. My brain was screaming at me to stop, but my arms and hands and mouth disobeyed and instead showed Aubin how much I needed him in a way I had never needed anyone before.

When it was over, I cried. I cried because I had nothing else to do. I cried for Toan and the pain I knew I would cause him. I cried for the years with him that I hadn't understood. I cried because we had never shared such a moment. I cried because Toan loved me, and Aubin loved me, and I the only thing I was sure of was that I didn't deserve either of them. And I cried because I was so happy lying in Aubin's arms with the warm grass under us and the sun spraying sparkles of light through the breaks in the leaves. I cried because everything was wrong and everything was right, and I couldn't decipher the solution to that problem.

Aubin seemed to know. He held me tightly and kissed my shoulder. He stroked my hair and wiped tears from my face. When I was spent, he kissed my lips and whispered "Thank you" in my ear. We sorted out our clothing and I fixed my hair back into a tidy tail in the back. Aubin's smile was frequent but shy, and I nodded when he said, "We should go," even though I think I would have given up everything to stay there forever.

I've never been back.

We walked from the park to the hover station hand in hand, each thinking our own thoughts but not trusting them to voice. I knew Aubin was happy because his smile stayed on his face, easy and natural. As time crept away from that moment, the knot in my stomach grew so that when we got to the station and had to separate to our different hovers, I blurted, "We have to go soon."

His eyes were surprised, but he nodded quickly and said, "Whenever, Hessa, whenever you're ready. I'll do whatever you want to do."

"I don't know what I want, but we *need* to just go." He seemed to understand my vague reasoning, or he didn't care. He nodded and squeezed my hand. "I need to tell Toan." It was only because his smile fell that I knew I had whispered those words out loud.

"When?"

"Now. Tonight. When I get home."

"Do you want me to come?"

I hadn't even thought of him being there. I wondered for a moment if it would help. Toan would be terribly hurt, terribly angry. Learning of my betrayal in front of Aubin could only make it worse. I couldn't do that to him, not now. "No, I think I should do it alone." Aubin nodded and squeezed my hand again, and I walked toward my hover platform.

I was three paces away when he called after me. "Wait! Here, I almost forgot." He dug into his pocket and pulled out a yellow envelope, bent at the corners. My hover slid into the station behind us, and I had to run to catch it. I snatched the envelope as I left and yelled "Thank you" over my shoulder. I knew he stood there watching, even though I didn't look back.

I found a seat on the hover and shifted my bag to my lap. I opened the envelope and unfolded the paper, needing to see his familiar handwriting.

Hessa,

Your times are dark, painful, I know. Lean back when you must, and my confianza will hold you up. Save and shelter you. Keep you strong and fill your need.

Our meeting, a tjotjog, one extraordinary star in a sea of lights in the night, making my tenalach respond to the life around me. Let me surround you with the light you have given. The love you have given. The life you have given. A.

After his inscribed 'A', he had written in a hasty, messy line as if in after thought: *We'll be okay, Hessa, it'll all work out.* I slipped the envelope into my bag. His note made the storm in my middle settle just a bit. With the bolster of his note, I knew I was right to tell Toan that night. There was no point in waiting any longer.

When I got home I could see the lights on in the house, which meant Toan had beaten me home. My conviction drained instantly, and I stood shaking on the sidewalk. Then his face appeared at the window of my office, the room he usually only entered to talk to me. I jumped, startled, but I forced a smile and waved up to him. His face didn't change, and the heavy pit in my stomach grew bigger. Even from three stories below I could see his eyes were angry before he disappeared from the lit square. His sudden absence propelled me forward. And then I couldn't be apart from him, I couldn't let him stay out of my sight. I was in the house and up the stairs before I could reconsider barging into his wrath.

The door to my office slid open, and he was there waiting for me, still dressed in his work clothes, his dress shirt pulled haphazardly from the waist and his sleeves shoved up past his elbows. He leaned back against my desk, his arms folded. His face was stone. Beside him on the desk was dumped out the box I had kept hidden. Months of correspondence between Aubin and I were piled on the desk; all of the notes I had known I should destroy to protect us from this exact moment. My face burned and my stomach twisted. My hands shook at my sides. Toan was silent. His face and his stance demanded an explanation, but he gave me time to absorb the sight of him standing with my secrets spilled around him.

"Toan," I whispered, pushing the sounds painfully through my throat.

"What do they say, Hessa?" His voice was controlled,

178

though I could tell from the flash in his eyes it took great effort for him to keep it that way.

My mind raced, flashed images of each paper, the words and the dancing letters. "They … they are poems about different things." It was impossible to summarize the months of writing into a simple explanation.

"Poems." Toan nodded with his lips pressed together. His jaw worked under the shadowed skin of his face. "Are they *love* poems?" He sneered when he said that, with an ugly tone I had never heard before in his voice. At least not toward me. My eyes welled up, and hot tears spilled over my cheeks.

"Some of them, yes." I was falling, as if I'd just stepped off a cliff and there was no way to stop the gravity pulling me down. No bottom to the gravity, no end to the fall.

"Who wrote them?" Toan's quietly even voice was more cutting than if he had screamed or cried.

"I did." I forced the truth out; it burned like vomit.

"And?" Of course he already knew.

"Aubin Wallace." I forced myself to look at him when I said his name. My intention was not to be defiant or defensive or challenging. It would have been cowardly to look away in that moment, the moment when the full impact of my betrayal hit Toan, *my* Toan, and his face and body reacted. His pain was my fault. I needed to feel it. My witness was my punishment.

His stony face faltered, cracked and fell. His eyes blinked, fast and hard, but not quickly enough to stop the single tear from falling from his right eye. It glanced on his cheek and dripped to his chest before he swiped viciously at its glistening trail. His lips winced and then pressed together, his jaw shifted behind his closed mouth, the muscles lifting under his cheeks. His arms refolded, his fingers gripped the opposite bicep so that each digit turned white. He said nothing, and I couldn't stand it.

"Toan." My legs shook when I stepped toward him, and my knees buckled. I fell into the chair in front of him. He looked away.

"Did you— Did you sleep with him?" His voice cracked, and he shuddered.

There was nothing left to hide. "Yes, once." I didn't tell him that hours made the difference in that truth; I couldn't bear for him to know. He peeked up at me from the corner of his eyes. I resisted the urge to hold him. My memory flashed: him leaning away from me in the car years ago, when his heart was breaking and I felt helpless to do anything about it. Now I was the one who had broken him.

"When he came here and had supper in our home…" His voice trailed off as if he couldn't finish the thought.

"No, not then. We were just friends then. I wouldn't do that, Toan."

He glared at me. "I don't know anymore what you would and wouldn't do, Hessa." His words spat out and pierced me, cut through me to my core and stayed there burning.

I stood up and took a step toward him, he took a step back. "Toan, I'm sorry. I'm so, so sorry. I didn't mean for this to happen, it just — "

"You sure as hell didn't do anything to stop it, did you?"

We stood there for a long moment. I wanted to leave, to escape from him and run to Aubin, who could make everything feel right again. At the same time I wanted to step closer, wrap myself around Toan and take it all back. I wanted to take away the anguish that I was causing, to make him better, make *us* better. I couldn't do both, so I did neither. I stood and waited.

"So what do you want? What are you going to do?" His voice was broken and resigned, not defensive.

"I don't know." But I did. I just couldn't say it to him.

"Then I do. That's answer enough."

He unfolded his arms and ran his hands through his hair, leaving tufts of it standing up in all directions. It was a gesture he had made for years, the same one that led me to tease him, laughing and calling him names, and I had to bite my tongue to stop myself from doing just that, just then. Sometimes he would mess it up further with an impish smile. It was unsettling how that movement and my instinctive response stayed the same when everything else between us was different. His eyes met mine, and I was sure he knew what I was thinking. He raised one hand slowly and leveled the unruly hair.

"I'm going to go," he said, his voice flat again.

"Where, Toan? You don't have to."

"Yes, I do. I'll go to Mom's." My stomach sank. I don't know why, but I hadn't expected him to leave. Not tonight. "Don't worry, I won't tell her." His voice was sarcastic.

"You don't have to go." I could only manage a whisper.

"I do. I can't stay here. Not tonight." He didn't look at me again. He stepped past me through the hall to the stairs. I followed him up and waited in the hall while he banged around and then emerged with a bag and walked past me. I followed again as he went down the three flights to the front door. I stood shaking and silent as he put on his street boots, took his jacket from the closet. He shouldered his overnight bag and then his work bag over top and touched the panel to open the door.

"Toan," I whispered, and it made him stop on his way through. But he didn't look back, and I had nothing else to say.

"I'll write you soon," he said. He meant a text on my communicator or through the network panels, but the word echoed in my ears. He stepped through the door, and it slid shut behind him. I watched through the glass as he turned, walked down the street and disappeared around the corner before I slouched to the floor.

20

Gallie – Your medical records indicate that you were subjected to a Random Routine Health Assessment on Ten 28?

Hessa – Yes.

Gallie – Were you expecting it?

Finch – By definition, Random Assessments are unexpected.

Gallie – Had you been subjected to an RRHA before?

Hessa – Once in senior class.

Gallie – Were you following the healthy lifestyle regulations?

Hessa – Yes, of course. I'm sure your records show that.

Gallie – In fact, yes they do. You completed your compulsory run an average of six days out of seven, fulfilled the grocery ration as dictated. I see you regularly had credits left over for food and alcohol luxuries. Is this all accurate?

Hessa – I would assume so. It's government record.

Gallie – So you had no reason to expect anything to come of your RRHA in Ten?

Hessa – No.

Gallie – What did you expect when the Medic asked you to come into his office on Ten 30?

Hessa – I don't remember.

Gallie – You don't remember? Being called into the Medic's office is not a common occurrence, is it? Especially for one as fit as yourself.

Hessa – No, but I don't remember worrying about it. I was probably thinking about my course work or something.

    Gallie – Were you alone at your meeting with the Medic?

    Hessa – No.

    Gallie – Who was there?

    Hessa – Toan was in the waiting room when I got there.

    Gallie – Were you surprised to see Mr. Whitley waiting as well?

    Hessa – Yes.

    Gallie – What reason did you think Mr. Whitley had for attending your meeting?

    Hessa – I didn't know. I guess I assumed he had an issue with an RRHA as well. Maybe we were doing something wrong together.

    Gallie – A plausible explanation. Had Mr. Whitley been subjected to an RRHA?

    Hessa – No, but I didn't know that.

    Gallie – Why didn't you know that at the time?

    Hessa – Toan had been visiting with his mother for a few days.

    Gallie – Did Mr. Whitley participate in your meeting with the Medic?

    Hessa – Yes.

    Gallie – So he was there when the Medic informed you of your pregnancy?

I threw myself into my work. Work let me hide from Toan's absence from our home and distracted me from Aubin's expectations while we prepared to leave. We had days, maybe a week to endure until we could safely get away. If the Authority discovered that my match was broken, we would miss the opportunity to disappear into an oddout community. I'd be moved to another Quantifier position, and Aubin's ability to follow me there was limited.

When my communicator flashed the request for me to meet the Medic in his office, I was entrenched in planning for a progress assessment for my students. I was frustrated by the interruption and spent the time it took to walk to the Medic's office running through the topics I needed to include on the test in my head. I met Toan in the waiting room, and fear clenched tightly around my heart. I felt cold. They knew Toan had removed himself from our home and that I was breaking our match.

Toan looked up when I entered the small room, and I stopped at the sight of him dwarfing the small couch that filled the space. The list I had compiled in my head slipped away. There was Toan and his familiar dark eyes watching me with an expression I didn't recognize.

"Hi, Hessa," he said. His voice was soft and calm but not quite friendly. My stomach twisted at the sight of him, or maybe that was because the scenters emitted too much lavender.

"Hi." I walked toward him and dared to sit on a chair beside him, hoping he wouldn't move away. He didn't. "I've missed you." I held my breath after I said it.

He sighed first and then said, "I've missed you too, Hessa." He smiled a little, and I wanted to hug him, but I worried that would be pushing too far. "Do you know why we're here?" he asked.

"No, did you have a RRHA too?"

"No. You did?" I had just enough time to nod before the Medic's office door opened and he stepped out in his light green uniform.

"Hessa Black?" I nodded. "And Toan Whitley?"

"Yes," Toan said beside me.

"Well then, please come in. This will only take a few moments if we are efficient."

Toan stood, but for some reason my legs wouldn't work. Dread had started to creep in, and my weight was frozen heavily on the chair. Somehow I knew the Medic had only bad news to report. I was immobile in sudden fear until Toan, a step ahead of me, turned and offered his hand. I took it, warm and solid, and he squeezed, causing tears to fill my eyes. I stood and followed him into the small office.

We sat in the two slippery polyleather chairs offered to us, facing the Medic with his large steel desk between him and us. Toan let go of my hand when he sat, and I felt cold in its absence. I forced myself to sit slowly in the chair beside him when

my body threatened to fall. The chair had a round warm spot
where someone had recently sat. The office had one small window with a blind that blocked all of the sun but a square of
sharp light that surrounded it. The sharp, light lines seemed to
fit with the sharp scent of antiseptic and the Medic's sharp stare
down the end of his sharp nose. The Medic flipped through images on his screen until one appeared with my name in bold text
at the top, *BLACK, HESSA: QUANTIFIER*. I was holding my
breath again.

"Let's get right to it then, shall we?" the Medic asked,
though he obviously wasn't looking for our input. "Hessa, the
results of your Health Assessment indicate that you are three
days pregnant." The breath I had been holding fell out of me
with an audible gasp that sounded like I had been punched in
the stomach. I didn't dare look at Toan beside me but could
sense his body stiffen. "The complication of this situation, of
course, is that you have not applied for a Procreation Permit. Is
this correct?"

I fumbled but couldn't speak. Toan saved me the effort.
"That's correct, we have not."

"My records show that you have not completed the probationary two years necessary before applying for a Procreation
Permit."

"It will be two years next Seven. We were matched on Seven
17 last year." His voice was steady, even. I wondered if the Medic
could hear the restraint in Toan's voice that was so obvious to
me.

"I see. I'm sure you are aware of the Recovery of Fertility
Act. With you being First and Second Stat, the likelihood of
your offspring having high aptitude prohibits termination." He
looked up at us from over his screen as if to make sure we were
listening.

Toan assured him, "We know," and I managed to nod.

"So that leaves you with two options. You can place the in-
fant for adoption with a Quantifier couple that has been verified
as infertile. That will entail apprehension of the fetus at thirty
weeks for external incubation. Or you can pay the fee to have
the probationary period waived and the Procreation Permit ex-

pedited. Either way, you will be required to acknowledge liability in the unapproved pregnancy. Which of you was prescribed the contraceptive?"

"I was." Toan's voice remained strong. I didn't dare look at him.

"And which contraceptive were you using?"

"Preventa, by weekly dosage."

"Interesting. That has a statistical success rate of one hundred percent."

"Yes. But I missed a dose." His voice didn't provide any indication that he was lying. I opened my mouth, but Toan slipped his foot sideways to brush against mine, and I shut it again, clenching my jaw tight until it hurt. I knew for a fact that Toan hadn't missed a dose. He was never that careless.

That was the first of three times Toan saved me, in spite of everything I did to him.

"That would explain it. Which dose was that?"

"I was supposed to take one Friday night, the twenty-second. I fell asleep watching a show on the panel, and when I woke up I went right to bed."

"Why didn't you see a Medic about an emergency dose?"

"I honestly forgot all about it until Monday after we ... I just hoped nothing would come of it."

"I see. Well, that was a foolish choice, wasn't it? It explains the unplanned pregnancy, though, as it corresponds with the hormone levels indicated on the results of Ms. Black's RRHA. You will have to report to the Judicial office for a citation and fine sooner rather than later, as my report will be submitted this afternoon." The Medic returned to the screen and flicked his fingers through the hologram floating above it. "As for the pregnancy itself, you have four days to come to a decision on whether to file for an Expedited Procreation Permit or allow apprehension of the child."

He looked up at us again, as if surprised to see us still sitting in front of him. "Ms. Black, perhaps you might learn from this situation and in the future secure responsibility for your fertility health, since Mr. Whitley has proven to be unreliable?"

186

I opened my mouth to argue, but Toan beat me to it. "Yes, he's probably right, Hessa. I'm sorry." I couldn't help but look at him. I couldn't comprehend how he managed to glare at me while looking so sad at the same time.

"I guess," I managed to mumble.

We left the Medic's office together but silent. My mind was spinning from the information and from Toan's reaction to it. It took several paces until I could find the breath and words to challenge him. "Toan, why did you do that?"

Toan stopped and looked at me hard in the eyes. "I'm sorry I didn't tell you I forgot the dose. You deserve the choice." His voice was intent, asking me to read between his words. His eyebrows rose slightly. I realized he was talking for the sensors and the personnel on the other side of those sensors, not for me. "I'll be home tonight. We can talk about it then." With that he turned and strode away from me down the hall.

And with his abrupt exit, Aubin entered my mind. I needed to see him, but lunch was still a half hour away, and my class was waiting for me. I forced myself to go back to my room. I apologized to the class for my tardiness and asked them to continue with their individual studying. I sat at my own desk trying to look busy to ward off any interruptions, trying to keep the panic closing in from crushing me. I sent a message to Aubin. The need to talk to him alone was greater than the risk.

As soon as the intercom chimed the start of lunch break, I left the noisy students behind and hurried past Aubin's classroom. He stood in the doorway, seemingly watching the students but waiting for me, a look of concern frozen on his face. When I walked past him he hurried to fall into stride beside me as we walked down the hall to the closest exit and away from the building.

"What's wrong?"

"I'm pregnant." He stopped in this tracks, but I kept walking, leaving him behind.

"Hessa! Wait!" he called from behind me.

I couldn't stop. Suddenly I needed to get far away from the school, from the Medic and the administrative authorities with their sensors. From Toan. And maybe even from Aubin. But he

caught up, his heavy boot soles beating on the pavement until
he fell back into step beside me. His hand slipped over mine,
and he squeezed. My fingers curled between his, and I didn't try
to stop them. We walked in silence for several minutes more
until the instinct to run subsided and I let my heart and feet
slow. Finally he tugged at my hand and led me to a bench,
where we sat silent for what seemed like forever.

"Hessa? Is the baby mine?"

I shouldn't have been angry at his question. Unlike Toan, he
was well aware that he was not the only man I had been with. I
bit my cheek to check my angry response and just nodded. Metallic blood seeped against my tongue. Then, as if someone had
opened a door and let in a bright spotlight, the answer was clear.
I couldn't speak fast enough. "Let's go now. Right now, this afternoon. If we leave now, we could be long gone before anyone
even knows we've left. How long would it take us to get to a
new district? We should probably go three or four away so no
one knows us. We'll find a Chosen oddout community, and
they'll help us get some jobs. I'm sure we can get settled before
this baby comes. We don't need much, right? Just a small apartment that will fit three of us. I could learn how to clean. It can't
be that hard. You could try cooking, like you said? If you want.
Or something else — anything else. When some time has gone
by, I could get a note to Toan to let him know I'm okay, and
maybe by then he'll forgive me. Maybe." Aubin sat beside me as
I rambled, his face hidden behind his hands. Silent. I was sure
he was listening to my plan, thinking through the holes and
weaknesses, trying to find solutions. It was what he had wanted
all along. He didn't say anything when I stopped talking, so I
pulled his hand from his face and prompted, "Well?"

He looked up to stare straight ahead, not at me. His blue
eyes shone bright against his paled face. "You have to go back
and talk to Toan."

I winced and groaned. "I know I should. I wish I could, but
I think it's safer if we go now, without him knowing. He said the
baby is his. He told the Medic that. If the Authority thinks I'm
stealing his baby, taking a First Stat child into an oddout colony,
they'll never let us go. Maybe it'll even be easier for him if I just

go, you know, not draw it out."

He looked at me. The tears pooling in his blue eyes scared me. "That's not what I mean, Hessa. You need to go talk to Toan. You need to apologize and ask him to take you back. Or beg. Do what you have to so he'll come back to you. Stay matched."

"What? What are you saying?" My chest tightened until it hurt to breathe.

"We can't leave. Not now."

"Of course we can. Nothing has changed! If anything, we have to go! We don't have a choice. We can make this work — you said so yourself! Who cares if we're oddouts as long as we're together?" My breath wasn't working with my voice and my words. It was coming too fast and I was dizzy. I wanted to close my eyes to stop the world from spinning, but I feared that when I opened them again Aubin would be gone.

"*Everything* has changed, Hessa. We can't … *trap* a child in an oddout life! Think about the risks! Oddout Donation Program, oddout Medical Experimentation. Those things are real, and you know it! If you and Toan raise this baby, he'll be safe from those."

"We could keep him hidden, keep him out of the system so they won't find him." I was shaking so badly, the words bounced and trembled as they spilled out.

"It would never work. They'd find him."

"It could," I whispered.

"Okay, say we *can* keep him hidden. Even if he can escape that, what kind of life would that be? I can only imagine how brilliant this baby of yours will be. To subject him to a life of menial work? How could we do that to our child? What if he gets sick? We'd only watch him suffer. How do we take care of him then? How do we find enough food? How could we live knowing we forced our baby into that existence for the sake of our own happiness?"

I felt everything slipping away, could feel the lessons and the truth he had shown me over the months crumble and blow away. "It's not a trap. Classification *is* a trap! You know that, *you* taught me that! Rules and roles and responsibilities? An oddout

189

can do whatever he wants! Only oddouts are free!"

"Free how? There are no opportunities, only limitations. He'd be restricted to a life that falls so short of his potential. Never to aspire or achieve anything that means anything? A life spent lugging other people's things around, cleaning up other people's garbage? An existence that hurts the body and smothers the imagination? How is that free? And that's if we can keep him hidden from the Protectors and the Deciders and the community that will turn him in for his turn for medical programs. How do we do that? We could choose that for ourselves, Hessa, but we can't force someone else into that life when he would have so much more to accomplish."

"Then you're just like *them*. Telling this, this *person* what he has to do, who he has to be."

Aubin tipped his head in thought. "Yes, I —— I guess I am. But later, he can decide for himself. He'll still have the choice. Just like you did when you started to write, *he'll* make his choice, not us. We have to give him the tools to have that choice; education and health and exposure to life. He deserves every opportunity, not a life of labor."

"We could teach him, Aubin. He would learn numbers and writing and be ... happy."

"That would be worse, Hessa, don't you see? That would only show him the life we cost him, the experiences he's not entitled to because we took it away. We made this mess. We owe him that much." Aubin's voice was a hoarse whisper that rattled on his breath.

I shook my head, and once I started I couldn't stop. I shook until it hurt inside. "No, Aubin. You can't say that. You can't mean that. You promised it would work out. You promised we'd be okay."

His smile was weak and sad through the tears that kept falling, but painfully sincere. "It *will* work out, Hessa, we *will* be okay. Just not the way we planned."

"No, no. Aubin, no."

He reached up and stroked the hair that was shaken from the ponytail, back behind my ear. "Hessa, it's the only way."

I leaned into his fingers then wrenched back away. "How

190

can you do this? How can you leave me now that I'm pregnant with your child? Toan won't want me. He won't want this baby. You're leaving me alone." I buried my face in my hands and cried. I heard him slide closer to me, and when he tried to put his arms around me, I fought him off — squirmed and pushed and screamed — until I couldn't fight anymore. I sagged against him, and he tightened his grip.

"Can't you see this is killing me too? You won't be alone. Toan loves you, Hessa. Not less than I do, just differently. He won't let you down. I promise."

I pulled away again and he let go. "You promise? You *promise*? What exactly is that supposed to mean? What good are your promises?" He cringed, and I was glad that my words hurt him.

"You're right. I guess I don't know anymore." He looked at me for a moment and then looked back at his hands folded in his lap. We sat silent, and the world kept turning in spite of the screeching halt I felt it should have made just then.

I was scared to ask him, but more terrified not to. "Don't you love me anymore?" My whisper was nearly drowned out by the breeze that lifted the wayward lock of hair and pressed it against my face.

I watched him shudder. He gasped as if hit in the stomach. He squeezed his eyes and his mouth closed and drew air through his nose with a fast sob until his shoulders and chest were raised high. As he blew it out, he turned to look at me with his wide, wet blue eyes. His hand shook as he reached toward me, taking a lifetime to cross the inches, to tuck my hair back again. I let him. "Of course I love you, Hessa. That's the only thing I'm sure of right now." He laid his hand on my leg. "I *hope* this works for the best, but we don't have time to wait and be sure. We have to act now. I have to go, and you — you have to talk to Toan." He took me by surprise and kissed me. It started hard and hurried and softened as his lips paused still against mine. The kiss lingered as if he was passing me information, as if he couldn't bear to let go, as if by sheer will he could change our dire circumstance. None of that happened, though, and the kiss ended, leaving me empty and sad and knowing he was convinced, even if I was not.

191

He rested his forehead against mine and started laying out his new plan so I would have the answers if asked. Each of his words dripped in my ear and fell heavy and toxic in my middle. "My mother is sick. I just heard this morning, and I need to go to her immediately. I anticipate her needing me there for quite a while, so I will request an employment transfer to follow me back to Toronto." With that he took a deep breath and leaned away to look at me with the intent I'd seen when he studied one of his words. He smiled and whispered, "You will be my yoin, to carry me forward and keep me true. For life we share a shih that cannot be lost or stolen or forgotten."

His words, with their familiar beauty, almost made me smile. "Walt Whitman?" I asked, trying to keep my voice light.

He smiled and let a chuckle fall just under his breath. "Aubin Wallace."

He stood and offered his hand, which I took. But once he pulled me to my feet, he let go. We walked back to the Educational Department building. We didn't hold hands or talk, though I desperately wanted to. It was if our delicate agreement hung in danger between us like a soap bubble; one touch or one word could pop its integrity, dissolving our resolution. More than once I tried to open my mouth to argue with him or instructed my hand to reach out and touch him, but it was as if he cast a spell over my body to ignore my mind's directions. My mouth and my hand remained uselessly idle, and our terrible decision stayed intact. When we reached the building, the door slid open and he paused to let me enter first. I mumbled "Thank you" out of reflex. I wish I had said something more, that those weren't the last words he heard me say to him. But maybe they were appropriate: what more could I have said for all he had done?

And as always, there was work to be done. I went back to my room and taught in a trance for the rest of the day. My students looked back at me with confused and bewildered faces as I stumbled through lessons and made mistakes. I apologized, blaming a headache that was painfully real by the end of the day. As the last class filed out of the room, I sat at my desk with my face resting in my hands propped up on my elbows. A nervous student muttered my name, her voice cracking under her timidity. Exhausted by the effort, I pulled myself up to look at her. She held a small yellow envelope with my name written on the outside: an evenly crossed 'H', tipped heart 'E', two synchronous 'S's and a long-tailed 'A'. "It was taped to the door," she whispered as if defending herself for interrupting me. I thanked her and waited until she left the room to open the note.

You will be my yoin, to carry me forward and keep me true. For life we share a shih that cannot be lost or stolen or forgotten. Always remember I love you. A.

He left me with that peace.

21

Ikkisa

Gallie – Why have you not felt obligated to inform the court of your pregnancy?

Hessa – It's pretty obvious by looking at me, isn't it?

Gallie – Is it a coincidence that Aubin left for Toronto the week your RRHA uncovered your hidden pregnancy?

Hessa – He left because his mother was sick. My pregnancy wasn't hidden, just unexpected.

Gallie – Unexpected by whom, Mr. Whitley?

Hessa – Yes, and myself.

Gallie – Did you apply for a Procreation Permit before conception of this child?

Hessa – No.

Gallie – My records show you are currently in your twenty-seventh week gestation, is that correct?

Hessa – Yes.

Gallie – And will you inform the court of your plans for this child, please? Did you secure a Procreation Permit, or will the fetus be apprehended at thirty weeks?

Toan had said he'd come home that night, but he arrived so late that I was doubting I had heard him correctly. Maybe I had only heard what I wanted to hear. Or maybe he changed his mind. I was slumped on a kitchen chair when my shaking legs wouldn't carry me any farther. I don't know how long I laid my head on my arms and cried, but when my eyes were empty of tears I just sat at the table; the sunlight slipped away from the window, and I didn't bother turning on the lights. When Toan came home, he found me sitting in the dark.

The central system announced his arrival, and I pulled my-self up straighter in my chair, trying to rally what was left of my strength to face him. "Lights," he commanded as he walked through the door. I heard the door slide shut behind him as a glare burst throughout the room. My eyes, accustomed to the darkness, blinked in dispute. His footfalls brought him into the kitchen, where he stood, startled, in the doorway. "Hessa! It was dark. I didn't think you were here."

"Where else would I be?" The question was biting, though maybe only to me, because I knew just a few short hours earlier how much I wanted to be anywhere else.

"Gone." His voice sneered and his eyes were leveled at me, carrying so much more emotion than the single word. Of course he knew.

Toan shrugged, as if shaking off an argument. He set his bags by the door, where he always did, and came into the kitchen. He opened the cooling system and stared with blank eyes for a moment before he closed it again.

"Did you eat?" he asked, and even that sounded angry. He started the tea program on the synth.

"I'm not hungry."

"You need to eat." He growled and then turned to lock his eyes on mine until I turned away to look at my hands on the table.

I tried to keep irritation from my voice; he was just taking care of me. As always. "I'm not hungry."

I don't think tea ever took so long to make. He stood across the kitchen, waiting for it while I stared at my hands on the ta-ble. Silence had never been unpleasant between Toan and I. From babies engaged in our own play side by side to students studying for hours, we had always shifted in and out of silence with easy transitions and an uncanny understanding of each other's needs. When we were younger I wondered if it was because we could read each other's minds. I made him try to send me one of his ideas. It hadn't worked then, but there were other times when I was sure it did. In the kitchen that night, I couldn't read his thoughts. He could have been miles away as easily as he was those ten feet. The silence hung sharp above us, threatening to pierce us when its suspension ended. My apprehension was so high that by the time Toan stepped toward me with his hands fisted around two mug handles, I startled in my chair. He put one mug in front of me on the table and said, "Drink that." It was not a request.

Toan sat across the table, and I felt his stare on me. I curled my fingers around the hot mug, breathing in smell of cinnamon. It soothed me a little. I forced myself to look up and meet his eyes. I was surprised that he wasn't glaring. Instead his look was softer, sad and more familiar. Closer to my Toan. "Where's Aubin?" he asked. There was a hint of a sneer in his voice, as if his effort to hide it, though great, was not quite enough.

I sucked in my breath and realized there was no longer any reason to lie. "He's gone back to Toronto." I hoped he heard my low voice. I didn't think I could bear to repeat myself. As it was, the words rang in my head, making their truth more real with each reverberation.

"Does he know?" The sneer had turned incredulous.

"Yes, he knows."

"Cowardly son of a bitch." That was said under his breath, so I don't think he meant for me to hear it.

"It's not like that!"

"How is it then, Hessa? He left you behind to face the consequences of an unpermitted pregnancy alone."

"He wanted the baby to have choices and opportunities, not stuck with an oddout life." I took a moment to watch Toan's face before adding, "And he knew I wasn't alone."

At that Toan's mouth curled up, but it wasn't like any smile I had seen on his face before. He nodded once and replaced words with a hard pound of his fist on the table. He stood, strode to the incinerator and threw his mug inside so hard that I heard it smash on the other side of the container before the heat absorbed the mass. He punched a hole in the wall and then stood with his hands on the counter, his shoulders heaving.

"I'm sorry, Toan." I knew it meant little, but there wasn't anything else I could say.

"Yeah, you've said that."

"I am. I know that's not enough, but I am." I waited for him to say something more, but he didn't. He came back to the table and sat across from me, watching his hands fold around each other and let go, only to fold them again. He rubbed his knuckles as they turned red. "Why did you tell them you missed your dose?"

He looked up at me, and I could see his eyes searching to understand what I had asked. He finally shrugged and shook his head. "I didn't think you'd want an investigation. We know the truth, that's all that matters."

I shuddered at that. I hadn't thought of what could have happened. Of course they would want to investigate why a drug with a hundred percent success rate failed, and that would include genetic testing of the baby. When they discovered that the baby was not Toan's but a Creator's child… I must have looked horrified at the thought, because Toan's hand crept across the table and lay on mine.

"I *am* sorry, Toan." I couldn't help but say again.

This time his eyes were softer and his smile was gentle. He took a deep breath and then whispered, "I know." The sneer had fallen from his voice. My Toan was back.

"Do you hate me?"

Toan's reaction was a snicker that was heavy with sarcasm but void of malice. He shook his head. "I couldn't, Hessa. I'm pretty sure I hate *him*. I hate what you did with him and what you did … to me. I think it would be easier if I could hate you. But I can't. I've always loved you. I don't know how else to feel."

And I knew he did. He loved me, not in the same way as Aubin, but not less. Maybe even more. Probably more. His eyes were steady on mine as mine filled with tears again. My throat was tight, thick and painful. The sips of tea I had managed swirled in my stomach. Not only had I betrayed that man who loved me so, but I had failed him by not loving him as much.

"What are we going to do?" he asked.

"We?"

197

He squeezed my hand. "We're still matched, Hessa. We're supposed to face challenges together. I think— We... I am willing to try if you are."

I found myself holding my breath, wondering what conditions were attached to his offer. I was scared to ask, but there was no moving forward if I didn't. "And the baby?" I whispered, hoping it was loud enough for him to hear.

"What do you want to do?"

I was gagged for a moment, unable to voice my fears. I couldn't ask Toan to accept a child that wasn't his, that was the product of my betrayal. But the thought of surrendering my child — Aubin's child — first to a biotech incubator and then to unknown parents? Impossible.

"I don't want ... I don't think I can give it up." I couldn't ask him, but my line was clearly drawn between the two choices.

He took a deep breath and nodded. "What's mine is yours and what's yours is mine, Hessa. The baby is yours. I will make him mine too."

And that was the second time Toan saved me. Aubin's love for our child drove him away; he wanted the baby to have what we couldn't give him. Toan's love for me was strong enough to come back. It was great enough to accept a baby that wasn't part of him simply because it was part of me. I think that was when I started to hope the baby had brown eyes like me and like Toan, not blue.

I wiped my hands across my face and tried to smile. "I do love you." My voice cracked, even at a whisper.

He nodded, but his smile was sad. "I know." I wondered if love could change. I'd loved Aubin with a fierce need, but it hadn't been enough. After everything that had happened, everything I had done, there I sat with my Toan, my childhood friend, my partner. I realized his boyish face had disappeared over the past week. His dark eyes looked older.

"Wait here a minute." I stood quickly enough to startle us both.

I went up the stairs two at a time and squeezed through the opening door of my office as soon as the space was big enough. My letters were still scattered on the desk, where Toan had dumped them. I shuffled through the papers until I found the one with large, wobbly letters. I started to leave but turned back, collected the rest of the papers in the box and picked up the box as well.

When I reentered the kitchen, Toan's eyes fell on the box in my hand, and his face hardened with narrowed eyes and pinched lips. I put the single paper on the table and stepped toward the incinerator. My feet dragged, heavy. It took every bit of will I had to keep moving forward. I willed Toan to stop me, screaming in my mind, hoping he could hear me with that telepathic connection I used to think we shared. He watched me silently. I hoped for a last-minute reprieve, a moment of sympathy or compassion greater than my treachery, but he had already given me all he had. In my tear-blurred vision the incinerator door opened, and I held the box in the hot air over the open space. Aubin's blue eyes flashed in my mind as my wrist turned and the box tipped. Folded papers and yellow envelopes rained down into the red heat, shriveling and curling at the corners for the briefest of moments before their delicate shapes, silhouetted black against the glowing light, disintegrated into nothing. I dropped the box in after, and with a flash of heat and light, my written words were gone. My eyes burned from the hot air wafting up out of the hole. My heart burned too, intense and acute. For a painful moment I wondered if I could go on. My eyes gazed unfocussed into the heat where the words had disappeared, and I wondered if I had gone with them.

From the table Toan said, "Thank you," which brought me back to our kitchen.

I went to the table and sat across from him again, lifting the surviving paper in my shaking hands.

"I wrote *this* one for you," I said through my tight throat.

"What does it say?"

I skipped Aubin's word, *'jayus'*, and its definition at the top, and started where Toan came into my writing:

"'*We are two halves of an imperfect whole, so that I don't know where he ends and I start, or where he starts and I end. Around and around we spin, locked together in an embrace no one can enter, no one can share, no one can break. Comfort and shelter and insight beyond senses, we each know the other. We are shielded, a team of two against the rest.'"*

When I looked up, Toan was listening with his eyes closed and his face blank. It was impossible for me to read him, to know what he was thinking or feeling, which I hated. I waited for him to open his eyes and look at me.

"Is that true?" he asked when he finally did.

I couldn't lie to him. I didn't know who we were anymore. Who I was, who I was with him. Without Aubin. "It was when I wrote it." I touched his hand when he looked away. "I want us to be that way again."

For a long moment he stared at his hands, and I sat quietly resisted the surge of arguments and appeals that threatened to boil over in my desperation to convince him I was committed.

"Did he ask you to go with him?" Toan's voice was tight. I knew he hadn't wanted to ask that question and probably didn't want to know the answer either.

I thought of my rambling proposal to Aubin and wondered how it was possible that only hours had passed; it seemed like a lifetime at least. I wondered if I would have gone through with it, if I could have left everything behind. Sitting with Toan across from me, my fingers resting on the back of his hand, I couldn't imagine how it would have been possible. Incomplete truths are dishonest, but sometimes they are kinder.

"No, he didn't." I left it at that.

22

Èr shièr

Hessa – Toan and I applied for an expedited Procreation Permit, of course.

    Gallie – And was it granted?

    Hessa – Yes.

    Gallie – Congratulations.

    Hessa – Yeah, thank you, I'm sure.

    Gallie – Have you heard any more from Mr. Wallace since he left?

    Hessa – No.

    Gallie – Not at all?

    Hessa – No.

    Gallie – That seems peculiar for someone who was a good friend of yours.

    Hessa – I'm sure he was just busy.

    Gallie – Perhaps you weren't as good friends as you thought.

    Hessa – I suppose not.

I hoped to hear from Aubin, a note on my communicator at the least, but I also hoped I didn't. Toan and I fell into a new routine, as if we were just getting to know each other. It felt like we were strangers living in the same space, but the stranger looked and smelled and sounded like my best friend. There was a careful shyness between us that had never been there before.

We ate breakfast together through silence or stunted conversation about our plans for the upcoming day. We rode the hover and walked to work. When he finally reached for my hand one day, my stomach fluttered with relief and my eyes welled with tears. I held tight so he would know I didn't want him to let go.

He smiled, and it was Toan's smile back again. Toan didn't stay late at work anymore; sometimes he was even waiting for me in the lobby when I came out. He left with me each day, riding the hover beside me and reading the news on his screen. He heated the suppers and I cleared our dishes, and each time I dropped them in the incinerator I could see thinning papers spinning in the red heat that were no longer there. We did our compulsory run together, and I felt his eyes watching me. He said he was worried the run would be harder for me with my pregnancy, and he was worried we wouldn't be okay.

And little by little the shyness slipped away. Toan still had sullen, angry moments. I'd catch a frown or a glare in his eyes. I learned quickly not to ask him about it but instead find a reason to leave the room and leave him alone. I'd retreat to my office to putter at an outstanding task until he came looking for me.

Toan tried, too. He met me for lunch. Not every day, but a few times a week, at least. He still couldn't talk about his work, but he said more than he should in our hushed house, more than he should but just enough to let me in.

A month after Aubin left, I received a letter at work with a return address from Toronto. I sliced through the top of the envelope, hungry to see Aubin's handwriting, but when I pulled the paper out it was lined in even, perfect type. The type created a formality, a barrier between us that his notes had never possessed. In my hasty pursuit of Aubin through his letter, I hit that wall hard enough to knock the wind from my lungs and tears from my eyes.

Hessa,

I'm sorry I have not been in touch sooner. My current commitments leave me too short on time to attend to what I left behind. My mother is doing well and happy that I'm staying in the city nearby. I have been placed at a local school teaching the Proof class about language structure in literature. My family has arranged a match to be completed in the new year. I wanted to repay the money spent on my behalf. Please accept this notice for funds transfer to cover the expenses you incurred. I hope things are well with you.

Aubin

Somehow even his full name typed at the bottom where his

tailed 'A' should have been was an obstruction blocking him from me. I hoped he was being careful, not callous, and that his formal words were out of concern for security and privacy for our secret. He was the one that left, after all. I wanted to believe his letter was code for 'I miss you, but it hurts to look back', but that was a selfish thing to hope. When I read it again, I was glad the letter was typed; seeing those cold words in Aubin's hand-writing might have been too much.

The funds transfer notice was a significant amount; it covered Toan's fine for liability of my unapproved pregnancy and the fees associated with our expedited Procreation Permit with a little left over. Toan didn't want to accept it. He was angry when I showed it to him and muttered something about "too little, too late" between curses. In the end I convinced him that Aubin was trying to make things as right as he could, and the money would help us prepare for the child. He agreed to take it, though I suspect our financial need was a greater reason than Aubin's conscience.

And so Toan and I moved forward, picking up the pieces of our match that I had tossed away. Late one night, when he slipped into my room with his face wet and his eyes frightened, I lifted up the covers and held him in the dark. I forced away the memory flashes of Aubin and the clearing and found a new want for Toan that I hadn't felt before. When he asked me afterward why I was crying, I couldn't find the words to explain it. I just nestled in closer against him and found the safety I had known all along was mixed with a new feeling that was growing as we healed together.

That's how it went for months, taking small steps closer by rebuilding our routines and our trust. Until that dark night when Toan left for a meeting and I was alone in the house and the Protectors in the private vehicle came and took me into custody. I wonder if I should have expected it. We had rebuked the Authority's rules and customs. We crossed the boundaries they built for the good of the community. We disregarded the gifts we were given, the skills we mastered. We kept secrets. We made choices that weren't ours to make, at least according to them. And we thought we had gotten away with it. So maybe I shouldn't have been surprised when they arrived to hold me accountable.

Aubin was dead. I had tried to leave him in the past, for Toan's sake and for my own sanity, but I still don't understand how he could leave this world without my knowing, feeling or sensing him gone. And I knew it was my fault.

23

I hope Gallie's amplified voice and the clicking of her heels on the floor cover the sound of my shifting in the uncomfortable seat. She asks, "Please remind the court of when and how you learned Aubin Wallace was dead." She stops pacing long enough to look at me when she finishes speaking, and the halt in her motion punctuates her sentence. The bottom half of her is colored by the light coming through the stained glass window, while her shoulders and head are not. I've been watching the stripe of stained glass colors slide up and down her body as she paced in the space that separates the Judician and I from the rest of the people in the court, amusing myself by anticipating when the colors might reach her face.

I am so tired of answering her questions and know the hard ones are yet to come. This one opens the door, I guess, to the reason we're here. Aubin. I am exhausted by the effort of filtering my answers, keeping the two truths separate — the one I need to tell from the one I need to keep hidden. I take a deep breath and try hard to keep my contempt for her out of my voice. "You and Counsel Finch told me last week, when you came to see me in my cell."

"So you had no notice of his death before that?"

I hate her reiterated, reworded, rephrased questions. I hate answering the same thing over and over. "No." I keep the argument *How could I?* to myself. It doesn't help to be impolite, though sometimes it feels better. I look from Gallie to Toan, who still sits ramrod straight in the first row behind Finch. He gives me enough of a smile to remind me he's there.

"And are you aware that the Medics ruled his death a suicide?"

The word cuts as sharply and as real as if I sliced myself

with a knife. "Yes, it was ... it was in the documents."

Gallie nods and steps away from me toward the desk she shares with Finch. The colors slip off her legs as she steps out of their light. She picks up a piece of formal-looking paper and holds it up to show me. "This is the Medic's report. I have high-lighted the comments regarding his cause of death. Could you please read that to the court?" As she approaches, the colors climb her body, stopping just before her eyes are submerged.

I want to say no. I don't know why I need to be the one to read it aloud. The court would learn the same information if it is read by Gallie or Finch. I suppose hearing the gory details in my voice adds power to their conviction. I look at the paper, and my sight blurs. I blink away tears and see the words 'self injec-tion of Euthanix' floating in a streak of yellow ink. When I open my mouth to read, nothing comes from my dry throat.

"Ms. Black? Please read the cause of death."

I nod to show I understand and work my tongue around my mouth to find some lubrication. With a deep breath I force out the sharply thorned words. The court is silent, though not in shock, more in apathy, I'm guessing. No one but me seems to react to the gruesome words. A few of the reporters flit their fingers over the screens in their laps, but most stay still, with blank, staring eyes, as if their minds are far from this stuffy room.

"Do you know when and why the medication Euthanix is typically prescribed?"

Gallie's eyes are trained on me, intimidating me to answer. I'm so angry, but my only defiance is to answer her questions so specifically that I do not give her what she wants. "Yes." I stare back.

"Please tell us, then."

"It's prescribed to end life sooner when someone is suffer-ing and dying."

"To commit suicide."

"Yes." I keep my eyes locked on her, even though every part of me wants to look away. I want to see Toan. I need his reas-surance, but I can't be the first to break contact. Holding my breath helps my resolve, and I relax both my eyes and my chest when she turns back to her desk.

"Do you have any insight as to why Mr. Wallace would be compelled to end his life?"

"No, I don't," I lie.

Of course, I worry that I know exactly why. I don't know what I could have done to stop it, even though it is my fault. Sure, Aubin left me, not the other way around. But now I'm safe, finding my way again with Toan, anticipating a baby that we are both learning to love in a way we never expected. Aubin was alone.

Admitting to the court that I fear he was lonely enough to… It would be admitting that our relationship was more than just as friends. And that would lead to questions about us and about the baby that I can't answer without risking the future of his child. They can't doubt that Toan and I are the surprised but thrilled parents of this unplanned pregnancy, something that is becoming true anyway.

"This letter was left with Aubin's body," Gallie says as she turns to face me. I must not have heard her right. No one had said anything about a letter left behind. "Have you seen it?"

"Of course not," I spit out before I can restrain myself. At least it is the truth. There is a subtle sound of shifting in the courtroom. The people lean closer, and the space around me seems to shrink. I'm trapped.

"Did you know a letter was left behind?"

I swallow my anger before answering, "I only know what you've told me. You didn't tell me about a letter."

"You seem upset. Why are you concerned about a suicide note, if you are not to blame for Aubin Wallace's death? Could this letter implicate you?"

I remind myself to take a second before answering. I glance at Toan, and he gives me a discreet nod that pushes me forward, but Finch interrupts before I can answer. "You are not request-ing facts, Counsel Gallie, you are asking opinion." He shoves his glasses farther up his nose.

"No one told me that there was a note," I almost whisper and earn a glare from Finch in his chair.

207

"The court permits some information to be withheld until the summary narration in order to obtain the most natural and truthful reaction for our judgment." Gallie's tone is condescending, as if she is telling me something I should have known all along. I want to say, "that's not fair" or "of course you do" or swear at her, but I don't say anything at all.

Gallie walks towards me with an envelope lifted in her right hand. I resist the urge to lean back in my chair. It is like she's holding a flaming torch toward me with my clothes soaked in fuel. When she stops with her face covered by a grotesque mask of angry red, orange and yellow light, the envelope hangs suspended in her fingers between us. I am terrified to touch it. "Read this to the court, please, Ms. Black," she says, thrusting it forward.

I will my shaky hand still and grasp the envelope. It is yellow and small, painfully familiar. I pinch it between my thumb and two fingers. When I turn it over, the air in my lungs falls out of me in an audible groan.

"Ms. Black?"

On the front the scrawl says 'Hessa' in capital letters. The 'H' is straight and perpendicular, the 'S's curve uniformly upright, the 'A' an even triangle with the point in the middle of the base. No tail. The 'E' is three sides of a nearly square, dissected in the middle by a line growing from the left. Not a tipped heart. I look at Toan and see him frowning in his effort to read my expression.

"Ms. Black. Read the letter please."

I pull the note from the envelope. It is typed, which is wrong. I read it anyway.

Hessa,

I am sorry to take the coward's path, but I cannot go on without you. My life was over when you left me. I hope you find the happiness you deserve.

Aubin.

I stare at the letter while Gallie's voice rings and echoes in my ears so that I can't understand what she is saying. The note is not from Aubin. And if he didn't write it, he didn't take his life. I'm certain.

208

"Ms. Black!" Gallie's insistent voice draws me out of my trance.

"I ... I need a break," I hear myself say.

Finch's chair scrapes against the floor as he stands behind Gallie. "It is nearly eight. It is a reasonable time to break for the night."

Gallie ignores him and focuses her scowl on me. "I thought you wanted this to end as quickly as possible? I have only a few more points to summarize. Surely we can finish this tonight." Gallie's voice is sharp, her arms crossed and her foot actually stomps on the spot. I don't care.

I force all the sweetness I can muster into an insincere smile and say, "It's not wise to rush through a Court Summary."

Gallie's lips slither back with an equally disingenuous look. "So right, Ms. Black," she says.

Finch clears his throat and says. "I request a recess by the court and to reconvene tomorrow morning."

The Judician mumbles something under the heavy bang of his antique hammer, and the people in the court start to shift and stand and move to the exits. Toan sits still in his seat, and our eyes meet. I can tell he is trying to read me, to figure out what I am thinking. My head hurts from trying to send him my thoughts, but his frown means he has no idea.

"May I visit with my match?" I ask. I don't know the rules. Toan visited me twice in the week I was detained and said he was only allowed to stay a few minutes.

Gallie looks at me, the irritation clear on her face. She turns and studies Toan for a minute. "I think not, we're in the middle of a summary."

Finch's heavy steps move around the table he sat behind all day. "I'm sure it won't matter at this point. What damage can he do?" Both Counsels look to the Judician and wait. I stare at Toan.

"Thirty minutes," is mumbled from behind and above me, and Gallie tosses her hands out in disgust.

Finch smiles, looks pointedly at me and then says, "I will see you tomorrow." It sounds like a threat, even coming from him, but I'm just relieved I'll have an opportunity to explain my thoughts to Toan.

The oddout guards appear out of the thinning crowd and usher me out of the courtroom. I hear Toan call out, "I'll be there soon," behind me. We walk down the gray corridor to my detention cell. It is just as I left it this morning, though there is not much in here that could have changed. The bed is unmade, the red blanket thrown back as it fell when I was woken by the oddouts on the morning shift. The table is bare, but I have no possessions with me to keep on it. The oddouts leave, and the door slides heavily shut behind them. I sit on the bed counting the knocks inside my ribs and wait for Toan.

It's dark before the door slides open again, and I'm propelled to my feet. Toan pushes his way in before the door is all the way open, and a disgruntled oddout mutters "Thirty minutes" as the door slides shut in his face. Toan puts his arms around me, and I press my face to his neck, breathing in the scent that is unique to him. My heart, pounding between us, starts to slow.

"I'm sorry it took so long, Hessa. I've been waiting out there since the court ended. They wouldn't let me back, just told me to wait. I was worried they were going to find a reason why I couldn't come like last week— " I kiss him to stop his words.

"We don't have time," I say, shaking my head and pulling him to sit on the bed close beside me. "Aubin didn't write that letter." I whisper as low as I can, because I know Toan isn't the only one listening.

"I know. You didn't leave him. He left. But you can't tell them that."

I nod and try to ignore the pang of guilt that always pierces me when Toan's voice sounds wounded. "The way my name is written on the envelope. That's not his handwriting." Toan winces, and I know it's painful for him to think of how familiar I am with Aubin's handwriting. And why. We haven't talked about it in months, but the reality is still there between us. "But I burned his letters. Everything. I don't have any proof." I have regretted destroying Aubin's letters many times, but it was the only way I could show Toan that I could move forward with him. Now new regret burns for a different reason.

"If he didn't write the letter, he didn't take the Euthanix." Toan's face is puckered in thought, and he squeezes my hand. "I'm going to go." I think I see remorse flash in his eyes before his steely resolve to mask his emotions clouds over. I can't imagine what he has to feel guilty about.

"What? You can't! You just got here, and we still have time left." My chest constricts, and my heart skips faster at the thought of being left alone. I hate the nights when the small line of light is gone, and I'm left to lie in the dark, tormented by thoughts that keep me awake.

Toan kisses me quickly. "I've got to go," he says as he stands and pries my hand off of his. "I'll see you tomorrow." He presses the palm panel, and the oddout's face appears in the small window before the door slides open. Toan turns and looks at me one last time before he disappears around the corner into the hall. I blink back my tears. His sudden departure leaves me too confused to say anything before he is gone. I try to call out a goodbye, but my voice is caught in my tight, dry throat. In his place my Butler appears. When he sees my tears, he smiles just a bit and shuffles the few paces to lay my meal flask on the table. When he turns and leaves, the door slides shut behind him, leaving me alone to my thoughts and the dark.

24

Twenty-Four

I'm startled out of a nightmare by the door sliding open. The oddout guard shouts the wakeup time from the doorway until I sit up straight in bed. I look around the room as the shadowed torments from my dream dissipate in the corners. I don't remember what I was dreaming, just the feeling of fear, of being chased and trapped and of losing control and slipping away. Flashes of lights and blurs of shapes, blue eyes and brown eyes are all I remember seeing. When the guard steps back, the door slides closed and I lie back on the pillow and start to cry.

I'm still curled up on the bed and my hair on the pillow under my head is wet with tears when my Butler shuffles into the room with my breakfast. I don't move. He nods just slightly and holds up the flask of nutrients before placing it on the table. When he turns to back out of the door, he looks at me. His eyes meet mine for too long, and it makes me feel uncomfortable. I close mine and hear him sigh before he shuffles out.

I want to stay on the bed, not move, not talk to anyone, but I know that's not an option. I wonder where Toan is, if he's made it to the courthouse yet or if he's still on the hover. I worry that he missed the hover and will be late, but he has never been late before. It takes all my willpower to push myself up off the bed and across the room to the table. I abhor using the toilet, but I know it's only a matter of time before it becomes a necessity. The thick, bland breakfast drink coats my tongue and triggers my gag reflex. I concentrate on swallowing and keeping it down in my churning gut. I don't want to drink it, but Toan's voice echoes in my mind, gentle and firm. "You have to eat."

Yesterday the Court Summary started early. I was taken from my room before eight in the morning. So when I see the glowing numbers on the wall shift to 10:00, I am worried something has gone wrong. I sit at the table, making letters on the smooth surface. If I press my finger hard enough, a dull smear stays on the table just long enough to show the letter before it fades. In this way I've written Aubin's alphabet over and over until I've lost count. As hard as I think, I can't reason a cause for the delay, just a droning, tingling in my chest and head that something isn't right. Of course nothing has been right for a while now.

At 10:43 the door slides open without notice, and I jump. An oddout appears at the door and grumbles an order that I assume means "Let's go." He waits while I stand on jelly legs and meet him at the door and then turns down the hall without checking to see if I follow. The hallway is pocked with solid doors, all closed, identical to the one I have watched for a week, and has intersections at irregular points. All of the walls are metallic and gray, and the ceiling glows with sunlight transferred from the outside. I run my fingers along the wall for balance, to stay grounded and to know which way is sideways, which way is up. It keeps me from falling over. For a moment I consider slipping away from the guard down a different hallway. If I could slip his presence, maybe I could find a way out and escape from the prison, from today. But the impossibility of the idea follows so closely that I almost laugh out loud. Even if there weren't oddout guards slinking through the halls, I would never find my way out of the maze.

The oddout stops so short at a door that I walk into his back. "Excuse me," I say, stumbling. He grunts. He puts his hand on the palm panel, and the door slides open. I'm hit by the noise of people killing time, clashing of words at volumes and intonations competing to be heard. Over it all, I hear Toan call my name. I scan the faces for his and find him sitting near the front. His smile soothes the pressure in my chest, just a little bit.

The oddout escorts me to the same chair I occupied all day yesterday, as if I might have forgotten where my place is. Without a word he turns and leaves through the same door. The Judician bangs his ancient wooden hammer on his desk, and a near silence falls immediately, leaving only the moving of chairs and shifting of bodies and the occasional low whisper. Then

213

Finch is beside me. I didn't see where he came from and wonder why he is out of the chair he ensconced himself in for the previous day. Gallie is in her chair, glowering at both of us from under her tight hair.

"Good morning, Ms. Black. How was your night?" Finch says.

"Delightful," I say with as much of a smile as I can force out. He is standing to my left. I want him to move closer to my right so I can look in his direction and still see Toan.

"I apologize to you, Hessa, and to the court for the late start this morning. I had a visitor waiting at my office door when I arrived this morning, and he was quite insistent that what he had to say was worth delaying the start of our summary."

I remember Toan's hasty exit last night and know he is talking about him. I want so badly to look his way and confirm I am right, but somehow it feels like tipping my hand if I do. I train my eyes on Finch and concentrate on keeping my smile blank and ignorant.

"Do you recognize this?" Finch holds the yellow envelope up between thumb and finger for everyone to see.

"It's Aubin's note." I'm tired. I loved Aubin. The note was not his. If I tell the court how I know it's not his note, I have to admit at the very least that I learned to read his handwriting. I guess I should have confessed that at the beginning, the lesser of my offences. Maybe then I could have convinced them our relationship stopped with a few lessons and innocent notes. But if they find the truth about it now, the rest of my lies will unravel behind it. I'm caught in my own web, and I start to realize maybe the court is right. It *is* my fault.

"Did you ever admit to having an affair with Mr. Wallace? Outside of your legal classification and your own match with Mr. Whitley?" Finch asks.

He paces to my right so I can catch a fleeting look at Toan. I feel beaten and lost and ready to give up, but he shakes his head just enough for me to see. "No." In my effort to make my voice strong, it comes out louder than I wanted. "Aubin and I were just friends."

"So this note? What is your explanation?" Gallie says from

the desk, drawing a stare from Finch.

"You had the floor yesterday, Counsel Gallie. This is my line of questioning." Finch says, as if he's declining an offer of tea. *He didn't write it* echoes in my head, but I can't say that out loud. I look at Toan again, and he nods. I wish I knew what he was thinking. I think of the times we tried to share our thoughts. I wish we could do that now.

"An explanation was brought to me this morning. I would like to hear your thoughts on the plausibility of this account." I turn from Toan back to Finch and see him holding a second yellow envelope in his hand. I know it instantly, and my stomach lurches. My heart instantly races. It's not the clean, new one Gallie handed me the day before. This envelope has curled corners, their points softened and dulled from being pocketed and handled. As Finch holds it to me, I see 'HESSA' clearly on the front, the letters leaning to the right. A tipped heart and a long tail.

It's my letter. It's Aubin's letter to me. It was forgotten in my pocket when I destroyed the rest of the notes in the incinerator. When I remembered it was there, I couldn't bring myself to burn it. Instead I hid it away in my office. In the weeks after he left, I read it so many times, I can still see his handwriting on the inside of my eyelids when I try to sleep some nights, even now that it's been months since I read it last. *I am not sorry I kissed you … you kissed me too … and I love you.* It was his admission, his declaration to me of his feelings and his intent. And wrapped up in his assertion, he names me as his accomplice. I kissed him back. I loved him too.

I stare at Toan, trying again to read his mind. He must have found the note and brought it to Finch. This note proves Aubin did not write the letter and could remove me as the cause of his death. But it also confirms our affair. My ears and thoughts roar. They will investigate the baby. They will find out he is not Toan's but a Creator's unpermitted child. Aubin loved the baby so much, he was willing to leave to save him. It shouldn't be surprising that Toan is willing to sacrifice the baby to save me. I want to loathe him. I remember his words, *'It might be easier if I could hate you'*. I glare at him, and he blinks and looks away.

215

"Who wrote *this* letter?" Finch asks.

"Aubin," I whisper. I meant to say it out loud, but I don't quite manage it.

"Please repeat that, Hessa."

"Aubin. Aubin Wallace gave that note to me."

He hands me the note, and I resist the urge to clutch it against my chest.

"Read it, please." And everything is falling apart.

"I ... I can't."

In one step, Finch steps toward me and holds out his hand. "I will then." His voice is strangely gentle.

I can't watch him open my letter. I can't look at Toan. I can't stand all of the eyes in the room on me. I stare at my hands, squeezing them together until the bones in my fingers glow white under the taunt skin and hurt from the pressure. The pain makes me focus. It makes me feel better somehow. I don't want to hear Finch speak his words, but I need to. I don't want to listen, but I have no other choice.

Finch reads: "*'Hessa, Please accept my apology that I missed our appointment at lunch today. My class ran late, and by the time I made it to the lounge you must have gone back to prepare. If you still want some direction on how to delegate tutoring opportunities to your stronger students, I'd be happy to help. I'll see you later this week. Aubin.'*"

While he reads, my eyes float from my white-knuckled hands up to Toan's eyes in the spinning room. He is holding his face in the mask that only I know shields his true thoughts and emotions. Others would think he was passively listening or maybe not even paying attention at all. His eyes lock with mine, and one lid blinks down so quickly, I wonder if I imagined it.

"So Mr. Wallace wrote this note to you?"

"Yes." My voice is stronger again, renewed.

"How did you recognize it when I first showed it to you?"

"His handwriting on the outside."

"I didn't realize you can read handwriting, Ms. Black?" Gallie says as she stands behind the table, and I feel like she's reeling in a trap.

"Just my name." I smile. I can see Aubin's hand in my mind,

pointing to the letters in my name. "He taught me how to read my name because he thought I'd be interested in it."

Finch steps between us and stares at Gallie until she sits back down. He turns back to me and asks, "What is so distinctive about a short name, five letters, that you can recognize this writing as his?"

I hold my hand out, anxious to have my envelope back, even though the letter I love is gone from it. I point at the letters. "His letters lean this way. His 'A' has a long part that hangs down, his 'E' is round, not square."

Finch hands me the other yellow envelope, the one that still had sharp pointed corners. "And this one?"

My words tumble out fast and cluttered. "The letters here on the front are all wrong. They're too, um, straight up and down, see? The 'E' is like a square and the 'A' has an even base. Aubin didn't ... he didn't write that note."

"What does this matter?" Gallie bellows from behind her desk.

Finch smiles at me a second before turning to address Gallie. "As I started off by reporting this morning, the appearance of this earlier letter caused a delay in this morning's summary session. This second letter to you was presented to me, along with three other documents shared by the Education Department. Investigators for the court compared the documents and confirmed all were written by the same person. The conclusion must be that Aubin Wallace did not write the note found with his body."

He turned back to me, tipped his head to one side and raised his bushy eyebrow over his glasses. "Why do you think someone would go to the effort of writing a fraudulent note that names you as the cause of Aubin Wallace's suicide?"

"I don't know." I wish I did. Or maybe I don't.

I sit for a minute, letting Finch's words sink in, and it all starts to make sense. All these months we thought we had them fooled, thought we had gotten away with our prohibited love, if only for a few weeks. We thought we had survived our choices and moved on. Toan was trying to forgive me, and Aubin had entrusted me with his baby to protect. I had started to believe

what Aubin had promised; we'd be okay. Things would just
work out differently than planned. But someone knew. Someone had found out and wanted to punish me, punish us for the
past. But with him dead and me detained, the baby apprehended
and Toan, our reluctant accomplice, left alone, the secret we
kept would be our undoing. Toan stopped it with the letter I
hid.

I don't know how, but Toan has saved me again.

"I do," Finch says, his voice close. My heart skips a beat because I almost forgot he stood there. "When the evidence was
returned to me this morning, I asked Investigators in Toronto
to speak to those who would benefit from the death of Aubin
Wallace. His new match received widow benefits, so they inter-
rogated her again. While she refused to admit to Mr. Wallace's
murder or forging the note, she conceded that Mr. Wallace had
recently requested they break their match, putting her in position of imminent Hazardous deployment as her second attempt.
While those facts are not enough to find Mr. Wallace's match
guilty, they certainly carry enough doubt to unfetter Ms. Black.
Do you not think so, Counsel Gallie?" As I try to sort out the
spinning facts, Finch walks slowly to his seat and settles into the
chair.

Gallie watches him, her mouth slightly open and her eyes
wide. "I have not been privy to this new evidence."

"I have." The Judician's low voice rumbles from above me,
and it makes me feel small. "The court has heard the testimony
of Hessa Black and needs no further information. The letter that
implicates Hessa Black has been determined to be fraudulent.
From the remaining information and reports given, doubt re-
mains that Hessa Black is responsible for the death of Aubin
Wallace." It sounds to me like a conclusion, but I don't have any
more answers than I did before it started. The Judician bangs his
hammer against his desk and the sound bounces through me. I
think that's why he uses it, to keep people in the room unsettled.
"This court thanks you for your time and your honesty, Ms.
Black." His hammer falls again, ending the summary but not my
guilt. It was my fault. I kissed him back.

The people in the room shift and stand, and hushed voices

raise as people converse. I look for Toan, but he is gone from his seat, and I can't find him in the crowd. Not seeing him scares me, and my chest tightens in the knot that has become familiar over the past week. An oddout appears at my side and ushers me from my seat. As we pass Finch's desk, I spot the rounded corner of my love-worn envelope peeking out from under his screen. It takes all I have left in me not to lift it from his desk. I follow the oddout closely so as not to be separated in the crowd. We finally step out of the old building to the wide, steep stairs out front. I suck in the air, unprocessed and spring-cool. I forgot how good it felt. The oddout doesn't allow me time to revel, though. He pulls me forward with a tug at my elbow, and we walk on until we are at the curb in front of a long black car. Toan is waiting inside.

I slide in beside him, and the door swings down to close. He watches me watch him for a moment, and I realize how much I've missed him. The urge to kiss him is so strong, it doesn't matter who is watching. I just do. I feel his smile against my lips, and when he pulls back, he takes my hand.

I have so many questions I don't know where to start. "Toan—"

He cuts me off with a slight shake of his head, and his finger touches his lips just long enough for me to see and understand. He raises his arm, and I'm content to curl up beside him instead.

I wake up when the vehicle stops, rocking me forward and then back with its sudden loss of momentum. Toan's arm, strong around me, stops me from slipping from my seat, and he kisses the top of my head. He pushes up the door and climbs out then reaches back in to offer me his hand. I can get out by myself, but it's nice to accept his help.

I am not ready for the flood of relief that hits me when I walk into our house. The scent is familiar in a way I recognize without even knowing it was there. My things clutter the surfaces of the tables and counters, a sweater tossed over a chair, waiting for me to come clean it up. I'm crying, but I don't remember when I started, and I turn back to hug Toan around his waist. I feel safer already, the way I always have with him.

Toan doesn't let go until I've stopped crying. Then he pushes me away, and I see his face. "What's wrong?" I ask. I know something is. His eyes are worried, his mouth turned down and pinched.

"I have something to tell you, Hessa."

"What is it?" I can't think of anything worthy of him looking so upset.

"I kept something from you. I'm sorry. I thought it would be better for us, but I only made things worse."

I hate to hear him apologize. I've hurt him so badly, sometimes I think he should never have to apologize again. It will never be even, never be fair between us, no matter what he does. I shake my head, but my throat is too tight, to thick to say anything. Toan takes my hand and leads me up the stairs to his office. I stand in the doorway as he opens a drawer and lifts some things aside. He pulls out a folded paper and a small yellow envelope, and I almost throw up right there.

He handed me the folded paper that was missing from the worn envelope. "I found this in your desk one night weeks ago. I shouldn't have taken it, but I didn't want you to have it. I wanted to burn it but when I tried ... I — I couldn't. I'm glad now that I didn't." I unfolded the note, and Aubin's letters slip into me as a salve on my stinging eyes. "When you told me it wasn't his handwriting, I knew I had proof. I typed up a note that seemed plausible and put it in his envelope. I talked to the director of literacy at the Education Department. He wasn't impressed that I interrupted his evening, but when I told him what I needed, he was able to give me a few pieces of paper from Aubin's file. Scribbles, really. I couldn't read them, but it seemed like enough to show." I nod. Aubin's letter is heavy in my hands. "I'm sorry, Hessa, I shouldn't have taken it."

"But if you hadn't..." We leave the possible ending to that sentence hanging between us.

"What is that one?" Toan is still holding the yellow envelope in his hand, less as if he forgot it and more as if he wants to keep it to himself.

He looks down at it and thrusts it toward me. My name and our address are typed on the outside. "This came in the mail in Two, five weeks after Aubin sent you the money. I knew it was from him by the Toronto address." I take it and my hand starts shaking. The top of the envelope is ripped open. I run my fingertip along the jagged triangles. "I opened it, but I couldn't read it. Hessa, please understand, things were just starting to get better between us, even better than before, I thought. I was sure he would call you away. And if he asked you to go … I … I was scared you wouldn't say no." Toan's voice is broken and hoarse and hurt. I wonder if the hurt I caused will ever go away.

It takes a few shaky tries, but I finally pull the folded page from the envelope through the seam Toan tore weeks ago. When I open it, the familiar letters are dancing across the page. I thought I had heard the last from Aubin Wallace, the last of his secret ancient words, his coded thoughts. But here he is again, whispering to me even after he's gone. The letters start to swim as my eyes fill with tears.

"I'll let you read it alone," Toan whispers, and before I can stop him he is gone and I'm left in his room alone with Aubin's letter.

Dear Hessa,

I find I'm only saying 'I'm sorry' these days. I'm sorry my last letter was so cold. I typed it hoping you would realize the words were not what I wanted to say to you. They weren't mine. My family arranged a match, and we had the ceremony last month. But she is not someone I can love. I've told her it won't work, and she asked me why. And here I have to say 'I'm sorry' again, because I thought I owed her the truth. I told her about you and about us. I didn't tell her everything, but enough for her to realize I still love you. Maybe I was wrong before, maybe we each only have so much love to give, and I gave all of mine to you. She doesn't understand why a good match isn't enough for me. But how could she, if she hasn't loved someone like that? And she is so angry. She says I am ungrateful and selfish. I realize now that I am and I that I have been all along. So I'm leaving again.

I'll go out West and see if I can't lose myself in an oddout colony like we intended. I hope you don't mind my going anyway. Maybe I'll even find someone to love again, and it'll be alright for all of us, just not what we had planned. It's strange, writing this letter to you now. I expected to be distraught by reaching out to you or terrified of my departure, but instead I feel zanshin, I feel relaxed in the face of this new challenge. It's right, I think. Or at least as right as it can be. Take care of yourself and take care of my baby. Take care of Toan. I am sorry we hurt him.

Never doubt I love you, A.

I touch the tail hanging down from his 'A' and almost wish I could touch him again. But even if he had asked, I wouldn't have gone. Not now, after Toan has forgiven and loved me. Finch's suggestions crept into my thoughts; could Aubin's match have been angry enough to stop his departure with a dose of Euthanix and a fraudulent note? Aubin is dead. It shouldn't matter how it happened, but it hurts a little less to know he didn't do it himself. Aubin was still full of words and light. He was still looking forward when he died. That is good to know.

By the time I finish reading the letter through a fourth time, Toan appears at the door. His head is hung low, as if he is trespassing and unsure of my reaction. He glances at me from under his brows and smiles just a bit. "Are you okay?" he asks.

I'm sure I look awful. I'm still wearing the bland gray detention uniform I was given for court. My dirty hair is pulled back, but strands have come free and tangled around my head. My face is wet, and I'm sure my eyes are swollen and red from crying. "I'm … okay," I whisper.

"I'm sorry," he says, and somehow I know it's not just for keeping the letter from me.

"I know." I echo his words from months ago. I step toward him and feel his weight as he slouches against me. "It's okay, we'll be alright." The conviction in my voice makes me start to believe the words.

"Did he ask you to go with him?" Toan's chest falls still, and he holds his breath after the words.

"No, he didn't." Toan's release of air presses his arms more heavily down on me.

"What did he say?" Toan's voice is hesitant, but as soon as those words fall out, he puts his hands on my arms and pushes me back, looks me in the eyes. "Never mind, you don't have to answer that. It doesn't matter."

He is trying so hard.

I smile, because I see my Toan there, his eyes unsure and soft. "He said he was breaking his match and moving away. He thought maybe he'd go to an oddout colony and try to start over."

Toan's eyes wander as he processes that plan, so different from anything he wants from life. His eyebrows raise, and when he says "Hmm," I suspect it's an effort to be polite.

I'm wondering if I should say more when the words fall out on their own, "He said to take care of you, and he's sorry he hurt you." Toan's mask falls, and I see his surprise for just a moment before he collects his features again. He nods and hugs me closer, but when he tries to kiss me, I push away from him. He looks down at me with hurt in his eyes.

"Sorry," he mutters.

"No, no. It's not…" I want to be close to him, but first I want out of the clothes I've been locked in for days. I want to clean the institutional smell from my hair. I want to drown away the past. "I just need a shower and some clean clothes, okay?"

He nods and lets me go. I walk upstairs to my bedroom. I stop long enough to tuck Aubin's letters into the top drawer of my dresser and then pass through to the shower room. I peel off the detention uniform and toss it into the incinerator. The heat from the atypically large mass flares up and lifts my loose hair and burns at my nose. I turn on the shower and step into the hot stream. Drip by drip, the past week falls away from my shoulders. Without that weight, I stand taller. I scrub at my hair first and then my body, brushing until my skin is red with heat and friction and a layer of me is gone. I stand in the shower long after I'm clean. I suppose I'm processing the events of the last day, the last week, the last months. Aubin's letter, the one Toan kept, is the first handwriting I've read since I burned his box of letters and my journal. I miss writing. I need it. I thought the writing was for Aubin, but it became a part of me. I've been trying so hard to prove myself to Toan that I've left that piece of me behind. I stand in the hot stream until Toan knocks on the door and asks if I'm alright.

"I'm coming," I call back and turn off the water. I dry myself and step into the bedroom. Toan's smile is sheepish, like when we were fifteen and he bounded into my bedroom without knocking first.

"I'll go," he says, though I know, because I know him, it's the last thing he wants to do.

"Don't." I stop him with my hand on his arm, and he looks back at me, unsure. "I want you to stay. I need you to stay," and I realize that both are true. And love *can* change.

"You do?" His doubt makes my arms and chest heavy, my middle speared by guilt, so I step closer and show him instead of answering.

I'm nestled against his side, his arm around me in my bed. I'm nervous, drumming my fingers against his chest but not saying anything. He laughs and asks, "What's up?"

"The letter.." I feel him stiffen.

"No, don't worry." I kiss his shoulder lightly, hoping to reassure whatever doubt he feels. "It's just ... I miss writing. I didn't realize how much until I read that letter."

My head on Toan's chest rises as he takes in a deep breath. "Then you should write." His voice is firm and sure. His fingers continue to drift on my arm, as if he hasn't said anything unusual.

"I don't have to—"

"It's okay, Hessa. It's important to you, I know that now."

"Really?" He doesn't say anything, but I feel his head nod against mine.

His shoulder lifts my head as he takes another deep breath. I hold mine, knowing he has more to say. "I think you should teach the baby handwriting too, when he's old enough." This flutters in my stomach and knocks the air out of my voice. I don't know what to say anyway. Instead I prop myself up so that I can see his face clearly. He smiles. "I agree with ... *him* ... on one point: I don't want this baby to be limited. We can give him all of the tools we have and let him decide what he wants to do."

And I don't know what to say, so I say something stupid. "Or her."

Toan smiles and agrees, "Or her."

I kiss his mouth and snuggle back down against his side. I feel safe again, and complete. And it's alright, somehow, as right as it can be.

224

Acknowledgments

It's daunting to write acknowledgments upon completion of a novel because so many people contribute, and I'm fearful of leaving someone out! At least there's no threat of cheesy music playing over me to usher me into silence.

Thank you to Fierce Ink Books for believing I was more than a 'one-hit wonder' and working with me to bring *Aptitude* to completion.

My sincere gratitude to the awesome Allister Thompson for his magic touch that stretched this story to its full potential.

Authors are notoriously hard on themselves, and a cheering squad of people who believe in the author when she has lost faith, direction, motivation, is essential. For me that squad includes: Colleen, Crystal, Kelly, Melissa, Jilly and Julie. The Head Cheerleader is my mom, Sue Corbett.

Thanks to the people who have taught me about many different kinds of love: my parents and parents-in-law, John, Sue, Ron and Diane, my children, Jack, Elliot, PJ and Wen, and my Aubin-Toan combo, Steve. My furry soulmate, Rookie, whose love was probably the purest.

Natalie lives outside of Halifax, Nova Scotia in a home filled with kids and fur. She is a Speech Language Pathologist, a job that allows her to share her love of language and words every day. Natalie spends her evenings and weekends trying to squeeze time for creative work like writing and drawing between trips to the rink or basketball court with her husband and four children. *Aptitude* is Natalie's second book; *Game Plan* was published by Fierce Ink Books in November of 2013.

The Wheres of It All

As a writer, all experiences are fodder for storytelling. Some are better than others, of course. *Aptitude* was born in a moment of procrastination on the Internet. One of those lists popped up on my Facebook feed, and I clicked on it instead of moving on to whatever work I should have been doing. It was a list of words in other languages that did not have a direct translation in English. One of the words was 'cafune' in Brazilian Portuguese. It's such a beautiful word, don't you think? And when I read the definition, 'The act of tenderly running your fingers through someone's hair,' I could clearly see Aubin and Hessa in the library, locked in a moment of intimacy so moving and so forbidden, it changed everything. I didn't know who they were or why they were so frightened by the deed, but I knew there was a beautiful story there that might come close to depicting the magic of words.

This story required more research than others I've written to date, and I had a lot of fun looking for words that would fit into Hessa and Aubin's shared story. I searched for words online and purchased a few books. The best resource by far was *They Have a Word For It* by Howard Rheingold (Jeremy P. Tarcher, Inc, 1988), which was a constant companion on my desk for weeks, filled with dog-ears and sticky tags. There were so many interesting words that didn't fit into the story. I love the way language is dynamic and organic. I hope *Aptitude* embodies that.

CPSIA information can be obtained at www.ICGtesting.com
Printed in the USA
LVOW11s0534100915

453526LV00005B/94/P